BEAR HUG

"*Bear Hug* . . . provides Doolittle with his broadest canvas so far. He fills it with sure strokes of local color that fast-freeze sharp images of urban and rural America and nail down indigenous characters in a single sentence. . . . Doolittle's mysteries go down as smoothly as anything in the genre."

— *Boston Globe*

"Guaranteed to generate at least a silent 'attaboy!' from readers! Superb hard-boiled fare in every sense."

—Wes Lukowsky, *Booklist*

STRANGLE HOLD

"Tom Bethany is some guy. . . . [Mr. Doolittle's] characters have heft as well as high-definition color."

—Marilyn Stasio, *The New York Times Book Review*

"Doolittle writes like Muhammad Ali used to punch—clean, sharp, and powerful. . . . You'll stay up all night to finish *Strangle Hold.*"

—Les Roberts, *The Plain Dealer* (Cleveland)

BODY SCISSORS

"A riveting political thriller written with an insider's savvy. . . .The Boston area scene is a lively backdrop, the dialogue crackles with fast repartee, and the characters make an assorted and colorful cast."

—*Washington Post Book World*

"*Body Scissors* lands Jerome Doolittle in the front rank of political thriller novelists. Written with wit, zest, and insight . . . Tom Bethany is a gem."

—Ross Thomas

Books by Jerome Doolittle

Body Scissors
Strangle Hold
Bear Hug
Head Lock
Half Nelson
Kill Story

Published by POCKET BOOKS

Praise for Jerome Doolittle and his latest Tom Bethany mystery,

KILL STORY

Praise for Jerome Doolittle's previous Tom Bethany mysteries

HALF NELSON

"Doolittle . . . ranks with Robert Parker, Elmore Leonard, Ed McBain, and Ross Thomas as a high-voltage storyteller, and that is exalted company."

—Charles Champlin, *Los Angeles Times Book Review*

"The fifth round for Doolittle's tough-talking, softhearted hero Tom Bethany—wrestling champ, Vietnam vet, PI, and lover of Hope Edwards, head of the Washington, D.C., branch of the American Civil Liberties Union—is bloody and intricate."

—*Publishers Weekly*

HEAD LOCK

"Bethany has no trouble defending his ideals. . . . Tough, fast-paced fun. . . ."

—*Chicago Tribune*

"Jerome Doolittle is [a] . . . terrific stylist. . . ."

—New York *Newsday*

"Solidly in the tradition of Spenser and Robert B. Parker. . . . *Head Lock* is well told and involving."

—*Ellery Queen*

"Doolittle tramples on some risky ground here, and he should be commended for it. . . . You'll be cheering in the aisle."

—*Rapport* .

KILL STORY

A TOM BETHANY MYSTERY

JEROME DOOLITTLE

POCKET BOOKS
New York   London   Toronto   Sydney   Tokyo   Singapore

This book is a work of fiction. Names, characters, places and incidents are products of the author's imagination or are used fictitiously. Any resemblance to actual events or locales or persons, living or dead, is entirely coincidental.

POCKET BOOKS, a division of Simon & Schuster Inc.
1230 Avenue of the Americas, New York, NY 10020

Copyright © 1995 by Jerome Doolittle

ISBN: 0-671-79981-9

First Pocket Books paperback printing November 1996

10 9 8 7 6 5 4 3 2 1

POCKET and colophon are registered trademarks of Simon & Schuster Inc.

Cover art by Dennis Ziemienski

Printed in the U.S.A.

To Jon

THE PAY PHONE WAS RINGING IN THE rear of The Tasty. Joey Neary could have come out from behind the counter to get it, except Joey was at one of those delicate points in the life of a short-order cook. If he took my two eggs off the griddle now, they'd be slimy and disgusting on top. If he answered the phone instead, they'd fry into white rubber with brown lace on the edges. Either way the loser would be me, so I got off my stool and answered the thing myself.

The woman on the line said she was calling about the ad about the bunny rabbits, so I told her she had a really wrong number. "Well, this is the number they ran in the paper," she said. "It says right here in the *Banner* classified. It says ask for Joey."

"Hey, Joey," I hollered. "You order any bunny rabbits?"

"Tell 'em hold on a second," Joey called back. "You mind?"

I told her and set the receiver down on top of the old

black coin box. Some weirdness had to be going on, or Joey Neary wouldn't have tacked on the "You mind?" Joey, the normal Joey, made it a religion never to be polite to a customer.

He slid my just-right eggs in front of me and headed out from behind the counter, while I tried to look busy with my *Boston Globe*.

"Oh, absolutely," he was saying. "Mickey's fourteen, very responsible kid ... Yeah, he's kept rabbits for years.... Well, they passed away ... Yeah, just from one day to the next, bang, they were gone. The vet still can't figure it out.... Oh, yeah, everything's all ready. Fresh newspaper down ... That right? You use a screen floor, huh? Let's the stuff fall right through the holes? Sounds like a good idea, Mickey should try that ... Three seventy-nine Harvard Street? Sure, I know where that is, Mrs. Bernstein ... Oh, *Ms.* Bernstein. Sorry about that.... Listen, I'm off work at one. A little after that be all right? ... Fine, see you then."

I made like I was still interested in my paper while Joey went back behind the counter. Let him think he dodged the bullet. Dream on, Joey, at least until I finish my breakfast.

"What did Ms. Bernstein want?" I asked when I had mopped up the last bit of egg yolk with the last bit of semi-toasted Wonder Bread.

"Hey, do I ask you about your personal calls?"

"Joey, Joey, you can talk to your old Uncle Tom. It's Julius Squeezer, isn't it?"

Julius Squeezer was the twelve-foot python that Joey's son, Mickey, kept in the basement. Julius lived in a glass-fronted cage the size of a steamer trunk, with his own heat lamp and Vita-Lite and a wooden box the size of a small suitcase in one corner for those times when he felt like curling up away from it all.

"Got to be the old Squeezer, Joey."

"None of your damned business, Bethany."

"Did Ms. Bernstein tell you what kind of lettuce to give the bunny rabbits for their little lunchie-poo, Joey?"

"I'm warning you, Bethany."

"Joey, you got nothing to warn with. Me, on the other hand, suppose I was to go over to Ms. Bernstein's around twelve-thirty? Maybe I'd tell her about what the old Squeezer himself eats for lunch. Or maybe I could check in with the classified department at the *Bummer*, mention to them about the bunny fiend they're running ads for."

The *Bummer* is what everybody calls the *Cambridge Daily Banner*.

"You wouldn't do that," Joey said.

"Possibly not," I said. "Talk to me, Joey."

"No big thing, for Christ's sake. You know how it goes."

"How, Joey? Exactly how does it go?"

"Sis and Junior get bunnies for Easter, all right? Couple weeks later the kids lose interest, Mom and Pop got to feed the goddamned things, shovel the shit out of the cage. Couple months, the whole rabbit bit gets pretty old. See what I mean?"

"It's all coming clear to me, Joey. Hello, classified? Lonely child, single, sensitive, loves music and long walks. Seeks bunny similarly inclined."

"Come on, Bethany."

"What do you do when you've cleaned out all the Easter bunnies in Cambridge, Joey? Troll for gerbils?"

"Not gerbils, you dumb shit. Gerbils are too quick for Julius. What you want is your slower animals. Your hamsters, your white rats, your guinea pigs."

"Joey, I'm not going to tell anybody about this . . ."

"Hey, why would you tell anybody anyway? Who would care?"

"Harry, Louise, Mick and Charlie, Bingo, Stretch, Joanna, the Corrigan brothers, Mel and Melinda, Chuck, Doc La-Porta, Ernie Gallagher—"

"All right, all right."

"But I'm not going to share this with our little group here at The Tasty, Joey. On one condition."

"Condition? What condition?"

"From now on, Joey, I want my Wonder Bread toasted on both sides, and I want to get it while it's still warm."

"What do you think, I got three hands?"

"Every day, Joey. Both sides. Warm."

The phone rang again, and I was over to it before Joey could even think about coming out from behind the counter. Maybe Ms. Bernstein forgot something.

"The Tasty," I said. "This wouldn't be Ms. Bernstein, would it?"

"Oh, Tom," said a voice like no other voice. "I hoped I'd catch you there. I tried your apartment, but naturally nobody was there. Since you're here instead."

Felicia Lamport was one of the few people who knew both my numbers, the unlisted one for my apartment and the one on the rear wall of The Tasty. She was a poet who had been my friend for years, ever since she caught me sneaking into a class she taught at the Harvard extension school. Being an outlaw at heart herself, she let me stay.

"I'm here, all right," I said. "Where are you?"

"I'm home, and I'd like to talk with you about something."

"Your place or mine?"

"It's far too nice a day to stay indoors. How about the terrace in front of Au Bon Pain? Order me an iced tea and I'll be there in ten minutes."

The terrace is on Mass. Ave., only a few yards up from The Tasty. In front of it is Harvard Square, and across from it is Harvard Yard. The warm May weather had brought out both the Harvard kids and the street kids. People poured in and out of the subway stop in the middle of the square, which was actually a triangle. Cars and busses and trucks jammed the streets and backed up at the lights, rumbling and fuming to be on their way. Except for cabbies at the cab stand, nobody ever parked in Harvard Square. Nobody except Felicia Lamport.

I waited and wondered, to see how she would pull it off this time. One time she backed her yellow Volkswagen bug halfway down the pedestrian passage that runs through Holyoke Center and parked in front of the Harvard University Press bookstore. She asked a security guard to keep an eye on things while she went to find the nonexistent men who were supposedly going to load her car up with donation books for the scholars in the Charles Street Jail.

This time she just pulled her VW over, next to a police sergeant. She looked up helplessly, cluelessly, a pitiful little old lady with snow-white hair. The sergeant leaned forward to hear what she was saying. He smiled and opened the car door for her, carefully shutting it after her. Then he stood out in the street with his back to the car, waving traffic around the obstacle. Felicia came toward me without a hint of a limp, so she couldn't have used her pathetic old cripple ploy on the sergeant.

"What did you tell the cop this time?" I asked, when she was settled at my table.

"Honesty is always the best policy. I told him I intended to break the law, and would he very much mind aiding and abetting a tiny misdemeanor. He said he'd be delighted. Of course it helped that the bishop presided at his confirmation thirty years ago."

Felicia's husband was an Episcopal bishop who was theoretically retired but still spent every day volunteering at a shelter in East Cambridge. He had founded the shelter so long ago that his clients were still called vagrants. Then they got a little brief respect in the early 1980s when the right wing of our single political party dignified them as the

Homeless. The point was to hang them around the neck of the extreme right wing, called the Republican Party, which was then taking its turn in the White House. But now that a Democrat was actually in a position to do something about the Homeless, they were back to being shiftless bums again. Clinton's plan, if I followed him correctly, was to retrain them all as computer programmers. Probably half of them already were, at least in Cambridge, so it looked like the bishop would be in business for the foreseeable future.

"You're telling me there's an Episcopalian in the Cambridge Police Department?" I said to Felicia.

"I don't imagine there could be many, but there's at least one. Who is this Ms. Bernstein whom you were so eagerly awaiting when I called you?"

When I told her about Julius Squeezer she said, "Yes, I like the idea of an Easter bunny recycling service. I think I'm in favor of your Mr. Neary. Although I do wish he'd find someplace else to spend his advertising dollar."

"What's the matter with the *Bummer?* One rag is pretty much like another."

"More and more is the matter with it. That's what I wanted to talk to you about. Do you know Linda Cushing?"

"No, but I bet you do." Felicia knew an amazing number of people in Cambridge.

"She's the widow of the man who used to own the *Banner.* Mike Cushing. I don't suppose you knew him, either?"

"Nope."

"He died at a Holy Cross football game, and not in a terribly dignified way, I'm afraid. A piece of Polish sausage lodged in his throat. Somebody tried whatever that thing is on him. The Hemlock Maneuver?"

"Heimlich."

"Exactly so. Heimlich. Anyway, apparently it doesn't work if you have a coonskin coat on, and so poor Mr. Cushing died in his season seat. Are you beginning to wonder what the point of all this is?"

"Not particularly. I'm just enjoying the ride."

"Aren't you nice. Nonetheless, there *is* a point. Linda inherited the paper, and sold it last year for a perfectly obscene sum of money to a perfectly revolting man named Thurman Boucher. He claims to be descended from Jonathan Boucher of Virginia, which is probably a lie and is in any case irrelevant. You do know who Jonathan Boucher is?"

"Sure. He was an establishment brown-noser just before the Revolution. Sort of a Rush Limbaugh for the Brits."

"I thought you'd know. It's the kind of thing I count on you for."

Facts stick indiscriminately to me, most of them useless. I would have remembered Thurman Boucher, too, if I had ever come across the name.

"Actually he didn't stay in Virginia all that long," I said. "He moved to Annapolis. Jonathan, not Thurman."

"I'm sure he did. In any event, Linda Cushing is terribly upset by the things Mr. Boucher is doing to her paper, but there doesn't seem to be anything she can do about it. So I want you to get Linda's paper back for her."

"I see. Why?"

"I told you. Thurman Boucher is a perfectly revolting man and he has upset Linda Cushing terribly."

"Oh, *that's* why. How about how?"

"I don't have the slightest idea, but it's exactly the sort of thing you do so well. As you think about it, bear in mind the obscene amount of money I mentioned. I imagine Linda would be more than willing to give some of it to you."

"I don't need money anymore." I had restolen quite a pile of it from a savings-and-loan thief a little while ago, so Reaganomics had finally trickled down even to me.

"I know that. But whatever scheme you came up with

might call for money, and you couldn't be expected to spend your own."

"Hold on, Felicia. Something just struck me. What did you mean when you said you *imagined* Linda would be more than willing? Did she ask you to help out? Does she even know you're talking to me?"

"Of course not. She's far too distraught to deal with practical matters now."

Someone was close to our table, making the little throat-clearing noise you make when you want to interrupt politely. The name above his pocket was Sergeant Ethridge, which sounded Episcopalian enough.

"Sorry to butt in, Mrs. Lamport," he said.

"Perfectly all right, Ben. Won't you join us?"

"Well, thanks, but I better not. What I wanted to say was that I happened to hear over the radio the captain's headed this way."

"And no doubt he would wonder what a yellow Volkswagen was doing parked in the middle of Mass. Ave.? As well he should. That's what captains are for, poor souls."

The sauna ought to be a good place to read, but it isn't. After ten minutes or so, for some reason, mental meltdown happens to the point where I can't concentrate enough to follow Mother Goose, or even the *Boston Herald*.

But ten minutes had been plenty of time to absorb the *Cambridge Daily Banner*. It was every bit as flyweight as I remembered, full of semiliterate syndicated gruel and local mush that was even less literate. Its guiding editorial principle seemed to be to load as many local names as possible into as many short articles as they could fit between the ads. There was no good reason that I could see to read the *Banner*, but then there's no good reason to bite your nails, and look how many people do it anyway. Like most papers in America, the *Banner* was just an irritating habit.

8

Not being a native of Cambridge, it was a habit I had never picked up. I had tried to read the paper a few times back in the early 1980s, when I was new to the area. It wasn't much good then, and I couldn't see that it had gotten either better or worse since. I set the paper aside on the bench of the sauna. The pages were lumpy where my sweat had dripped and dried.

Even though the season was over, half a dozen other wrestlers were in the Malkin Athletic Center sauna with me, kids on the Harvard team. We had been horsing around for an hour or so, staying in shape. I helped the coaching staff in season and out, in return for gym privileges and the chance to keep my own skills alive. I had been way above the Harvard level of wrestling in my day, but that was back in the late 1970s. I could still keep ahead of even the best Harvard kids, but now I had to rely on skill and experience to do it, instead of speed and strength.

"The hell you reading the *Bummer* for?" Tony Mastrangelo asked. "You out of toilet paper?"

Tony was a 160-pound sophomore who would be a pretty fair wrestler in a couple of years if he worked at it. He had the Boston area accent, but my ear wasn't good enough to make distinctions beyond that.

"How do you know to call it the *Bummer?*" I asked. "You from Cambridge?"

"Just across the line in Somerville. We take the *Bummer*, though."

"You ever read it?"

"Ann Landers. High school sports. That's about it."

"What do you think about this new guy that took it over?"

"Did some new guy take it over?"

"Last year. Where were you?"

"Hey, it wasn't in Ann Landers, okay?"

Tony Mastrangelo didn't sound any more enthusiastic

about the *Banner* than I was, even though he was a local boy. I wondered what made it worth an obscene amount of money to Thurman Boucher or anyone else.

When you live alone and don't have a job, it's easy to let go. Why get up with the sun, or even at all? If you do bother to get up, why bother to shower? Or shave? Why get out clean clothes? Why not just slip into some old sweats? Why wear shoes you have to shine? Who cares?

Nobody, unless I do. So there I was the next morning, rubbing Meltonian Cream into my loafers and taking a fresh pair of gray flannel slacks out of the dry cleaner's plastic bag, like some idiot Brit dressing for dinner in the jungle. Except at least the Brit could say he was setting an example for the natives and the only one I was trying to fool was myself. Sometimes it even worked, the same way you can sometimes trick yourself out of the blues by smiling. My theory on dressing was that if I wrapped the package neatly enough, maybe there would turn out to be something inside after all.

The phone rang, which seldom happened before breakfast. The number was unlisted, and under another name. Even information didn't know where to find Tom Bethany. So usually it would have been a wrong number, but this time it was Felicia.

"Are you dressed?" she asked, without even saying hello.

"Pretty near," I said. "Why?"

"I just got a call from Linda Cushing's maid asking what to do. Evidently Linda always leaves her bedroom door open a crack, but now it's locked from the inside and she doesn't answer."

"She should call the police."

"We don't know what's happened, Tom. Linda might not even be in there."

"What do you have in mind, then?" I asked, although of course I knew. She wouldn't be calling me just for advice.

"I've known Linda for years and her mother before her," Felicia said. "I've been dropping by most days for a visit, which is why Josephine thought to call me. Linda has been feeling terribly low, but she didn't strike me as suicidal. She even seemed pleased about something yesterday. I think we ought to find out exactly what's going on before we involve the police."

"We?"

"Of course, we. You don't expect someone my age to go around breaking down doors, do you?"

Josephine met us on the front porch of a large three-story house on Wendell Street. Behind her the old oak door and its big brass knocker had the soft shine that things get when you rub and polish them regularly for a lifetime or so. Josephine was a small black woman in her sixties. "I tried again just now, Mrs. Lamport," she said. "I still couldn't raise her." Her voice was steady, although her hands were working as if she were trying to wring her apron dry.

"You'd better show us up, Josephine," Felicia said.

Mrs. Cushing's bedroom was on the second floor. The door looked nearly as solid as the one downstairs. "Can you break it down?" Felicia asked me. I liked it that she didn't bother to holler through the door or knock on it, that she took Josephine's word for it that anything necessary along those lines had already been done. The knob turned, but the door didn't budge.

I gave it the shoulder and nearly lost my footing when the door swung open. The shades were down, but I could see a bed on the far side, with a shape in it. "Mrs. Cushing?" I said, but there wasn't any answer. I turned on the light.

"Lord God!" Josephine said behind me.

The woman's hands were crossed peacefully on a flowered

coverlet. Her upper body leaned against a backrest with cushioned arms. She might have fallen asleep reading in bed, except that a clear plastic bag covered her head. And the book lying facedown beside her was called *Final Exit*.

The bag was fastened around her neck with a rubber band. Moisture had condensed on the inside of the plastic, so that her features were blurred. Curls of damp hair stuck to the inner surface of the plastic. She was a small woman who seemed to be in her late forties or early fifties. Her eyes were closed and her mouth had fallen open.

Felicia picked up one of the crossed hands and then gently replaced it. "Cold," she said. "Poor thing."

She looked at Josephine, who was standing just inside the door. "We should call Serena," she said. "Would you do that, Josephine? No, I suppose I should. Do you have her number?"

"I called her before I called you," the maid said. "Nobody answered."

"So you did, and that's why you called me. I should have remembered. Well, we'll try again in a little bit."

"Who's Serena?" I asked.

"Linda's daughter. She's at Tufts Medical School, which is probably why she doesn't answer. Medical students are always off doing something or other."

Felicia picked up a glass from the bedside table and sniffed at it. "What would you say?" she asked, handing it to me to smell. "Whiskey?"

"I don't know," I said. "Something alcoholic, but I can't tell beyond that." The residue was tea-colored.

"Well, I don't suppose it really matters," Felicia said. "Let's look through the wastebaskets."

Only a couple of wadded-up tissues were in the one beside the bed, but the bottom of the one in the adjoining bathroom was covered with empty orange capsules. There was an empty pill bottle on the sink, with its childproof cap lying beside it. The name on the label said the prescription was for Michael Cushing. "What's secobarbital?" I asked.

"Seconal," Felicia said. "Sleeping pills. Those look like the hundred-milligram size. Is that what the label says?"

"That's it. The prescription was filled three years ago."

"Three years wouldn't affect potency much. The rule of thumb is to add ten percent to the dosage if they're more than five years old."

"Why would she have emptied out the capsules?"

"It speeds up the absorption. In addition to which, it's customary to dissolve the powder in alcohol. Alcohol can increase the potency of the drug by as much as fifty percent."

"You seem to know a lot about this stuff, Felicia."

"I should. The bishop and I have been members of the Hemlock Society for years."

"She just followed the instructions in her book, then?"

"So it would appear."

"Why would she commit suicide?"

"Who said she did?"

"You just did."

"I didn't at all. What I said was, 'So it would appear.' "

"Where are you going with this, Felicia?"

"Possibly nowhere. But I just find it curious that there doesn't seem to be any note."

"Not everybody leaves notes."

"True, but as you say, she apparently went by the book. In fact the book was right beside her, just to drive the point home. But the book says over and over again that you must always leave a note."

"Why?"

"In part to warn medical personnel not to attempt to revive you, but principally to ease the pain for family and friends."

"You're reading a lot into this note business, Felicia."

"I've known Linda since she was a little girl. She was the

kind of child who never colored outside the lines. And she would agonize for days over the thought that she might have inadvertently hurt some other little girl's feelings."

"She couldn't have been worried about hurting other people's feelings this time. Suicide itself is kind of selfish."

"Exactly," Felicia said. "And Linda was thoughtful. And don't you think she looks a little bit *too* peaceful?"

"She took sleeping pills. Wouldn't she have just dropped off to sleep?"

"Possibly. Possibly not. Frequently at the end there's a reflex attempt to tear the bag off. Not long ago in Connecticut a man's son had to hold the bag on before his father's second attempt was successful."

"Are you going to tell all this to the police?"

"Do you think I should?"

"I don't think it matters. I don't think they'd pay any attention to you anyway."

"Well, then, what's the use? And I could be wrong, of course. But it wouldn't be hard to force Seconal down a woman and then put a bag over her head once she fell asleep."

"Josephine," I said, "did you hear anyone or see anything last night?"

"I only come in days."

"Were any doors open?"

"No, sir. Everything tight the way I left it."

"When did you go?"

"After I done the dishes. Seven-thirty, right around in there."

"Somebody could have come by after that," Felicia said.

"She wouldn't have let in nobody she didn't know."

"How about the daughter?" I asked. "She live here?"

"Serena has her own apartment in Medford," Felicia said.

"So basically anybody could have come in," I said. "Anybody she knew, anybody who could get her to open the door so he could push in. Presumably the front door has a spring lock?"

"It locks by itself when you go out," Josephine said. "If that's what a spring lock is."

"Who would have wanted to do it, though?" I said. "Did she have enemies?"

"Thurman Boucher," Felicia said. "He promised to keep all her old employees on at the paper and then fired half of them."

"That's what these guys do, Felicia. Doesn't make him a murderer."

"Somehow he's behind it."

"He's got the paper. He's fired the people. He's won the war. Are you saying he's going around the battlefield shooting the wounded?"

"I'm sure it's exactly the sort of thing he would do."

"It's a pretty long jump from *would* to *did*. We don't even know if anybody did anything. All the actual evidence points to suicide."

"Yes, it does. I'm sure if I mentioned murder to the police they'd just laugh."

"Probably not out loud."

It would take a braver life-form than a Cambridge cop to laugh at Felicia. More likely they'd nod and pretend to take notes, and then forget about it. The deceased was under treatment for depression. If she was acting out of character, why not? Suicide itself was out of character. For the police, the shortest and easiest distance between two points was going to be to write the thing off as a suicide.

I couldn't think of any reason why I needed to stay around till the cops came. I don't like my name to be in any police files or any other government files. Besides, I had nothing to add to what Felicia and Josephine could tell the police. "I think I'll take off and leave the rest to you," I said to them. "I'd appreciate it if you wouldn't tell them I was here unless they ask."

"Why would they ask?" Felicia said.

"Good point. Don't ask, don't tell."

On my way home I detoured down Brattle Street to buy a copy of *Final Exit* from Wordsworth Books. It was a short book with big print, and in an hour I had gone through every word. Sure enough, Linda Cushing had followed directions like a good little girl—except for failing to leave a note.

Felicia was right. It was odd. I was right, too. Nobody but her would believe it was murder. And so far, that included me.

2

THE *BOSTON GLOBE* CARRIED A FIVE-inch obituary of Linda Cushing the next day. She had "attended" Tufts, which probably meant that she quit to get married. She had been active in various Catholic women's organizations and Cambridge charities. Her daughter, Serena, had graduated from Harvard and was a student at Tufts Medical School. Mostly, though, Linda Cushing had been the widow of deceased newspaper publisher Michael Cushing. Plainly that was the only thing in her life that made her death even marginally newsworthy to the *Globe*.

The *Daily Banner* did better by her, of course. The story was on the bottom of the front page, below the fold, and it was continued inside. Still, there weren't very many more details of Linda Cushing's life than the *Globe* had run. The story was padded out with quotes from family friends, Cambridge politicians, and *Banner* executives. One was from the paper's new publisher, Thurman Boucher. "Linda Cushing was a lady with a penetrating mind and a great sense of humor," he said. "She was a tough negotiator with one of the keenest business minds I've ever encountered. I was fortunate enough to come to know her very well before her untimely death. The Cambridge newspaper world will miss her."

There were studio shots of Mrs. Cushing and her late husband, who looked as if he would have died of a coronary if that Polish sausage hadn't got him first. He had the kind of fleshy face, smiling but not really humorous, that you'd expect to see sticking out of a coonskin coat at a Holy Cross game. Linda Cushing had the sort of face that English has no word for—not a pretty face, but an attractive one, as alert and curious as a monkey's. The French call it *jolie-laide*—ugly-pretty.

Another picture showed her in profile, a standard grip-and-grin shot of her shaking hands with the man who had just bought her out, Thurman Boucher. He towered over her. Boucher was bending slightly toward her, as though she were saying something he didn't want to miss. His head was smooth and sleek like an otter's, with dark hair slicked back straight.

The story said the body had been discovered by Josephine Burton, an employee of the deceased, and a family friend named Alicia Lambert. To be fair, the police were probably the ones who got Felicia's name wrong. The reporter had probably just copied it from the réport. Linda Cushing's death was presumed to be suicide, since a manual on self-deliverance was found near the body. Death was by an overdose of sleeping pills, combined with alcohol. The patient had been under psychiatric treatment for several months.

The story gave the time and place of the funeral services. I had no plans to go. I didn't even know the woman, not that I would have gone anyway. I wouldn't go to my own mother's funeral, and didn't. I hate funerals. I even hated my father's, not that my heart was exactly broken. But I hated to see him go before I got big enough to whip his ass.

And so my life went on.

Poking around in Widener Library. I've been making endless notes for a book that would lay out a unified field theory of political economy. This is the literary equivalent of working on a perpetual motion machine, and should keep me harmlessly occupied till I die. At least that's the way it worked for Henry George, although he missed the whole point when he started actually writing stuff down. The idea of grandiose literary ambitions isn't to do work, but to put it off indefinitely.

Rowing. I had just taken up sculling that spring, partly because I got clubbed on one heel a while ago, and it gives me trouble running. But mostly because Hope Edwards, my long-distance friend and lover for all these years, is an expert oarswoman. If I can learn the sport well enough, we can row together whenever she's in Cambridge or I'm in Washington.

Nerding. The information superhighway is sucking me in slowly. I found a wrestling bulletin board a few months ago, and I'm gradually moving on from there.

Hanging out. There may be better places to watch the freak show of life than Cambridge, but I don't know them. For sheer weirdness, day in and day out, Harvard Square beats the bar scene in *Star Wars*. As does the Harvard faculty club, where I drop in most days after lunch to skim the out-of-town papers. Nobody's ever thought to ask whether I was a member, which is another reason why I dress up a little.

So with one thing and another, weeks passed without my giving a serious thought to Linda Cushing, Thurman Boucher, or the *Cambridge Daily Banner*. Then one day an odd piece of mail showed up in my box at the Brattle Street post office. Odd for me, anyway. It was one of those squarish envelopes, smaller than a greeting card. The paper was ivory-colored and heavy. It was addressed by hand, in what looked like real ink.

Inside was a stiff card with "Felicia Lamport" at the top, engraved or embossed or whatever it is. The kind of printing that's raised, anyway. "Dinner Tuesday at eight, 2 Bond Street. You'll come, of course?" was the message.

Well, of course.

Two Bond Street was Felicia's home. It was a warm June evening, so I wore an open shirt under my seersucker jacket. I had a tie in my pocket, just in case. I had only met the bishop twice, and I didn't know whether a tie was in order or not. Hard to tell with bishops, since they don't wear the things themselves, even in church. Josephine Burton met me at the door, which threw me off for a moment. I connected her with answering doors, all right, but not this one.

"You're working for Mrs. Lamport now?" I said.

"Yes, sir," she said. "The Cushing house is mostly closed."

"So of course I hired Josephine instantly," said Felicia, who had appeared behind Josephine.

The battle for domestic help is ruthless in Cambridge, even though there's plenty of unemployment in the area. We lap up the most degrading abuse at home or at the office or shop or behind the counter at Burger King, but as good Americans we're far too proud to work in somebody else's house.

"Where's the bishop?" I asked.

"Oh, he's helping out at the shelter tonight. This isn't going to be his sort of group."

"Whose sort of group is it going to be?" Over her shoulder, I could see four places set at the dinner table.

"Your sort of group."

Then the doorbell rang behind me, and Josephine opened the door for two young women. "I don't believe you know Serena Cushing," Felicia said. "Serena, this is Tom Bethany."

She took after her father, unfortunately. His kind of large frame and fleshy face worked better for a man than for a woman. The joviality in Michael Cushing's newspaper photo had seemed a little false, but there wasn't even any false good humor in Serena's face. She was all-business. I couldn't imagine her going to a Holy Cross game, or bolting a Polish sausage.

"Of course you know Gladys Williams," Felicia said. I've known Gladys ever since she was a lab technician for the Cambridge Police Department. I'm the one who introduced her to Felicia.

"How come you got roped into this deal, Gladys?" I asked.

"Well, don't you see?" Felicia said. "Gladys and Serena are both medical students at Tufts."

"So you thought Gladys should drop by in case we needed a fourth for bridge?"

"I'm here to make sure you do the right thing, Bethany," Gladys said.

"I was afraid of that."

"It's for your own good, Bethany," Gladys said. "You vill enchoy zee ride ass long as you close your eyes, fasten your zeet belts, und do *eggzactly* ass you are toldt!"

It was the punch line from an old joke about a Lufthansa stewardess. I had told it to Gladys years before, since it summed up her relationship with the procession of men in her life.

"Come on, Tom," Felicia said. "Let's sit down and have a drink before dinner."

I had an India Pale Ale, which Felicia knew I drank. She and Gladys had wine. Serena had a bottle of some kind of two-dollar water, which actually made a certain amount of sense in Cambridge. The city water tastes like the runoff from Rocky Flats.

"I'd feel like I was being manipulated, except that probably isn't the exact right word," I said to Felicia. "Can you be manipulated by a bulldozer?"

"I'm the executor of Linda Cushing's estate," she said. "I'm just fulfilling my legal obligations."

"I see a couple of medical students and a poet here. I don't see any lawyer."

"Well, of course not. Lawyers always have these ridiculous objections to practically anything sensible. Except of course for your very sensible lady friend, Mrs. Edwards."

"I'm surprised you didn't drag Hope into this while you were at it," I said. Felicia and Gladys were two of the people I was fondest of in the world, and Felicia might as well have gone all the way by flying my long-term lover up from Washington.

"Oh, she's in it," Felicia said. "Hope found a broker for you to talk to."

"Broker?" My only investments were in bonds that I buy directly from the U.S. Treasury. You can't go wrong loaning your money to the guys that print the stuff.

"A newspaper broker."

"What for?"

"I told you weeks ago, Tom. I want you to get Linda Cushing's paper away from Thurman Boucher."

"That's ridiculous."

"Not at all. It's right up your alley."

"What do you expect me to do?"

"I don't know. It isn't up *my* alley, after all. I *can* provide any necessary funds, though. Apparently as executor I have the authority to do that, acting in Serena's best interests."

"She's in medical school. How is it in your best interests, Serena? If you bought back the paper you'd have to run the damned thing. Is that what you want?"

"Nothing would interest me less."

"Well, then?"

"Conversely, nothing would interest me more than getting it away from Thurman Boucher."

"Why?"

"I hold him responsible for my mother's death."

"Is this based on your theory, Felicia? That it was murder because there was no note?"

"I think Serena will tell you it was murder either way."

I turned to Serena.

"Mother wasn't a suicidal person before," Serena said. "If she killed herself, it was because of the way that man treated her. And if she was killed by a burglar, he would hardly have bothered to make it look like suicide. Boucher, on the other hand, would have been fully capable of such a thing."

"Why would he have wanted her dead, though? He already had the paper."

"I don't know, but I'd like to."

"Let's assume suicide, then. What did Boucher do to your mother that would have made her want to kill herself?"

"I don't really know that, either. It may have been what he did to other people."

"Which was what?"

"Firing all the people he did. Particularly Jonathan Paul. He was Dad's managing editor, and part of the sales agreement was that Boucher was supposed to keep him on."

"Poor Jonathan also carried a torch for your mother," Felicia said.

"He did?" Serena said. "I never knew that."

"Of course you didn't, Serena dear. Children never know anything about their parents."

"Did Mother know?"

"Oh, she knew. Why do you suppose she always referred to poor Jonathan as poor Jonathan?"

"Well, then, after Dad died, why didn't she, why didn't the two of them . . ."

Serena looked embarrassed, the way a lot of people seem

to get at any suggestion that their parents are capable of sexual intercourse. In my family we knew better, because the old man used to make a drunken point of leaving the door open. Not that we wouldn't have known anyway. With eight kids and two grown-ups jammed into a double-wide, there are no secrets.

"That I *don't* know," Felicia said. "I thought they might get together after your father's accident, actually. Jonathan was much more your mother's type than your father ever was." This time Serena frowned slightly, considering the matter. It had probably never struck her that her mother had a type.

"It's hard to imagine anybody killing themselves because somebody else got fired," I said.

"That's true," Felicia answered. "I just hold it out as an observed fact that Linda didn't seem particularly disturbed over selling the *Banner*, but she became severely depressed later. And that was after Boucher fired something like a third of the old staff. Including Jonathan Paul."

"Suicidally depressed?" I asked.

"I wouldn't have thought so, but her therapist might be able to tell you."

"Only probably he wouldn't," I said.

"She," Gladys said. "Dr. Elizabeth Estabrook. She lectures at Tufts. I took a course with her last semester."

"This is getting pretty incestuous.'"

"I was in the same course," Serena Cushing said. "Actually, I was the one who suggested that Mother see Dr. Estabrook."

"She can talk to you tomorrow afternoon," Gladys said. "She has a cancellation at four o'clock."

"So far you've got me fixed up with a shrink and a newspaper broker," I said. "Not bad, considering I haven't even said yes yet."

"You're fixed up with Jonathan Paul, too," Felicia said.

24

"His paper comes out on Thursdays, today, so he's free to see you pretty much anytime tomorrow."

"What paper? I thought he was fired."

"He started up one of those little papers they distribute free. Shoppers, they're apparently called. He's been doing reasonably well with it, according to what Linda told me."

"There's a big hole in the middle of this whole business," I said. "First of all, Mrs. Cushing is dead, probably a suicide."

"Probably," Felicia agreed.

"But we don't really know that."

"No, we don't."

"She had a lot of money, which she got from selling the paper. Presumably that money goes to you, Serena?"

Serena nodded.

"So now you have a big pile of money instead of a newspaper you didn't want anyway. People lost their jobs at the paper, but the chances are most of them found new ones. This Jonathan Paul seems to be doing all right, anyway."

"True," Felicia said.

"And yet you're willing to spend a lot of time and money investigating what seems to be a pretty normal business situation. Maybe even a pretty normal suicide. Most widows don't kill themselves after their husbands die, but some of them do."

"That's true, too."

"Why not just put it behind you, then?"

"Because we all think the same thing Serena thinks," Felicia said. "We don't know why or how he did it, but we believe this fellow Boucher is somehow responsible for her mother's death."

"And we know Mother wanted to get the *Banner* back so Jonathan Paul could run it as he was supposed to under the terms of the sale," Serena said.

"How do you know she wanted that?"

"She talked about it constantly," Serena said. "She even

made an offer to Boucher to repurchase the paper, although of course he laughed at her."

"So I'm merely trying to carry out the wishes of the deceased," Felicia said. "In my capacity as executor."

"Will you at least look into it?" Serena said.

"Do I have a choice?"

"None at all," Gladys said.

"She's right, Tom, you know she is," said Felicia. "Come on, then, let's go in to dinner."

3

IN THE 1980 CAMPAIGN I WORKED FOR both Kennedy and Carter. One of the things presidential candidates do is talk to editorial boards, so I've been to lots of newspaper offices, from big to pretty small. But none of them was as small as the *Cambridge Trader*.

It was part of the storeroom behind a drugstore near Central Square. One end was still piled with cartons of Pampers and Prell and Arrid. The other end had been cleared to make room for a collection of unmatched tables and desks and folding chairs. Old Macintoshes and recycled telephones sat on the desks, all linked into a web of wires and cables lying on the concrete floor. Big fluorescent lights hung from the ceiling on chains. The walls were unpainted cinder block. There were no windows.

Jonathan Paul saw me picking my way through the wires and got up from his computer. He was a lean man of middle height, with a head of curly hair so snowy white that it must have been red to start with. He looked to be in his middle fifties, probably a few years older than Mrs. Cushing.

"Mr. Bethany?" he said.

"Tom."

"Jonathan Paul, Tom. Let's go into my so-called office, where we can talk."

He led me back to the door I had just come in, and hollered to his staff to take his calls. The two men and one woman were talking into their phones. All three waved their hands, not bothering to look up.

"We can be private out here unless Doc Pritchard makes somebody wait for their prescription," Paul said, waving me to sit down on the bench in front of the pharmacist's enclosure. He took a seat beside me. "Serena tells me you're an investigator," he said.

"Not really," I said. "I'm kind of looking into things for her and the estate, but I don't have any kind of license. I'm retired, actually. Used to work for the government."

That was true enough. I spent three years in the army, and three more flying for Air America in Laos. Air America qualified as the government because it was a CIA front.

"Well, I'll help you any way I can," the editor said. "You come from Felicia and Serena, and that's good enough for me. What do you need to know?"

"A bunch of things that may not seem to be right to the point," I said. "So I better tell you what the point is. They want me to figure out some way to get the *Banner* back from Boucher."

"Serena wants to run it?"

"She wants you to run it. As far as the thinking goes now, the idea would be for you to buy it from her with her own money and pay her back out of profits."

"That's very generous, but Boucher's not going to sell it, believe me."

"Well, you never know. A man can change his mind

about just about anything, if you pound his ass deep enough into a crack."

"How do you plan to do that?"

"No idea. I'm just poking around kind of at random, hoping something will turn up. Tell me how Boucher came to fire you."

"He brought in a hatchet man from one of his other papers. Alan Fogel was the guy's name, supposed to be my deputy. But he reported directly to Boucher. Boucher would tell Fogel what I was supposed to do, and Fogel would tell me. Some deputy, huh?"

"I can see the problem, all right."

"So it's three weeks after the takeover, and this young hotshot comes in and tells me I'm supposed to fire two of my reporters. Christ, I only had four left by then. In I go to Boucher and tell him you can't put out a newspaper with two reporters, and Boucher says sure you can, I only got one and a half reporters at my paper in Middletown. I didn't even want to ask the son of a bitch what half-a-reporter might be."

"I was wondering myself."

"We'll never know, because he fired me on the spot."

"What about the sales contract with Mrs. Cushing?"

"Oh, sure. You can't fire me, I say. See? It's right there in the contract. Boucher says that's what contracts are for, to be broken. You don't like it, go hire a lawyer."

"Did you?"

"I talked to one. He said eventually we might win some kind of a settlement, but Boucher's attorneys could drag it out so long that legal fees would eat it all up. So I said the hell with it. Took out a home equity loan, hired the two reporters I wouldn't fire, and started this up. Later I hired Marie over there, too."

"How's it going?"

"Okay, actually. Everybody does everything. Answers the phone, takes pictures, sells ads, so it works."

"You use Macs, I see. Me, too. I do a little desktop publishing myself." It was publishing of a kind, anyway. Mostly fake ID.

"Then you know what these things are capable of. It's amazing what you can do these days. For a little less than fifteen thousand, mostly used stuff from the Boston Computer Exchange, I've got the equivalent of what used to be the whole back shop. Typesetters, compositors, everything. We write practically the whole paper, make up the pages, set type. Just the four of us, sitting in front of secondhand Macs. Everything else we job out, not that there's much else. Printing, distribution—that's about it."

"Making money?"

"Starting to. We're all from Cambridge, which is more than those bastards Boucher and Fogel can say. So we lean on the hometown angle pretty hard when we sell ads or go out on stories. We're not taking much in the way of salaries, and expenses are cut to the bone. So yeah, we're making a tiny bit of money. Next year it should be a living wage for everybody, and maybe enough left over so I can start paying my loan back to myself. It's driving that goddamned Boucher crazy."

"Why would he care? It sounds like so far you're barely in the black."

"From his point of view it doesn't matter whether we're in the red or the black. As far as he's concerned, a lot of our gross comes straight out of his pocket."

"Oh, yeah? How's that?"

"In a market this size, a good many of your ads are bought by relatively small businesses. They've only got a certain amount budgeted for advertising. If they drop a hundred dollars with us, that's a hundred dollars they can't spend with the *Banner*. So in a way Mr. Boucher is still paying our salaries. At least they come out of his pocket. I like that idea, frankly."

"You seem to be having a good time."

"I am. Tell you the truth, I never wanted to be a publisher. Let the Cushings have the headaches, was my theory. I went to work for Mike Cushing's father right out of the army, and I figured that was it. Stay on the *Banner* payroll till it's time for the gold watch and they wheel me out. But I'm liking it, actually. Putting something together and trying to make it run."

"And maybe you can drive your buddy out of town, huh?"

"Not a chance. It's practically impossible to knock off an established daily, no matter how bad it is. I might be able to pick up a living from what drops off his table, but that's about it."

"Tell me about Boucher."

"He's a mean, lying son of a bitch. One of the young reporters said he'd have to improve to suck."

"Is he smart?"

"He certainly makes money, but anybody could make money if his old man left him a bunch of newspapers. The only trick is to keep costs down, and you don't have to be smart to squeeze a nickel till the Indian hollers."

"A lot of people don't mind hurting Indians, but they don't have his kind of money."

"Well, that's true. He built a big chain from three small papers, so I guess he's good at getting money out of the bankers. But does that mean you're smart? Most of the bankers I know are dumb as stumps."

"Not so dumb they'd give *me* money," I said. "I don't know about you."

"Fair enough. They wouldn't give any to me, either, not until I put my house up as collateral. I don't mean to say Boucher's an idiot, because he's not. And certainly he's got a lot of energy, I'll give him that. He's mean, he's hungry, he's a natural-born liar, he'll run over anybody to win. Does that add up to smart?"

"In some circles. Was Michael Cushing smart?"

"No, you couldn't say that. He just stood off to one side and let the place run itself. He was smart enough to let himself be argued out of most of his bad ideas, but that was about it."

"Did you like him?"

"There wasn't anything about him not to like. Why?"

"I don't know. I'm just trying to read myself in on the whole situation. Did the guy even come into the office?"

"Oh, absolutely. He took long lunches and left early, but he wasn't an absentee owner."

"What did he do all day if he didn't run the place?"

"He played publisher, the way Reagan played president. Talked to the Kiwanis. Gave out prizes at the schools on sports day. Served on committees. Went to publishers' conventions. Gave graduation speeches."

"Did Mrs. Cushing have much to do with the paper?"

"A fair amount, but not on the business or editorial side. She'd give a staff picnic on Labor Day weekend and a big Christmas Eve party. She sort of tried to make the paper into a family. Remembered birthdays, sent flowers if somebody was sick, visited them in the hospital. If somebody was in trouble, she always knew it somehow and tried to help. Just a lovely, lovely lady."

"You're not married yourself, are you?"

"Divorced, a long time ago."

"Yeah, I'm the same. Let me ask you something that you can tell me it's none of my business. But I'm curious. Somebody said you might have had a thing for her."

"Well, it isn't any of your business, but I had a great respect for Mrs. Cushing."

"Did she know it?"

"She was a married woman, and I respected that. She was very loyal to her husband, and I respected that, too. It was a happy marriage."

"What about smart? Was she smarter than him?"

"I don't understand what you're getting at. Why does it matter?"

"I don't mean to be offensive, Jonathan, but at this stage I've got to be nosy. I don't know yet what matters and what doesn't matter, so I'm asking questions about everything. If I'm supposed to be getting the paper back from Boucher, I need to know how he got it."

"I don't follow you."

"Let's take an extreme case. Suppose one party to a contract is mentally retarded and can't possibly understand the terms of the agreement. That party couldn't very well be giving his or her informed consent to a legal agreement, and so there might be wiggle room to get out of the contract."

"Mrs. Cushing was far from retarded. She was a very intelligent woman."

"More so than her husband?"

"My opinion, yes. Much more."

"How did she get along with Boucher?"

"Fine at first. While negotiations were going on."

"Didn't see through him, huh?"

"Oh, he can turn on the charm. It's like the man said. Even horseshit shines on the outside."

"Did the charm work? Did he get a pretty good deal out of her?"

"I thought he overpaid."

"Maybe Boucher was right then, what he said in the paper."

"Which was what?"

"That she was a tough negotiator with one of the keenest business minds he ever encountered."

"You've got to know Boucher's sense of humor, so-called.

He was really saying she was a total airhead who didn't know the first thing about business."

"She must have known something if she got him to overpay."

"He overpaid because other buyers were interested, and he was desperate to get the paper."

"Why?"

"He liked the idea of Cambridge. A lot of people do. Lowell, Longfellow. The Harvard mystique. They don't know the real Cambridge."

Paul waved toward the front of the drugstore. Through the windows you could see the marginal shops across the avenue, the blacks and Hispanics and homeless, the trash blowing in the wind. It wasn't Flint or Newark, but it wasn't Longfellow's Cambridge, either.

"You said Mrs. Cushing got along fine with Boucher before the sale. What happened after?"

"I guess I happened, in a sense. She heard about the bloodbath in the newsroom, and she came down in person to protest. She went into Boucher's office, what used to be her husband's office, and she came out ten minutes later. You could tell she had been crying. That son of a bitch made a widow cry."

"What did he say to make her cry?"

"She absolutely refused to speak about it. All she would say is she never dreamed there were people like him in the world."

"We were feeling our way toward the Thurman Boucher relationship," Dr. Elizabeth Estabrook said. "But very, very slowly. At the point we had reached in Mrs. Cushing's therapy, a good deal of trust had been established, but not total communication."

"Trust between Mrs. Cushing and you, that is?" I asked.

"Of course, what else? Oh, I see what you mean. No, not

between Mrs. Cushing and Mr. Boucher. There had been trust there, or so I gathered, but it all disappeared on Mrs. Cushing's part after the sale was concluded."

"Why?"

"We hadn't gotten any further than her public version, I'm afraid. According to that, she felt he had broken their agreement by firing several longtime employees of the paper."

There was no couch in Dr. Estabrook's office. Patients presumably sat in the armchair I was in. I couldn't decide whether the therapist herself sat at her desk across the room, or in the second armchair, where she was sitting for her meeting with me. Apart from the desk, her office was furnished like a living room. The desk didn't spoil the effect much. It was mahogany, with gracefully curved and carved legs. The writing surface was green leather. The inkstand was green, too. It was made out of some kind of polished stone supported on little bronze fish tails, with bronze dolphins rising up from the green surface at each corner. It was worth plenty. I knew because somebody in my apartment building gets a magazine called *Antiques,* and it winds up in the laundry room every month. *Antiques* doesn't give prices, not even in the ads. *Antiques* is not aimed at the sort of losers who have to buy their silver.

Dr. Estabrook's silver had certainly come down to her, probably over enough generations so you couldn't even make out the monograms anymore. The nineteenth-century paintings on the wall hadn't been bought from a gallery, either. The frames showed wear. A chip had been knocked off the base of the inkstand, too. They were old family pieces, not arranged by a decorator but just shoved in wherever they fit. The office itself was in what had been a bedroom or an upstairs sitting room in a large yellow house on Linnaean Street, only a few blocks from the Cushings' house. Speaking of people who had to buy their silver. Mike

Cushing's grandfather or great-grandfather would have been lucky to make it out of Ireland with a couple of iron spoons and a jackknife to eat peas with.

"Did you go to Tufts yourself?" I asked Dr. Estabrook.

"No, I just lecture there. I did my undergraduate work at Wellesley and my graduate work at Harvard. Why?"

"I just wondered if you had known Mrs. Cushing there." They were about the same age.

"No, and she only went to Tufts for a year or two, as I recall, before she left to get married. Serena, the daughter, was the Tufts connection. She's in one of my classes at the medical school there."

"So presumably you didn't know her late husband, either?"

"I'm afraid not."

"Did you like Linda Cushing?"

"What an odd question. Yes, I liked her. She had led a sheltered life in many ways, but she was bright and curious."

"Was she intelligent?"

"Now that's a distinctly odd question. Yes, she was intelligent. Why?"

"I was wondering how easy it might have been for Boucher to take advantage of her."

"Probably quite easy, but that doesn't mean she was unintelligent. Incompetent, perhaps, although not in the legal sense, I'm sure. Incompetent at business. I'm sure I'd be incompetent at business."

"My impression is that Mike Cushing wasn't too competent at it, either. And probably not too bright."

"I never knew her husband."

"What was the impression you got of him from Mrs. Cushing?"

"She seemed fond of him. Almost protective of him. Yes,

you may be right. There was a distinct suggestion that he needed taking care of."

"His managing editor felt that way, too. The best he could say for Cushing as a boss was that you could argue him out of his dumb ideas most of the time."

"And of course he drank."

"Is that right? Nobody mentioned that."

"Oh, yes. Mrs. Cushing felt guilty that she didn't go to the game with him the day he died. He didn't drink so much when she was around, and she thought he might not have had his accident if she had been there."

"Did she usually go to the games?"

"No, she didn't care for football."

"So normally he managed to get through a game without choking to death."

"Exactly what I pointed out to Linda, of course. But survivors tend to feel guilt whether it's logical or not. And of course she was disturbed as well."

"How disturbed?"

"In hindsight, she was obviously very disturbed. But it wasn't obvious to me, I'm sorry to say. It's always a shock to lose a husband, particularly when it's unexpected like that. But I thought her principal problem was normal grief, and that my primary role would be to guide her smoothly through the normal grieving process."

"People do kill themselves when they lose someone, though, don't they?"

"Not normally. And Linda didn't strike me as abnormal in this respect or any other. I thought she was fundamentally strong, resilient, emotionally balanced. I didn't think she'd have any unusual difficulty working through her grief. The marriage didn't seem to be a love made for the ages. In fact I thought she'd be likely to remarry after the mourning period."

"Jonathan Paul?"

"You know about him? Yes, I thought it was entirely possible. Emotionally it would have been a very healthy outcome. If she hadn't sold the paper, there would have been almost no disruption, either at the office or in her own life. They had known each other for years, and apparently liked and respected each other. The fit was ideal."

"Did she love him?"

"I doubt if she would have admitted it, even to herself. It would have been disloyal to her husband's memory. It would be an admission that perhaps she hadn't really loved him, or at least hadn't cared for him as much as she cared for somebody else. Mrs. Cushing was a very conventional woman, anxious to do the right thing."

"Felicia said so, too. Said she was the kind of little girl who never colored outside the lines."

"I'm sure she didn't. One day I mentioned how nice her hair looked, and asked what she used on it. Just conversation at the beginning of the hour. She said all she ever did to it was shampoo twice every morning with some shampoo or other. Why twice, I asked her. Because the directions say to repeat, she told me. I found that quite extraordinary. Apparently it never occurred to her to ask herself why a shampoo manufacturer would put that on the directions."

"In a sense," I said, "couldn't you call behavior like that, well . . . dumb?"

"I don't think one should confuse naïveté with stupidity. Linda Cushing had never led a particularly dangerous or complicated life. Her father was a purchasing agent for the city of Cambridge, and he was a good provider. She went to good, respectable schools. She married a respectable young man who was in line to inherit a newspaper. Obeying the rules had been a rewarding pattern of behavior throughout her whole life. In her environment, being naïve wasn't dumb at all. It was the intelligent thing to be."

"Looking back over it," I said, "do you think the relationship between the Cushings might have been deeper, closer, whatever . . . anyway, stronger than you thought? I'm still trying to get at why she might have killed herself."

"No, I don't. My impression was that their marriage had the force of habit and affection and convention, but not much more. His drinking wasn't a terrible problem, but it was a continual, low-level one. And that kind of thing wears away at a relationship. Where I saw the possibility of something deeper was with her friend Mr. Paul."

"What pointed to that?"

"Nothing overtly sexual or improper in any way, I don't mean that. Nor was it anything that she herself was aware of. But his name came up often in our sessions, almost always as a kind of moral and intellectual reference point. Jonathan thinks this, Jonathan would never do that, Jonathan always said this. I was struck by it, and I had intended to lead her further into it."

"If anything," I said, "that would give her a reason to live, not to die."

"That's right. Her husband was gone, but a man she looked up to was still around. Available, too."

"Very available," I said.

"Why do you say that?"

"I talked to him this morning. He thought Mrs. Cushing was wonderful."

"I believe she thought the same thing about him. She was very agitated when Thurman Boucher fired him. Our next session, she was in tears over it."

"It doesn't add up, though, does it?" I said. "Not as a reason to kill yourself, anyway. He may have lost his job, but so what? He could have found one, and in fact he did. Went out and made one for himself."

"True."

"Besides, she was a rich woman. They were in their forties and fifties, in good health. She could have bought another paper for him to run. Or they could have retired to Florida. Anything."

"Of course they could have."

"Where does that leave us, then? What broke her up so badly? Something about the sale of the paper, you think? Doesn't seem likely. You might kill yourself over a business deal if it wound up ruining you. This one didn't, though. There must have been something else involving Boucher."

"I have no idea what it could be," Dr. Estabrook said. "Certainly the whole Boucher relationship was a very painful subject for her, but the reason why hadn't come out yet. I imagine the only one who'd know would be Mr. Boucher himself. And I don't suppose he'd tell you."

"He might, if I asked him nice."

Issues of the *Banner* were on file right around the corner from my apartment, at the main branch of the Cambridge Public Library. Like most papers, the *Banner* treated its own affairs as top secret, so there wasn't a word about the sale of the paper to an out-of-town buyer until the deal was complete. Then there were big stories, but only in one issue of the paper. The coverage had the kind of phony completeness you find in a packet of press releases or a corporation's annual report. Like a puddle of piss on a flat rock, as the sainted LBJ used to say. Wide but not deep.

For instance, we readers were allowed to learn that Thurman Boucher was the president of the Boucher Group, Inc., which owned twenty-one dailies, eleven paid-circulation weeklies, and eighteen free-circulation shoppers. We did not learn how he got them, where they were, how much they were worth, what percentage of net they returned on gross, what their circulation was, what their idea of news was, whether they backed Clinton or Bush or Perot. The Boucher Group could have been a front for the Moonies or Lyndon LaRouche, for all anybody knew.

Nor did we learn what Boucher had paid for the *Cambridge Daily Banner*, or very much of what his plans were for it. And what little we did learn had turned out by now to be a lie anyway. "There will be continuity of management," Boucher was quoted as saying. "What attracted us to the *Banner* was that it was a strong, well-managed paper with a long tradition of service to the community. We would be crazy to meddle with a winning team."

We did learn, though, that Thurman Boucher and his wife, Alison, had moved to Cambridge, where they were looking forward to taking part in the social and intellectual life of the community. Alison was standing beside Thurman in one of the pictures. She looked as if she might have been a model, but not the Kate Moss sexless waif type. More like the ones who wear tweeds and cashmere in the Talbots catalog. Mrs. Boucher filled out a dress well enough, if not spectacularly.

The stories didn't say where the Bouchers had lived before, or what their local address was. I set aside the newspaper files and tried the *Editor & Publisher International Yearbook*, but it only gave an address in Brewster, New York, for the Boucher Group. Thurman Boucher didn't have a residential listing in Brewster, as I found out by dialing New York information from the pay phone at the library. If you've lived on the cheap most of your life, one of the little things you learn is that information calls are still free on pay phones. The company figures you're about to make a call at the special, jacked-up rates reserved for people too poor to have a phone.

Next I called Cambridge information and learned that Boucher had an unlisted number. He wasn't in the city directory, either, which isn't the phone book but a privately published list of names, occupations, addresses, and phone numbers. He probably hadn't been in town long enough to be listed. If I wanted to find out where he lived, I'd have to go to City Hall and search the voter rolls or the tax list. Or try to con the information out of the electric company.

Or I could just drive out to the *Banner* and follow Boucher home. I had a rough idea where the newspaper plant was, out in East Cambridge not too far from M.I.T. I called Jonathan Paul to find out Boucher's schedule. "The son of a bitch generally leaves the paper between five and six," Paul said. "Check the lot for a Rolls-Royce."

The *Banner* was in an area that was as close as Cambridge gets to industrial. Heavy equipment sat in storage yards behind Cyclone fencing. There were sign companies and print shops and warehouses and contractors' offices. There were one- and two-story buildings with uninformative company names on the signs outside, names that ended with *-oid* and *-ek* and *-um* and *-us*. Tomorrow's high-flying high-tech winners, maybe. And in fact the headquarters of Lotus Development Corporation was nearby, as encouragement to dreamers.

The *Banner* was in a distinctly low-tech two-story building made of cinder blocks painted light green a long time ago. Nobody had bothered to fill the gaps in the row of yews outside, where dogs had pissed their favorite plants to death. The yews that had managed to survive were untrimmed. Trash lay under the ragged hedge, and a plastic bag had snagged on a branch. The bag was already starting to tatter, and would probably be gone in a year or two.

At one end of the building were loading docks, with unmarked trucks pulled up to them. No one was near the trucks, and nobody came in and out of what looked like the front door. After a while it occurred to me that the front door had probably been a design error. The door that people actually used was probably around back, convenient to where they parked. So I went around to the rear, and sure enough, it wasn't long before I saw people going in and out of a rear door in the building.

A Rolls is one of the few cars I can identify with any accuracy. If it's got a six-inch statue of a winged lady on the hood, it's a Rolls. The gray one near the entrance had to be Boucher's, since you don't get as rich as him by paying the hired help enough to buy fancy cars. It was four-thirty, and I settled down to wait. At five-thirty I was still waiting. Plenty of people had come out, but none of them had gone near the Rolls-Royce. I decided the hell with it. I'd wander over and get behind the car so I could make out the plate number, and then get Boucher's address tomorrow from Motor Vehicles.

Once I had the number, though, the Rolls kept drawing me closer. It was an elegant, shiny toy. Inside, the steering wheel was covered with padded leather and the dashboard was bird's-eye maple. The trim, inside and outside, was stainless steel. The hood and fenders were dove gray, gleaming rich and soft. You could see right down into the finish, it almost seemed. I touched the surface.

"Hey, you!" somebody hollered. "Fuck you think you're doing?"

The smart thing would have been to wave and walk away, but all my conditioning went against that. I looked at the man, measuring. He went probably a hundred and sixty, twenty pounds less than me. An inch or two shorter. About the same age. Nose lopsided and face a little lumpy, partly from old acne scars and partly from hard wear.

Years ago, when I used to go to the fights around Boston, faces like that were common. You'd see them on a whole parade of Irish lightweights and welterweights and sometimes middleweights, men with pale scrawny legs and arms and sunken chests. They looked almost pathetic in their baggy trunks, with big gloves ballooning from the ends of those skinny, corded arms. If you didn't know better, you'd think they were human sacrifices, punching bags shoved out there for the slick, quick brown or black fighters to pound on. But often as not those wiry, mean Irish boys would take those beautiful brown boys right apart.

"Nice car," I said to the middleweight.

I used to wonder, watching those matches, whether I could handle a really good boxer. What you'd have to do, I'd figure, was go inside him, get in close. Probably take a shot or two on the way in, but from then on he'd have to play my game.

Of course the other option would be to stay out of this guy's reach, and just walk away. And on second thought, this seemed like the better way. I turned and headed back toward the street.

He didn't exactly run, but he did that quick shuffle that fighters do, and it carried him in front of me.

"Fuck you think you're going?" he said.

"Home."

His eyes flicked at something or somebody over my shoulder, and then came back to me. Not to my face, but to my midriff, so he could get an early hint of which way I was going to move. There wouldn't be any more bullshit or bluster from this guy. Next would come the sucker punch.

The left jab came so fast it was unexpected even though I expected it. But that wasn't the sucker punch and neither was the second jab that came practically the instant I had slipped the first. The sucker punch was the right cross that caught me as I was moving away from the second left. It felt like a rock hitting me on the cheekbone.

Go inside, get in close, was all I could think. I kept on going down and shot for his left knee, while another rock hit me on the side of the neck. From then on I had my hands on him and I was on automatic and there was nothing to it. He was on his belly and I had his arm jacked up behind him in a hammerlock just short of a fractured arm.

I wasn't hot because I hadn't been hot to start with, and his punches hadn't begun to hurt yet so there wasn't anything new to get hot about.

"Take it easy, champ," I said. "I didn't hurt the car."

"He's right, Terry," a voice said to the boxer.

And to me, "You can let him up now."

So I did, moving away from Terry quickly in case he wanted to keep going. The man who had come up behind me was Thurman Boucher, to judge by the newspaper pictures of him. He wore summerweight blue seersucker trousers with red suspenders and a white shirt open at the neck. His necktie was a yellow silk foulard, loosened. He carried his suit jacket slung over a shoulder.

Terry was on his feet by now, focused on me.

"What did you plan on doing if he had hurt the car?" Boucher asked his man.

"He'd be sorry he did, Mister T."

"Really?"

Boucher just let the word hang there, while he looked in an amused way at Terry.

"Fucker used a trick on me," the boxer said at last.

"His tricks seem to be better than yours."

So the boss had Terry backed into a corner and there was only one way out for him. Since I saw that, too, I was ready this time. I slipped the punch he threw and went for a wristlock on his other hand. I still wasn't hot about anything, so I didn't break the wrist. But I put him on his knees and made him holler.

"That does it, Terry," Boucher said. "Two strikes and you're out."

So I let go of Terry's wrist.

"Give me the keys, Terry. I'll drive myself home."

"You got it, Mister T," he said, handing over the keys. "I'll be by tomorrow, usual time."

"No, you're through."

"But Mr. T—"

"Through, Terry. Get off the property."

The boxer's mouth moved a little, as if he wanted to say something. But he didn't. He turned to go.

"He's right," I said to Boucher as Terry walked away. "Those are just tricks."

"Some tricks," Boucher said. "That's Terry Dineen. You know who he is?"

"No idea."

"He killed a man in the ring, in 1982."

My neck and the side of my face were starting to hurt now. "I believe it," I said. "He's a heavy thumper."

"What's your name?"

"Tom Bethany."

"Ever drive a Rolls, Tom?"

"No."

"Like to try?"

4

BACK HOME, I CALLED HOPE EDWARDS first thing. She was home, too, surprisingly enough. She ran the Washington office of the American Civil Liberties Union, which meant she had to go to a lot of political cocktail parties in the line of duty.

"Oh, my God," she said when I was finished telling her about the business with Terry Dineen and Boucher's job offer. "How do you get into these things, Bethany?"

"This is a joke, right? You and Felicia and Gladys triple-teamed me, is how I got into this particular thing. This particular thing was totally you guys' idea."

"The idea wasn't for you to get into a fight with some homicidal prize-fighter."

"Hey, he hit me first. A man's gotta do what a man's gotta do."

"Bethany, you are *so* full of shit!"

"He hit me damned hard, too. I was expecting sympathy from you, actually."

"Think of this as my way of showing it. Toughlove."

"Besides, it got me a job."

"I can't believe you're going to work for that creep as a driver."

"I'm going to be a security consultant, actually."

"You're going to drive his car, aren't you? Isn't that a driver?"

"Hey, Paul Newman is a driver. He used to drive Nissans at Lime Rock Park. Nobody looks down on him."

"You're not going to be driving a Nissan."

"Damned straight I'm not. It's a Rolls-Royce Silver Spur II four-door saloon. You could buy a whole fleet of brand-new Nissans for what a Silver Spur costs."

"How would you know what a brand-new Nissan costs? You never even got into the high four figures for any of your cars."

"Couple years ago I did. You think they were giving those '87 Subarus away?"

"Well, chauffeur's probably a shrewd career move for you, Bethany. It's a step up from being unemployed."

"You're not unemployed when you live off government bonds. You're an investor."

"Whatever. When do you start this foolishness with Boucher?"

"Foolishness? It gets me inside the guy's gates, doesn't it?"

"I know it does, but it just seems so peculiar. Anyway, when do you start?"

"Next week. I couldn't start this week, could I? I'm coming down to see your buddy the newspaper broker on Friday. You want to drive out with me and see him together? We could spend the night in Luray and then head down Skyline Drive."

She agreed that we could, which was one of the nice things about our lives now. For more than ten years we had had to see each other on the fly, so to speak, because we kept up the fiction that her husband didn't know about us. We knew about him, since he had confessed to Hope after the birth of their third child that he was homosexual. But he kept his love life secret for the sake of his career and the kids, and we did the same with ours. A couple of years back, though, circumstances forced us to admit to him what it turned out he had known all along. With the air finally cleared, Hope and I became able to get together on occasional weekends, and even vacations.

"We could have dinner Friday night at the Inn in Little Washington," she said. Little Washington was Washington, Virginia, as opposed to D.C. It had been nothing much but a road sign till some out-of-towners moved in and started up a four-star French restaurant years ago.

"Do they have coconut cream pie there?" I asked.

"I doubt it."

"I feel pretty strongly about coconut cream pie."

"I know you do. We could find a truck stop somewhere."

"No, it's all right, I'll eat at the Inn. But I won't like it."

The newspaper broker's name sounded like an address, Ellsworth Court. "They're both old Rappahannock County names," Hope told me on our way toward the foothills of the Blue Ridge Mountains. "He'll ask you to call him Elzee, but start out with Mister. He's so old he can still remember what manners were."

She knew him through her husband, Martin. His law firm, Skaggs Philpott and Templeman, had represented one side or the other in various deals brokered by Mr. Court.

The old man lived in Sperryville, which I had driven past lots of times before without noticing it. It lay off to the left of Route 211, a village of a few dozen houses. Hope guided me through Sperryville and out into the country just south of it. "Can't be too many newspapers to buy and sell out here," I said.

"There aren't any 'too many newspapers' anywhere, when you think about it," she said. "By the nature of them, they're scattered all over. So a newspaper broker can set up shop wherever he likes. Elzee never liked anywhere but home. Wait till you see his setup."

Ellsworth Court lived on top of a high hill, with a road of hammered red dirt leading up to it. There was a mailbox at the bottom, with a number but no name. Class is when you don't need to advertise.

On the way up we passed an elderly black man digging in a garden. He looked up and touched the brim of his cap. We passed an elderly white man trimming weeds in a culvert, and he looked up and touched the brim of his cap, too. A yellow dog lay in the roadway and kept on lying there while I steered around him. He opened his eyes for a minute and then, satisfied, closed them. The dog had the same sort of polite, dignified, slightly remote way about him that the two old men had.

The main building on top of the hill was a two-story house, not terribly big. Around it was a small barn, a garage, a couple of sheds, a stable, and a one-and-a-half-story house painted dark red that had probably been for a tenant farmer once. Two cars were parked on the grass in front of it. A little girl was watching us from a rope swing that hung from one of the branches of an old beech. Initials and names by the dozens were carved into the smooth gray bark.

"His office is out there in the little red house," Hope said, and we parked by the other two cars. Inside the door a very fat old woman in a flowered dress sat at a desk in the hallway, and made to get up when we came in.

"Don't you get up, Laura," said an old man who was standing in a doorway down the hall behind her. "I've already got up for the both of us." He was leaning on two canes.

"Come on in, Hope, so we can sit down before I fall

down," he said. "Mr. Bethany, sir, it's good to make your acquaintance. You arrive at my door with the best possible recommendation and, I might add, the most lovely one. How have you been keeping, Hope?"

"Very well, Elzee."

"The result of a clear conscience and clean living, I'm sure. Keep on that way, and the Lord will reward you by making you as old and useless as I am."

He had maneuvered himself in front of a heavy oak chair, and now lowered himself into it with the assistance of his two canes. "The only way I can get around anymore is in my car and my plane," he said. "You fly by any chance, Mr. Bethany?"

"I used to."

"What did you fly?"

"Mostly a Porter Pilatus. Piper Cubs a little bit."

"Bush flying, then?"

"Sort of. Laos and Alaska."

"I fly a Cessna twin myself. I can still manage the controls and my eyes are just barely good enough. Without the plane I'd have to retire and turn into a cabbage. Well, Laura will be bringing us in some coffee as soon as it's ready and meanwhile I'm at your disposal as regards our friend Mr. Boucher. What did you want to know?"

"Anything at all, Mr. Court."

"Elzee, please."

"Elzee, yes, sir. I'm Tom."

"Anything at all, Tom? May I ask whether this is in furtherance of any plans to buy properties from the Boucher Group or sell properties to it?"

"The people I represent hope to buy a property from it."

"I didn't know Mr. Boucher had anything for sale at the moment."

"I don't know that he does, either. We're just looking into the situation."

"If something does come on the market, I'd hope you'd let me know about it. Not to get the business, but simply because I like to keep informed. If you should decide you need a broker, I might be able to steer you to someone who's willing to touch Mr. Boucher with a ten-foot pole."

"But you wouldn't yourself?"

"No, sir, I would not."

"I'd be interested to know why that is."

"Well, Tom, Hope and Martin tell me you're to be trusted, and I know I can take their word to the bank. I believe they'll tell you that I have a certain reputation for discretion, too."

"They already have."

"Then we can both speak freely with each other. By that I don't mean that the information can never leave this room. Information isn't worth a thing if you can't use it when you need to. What I mean is that I am assuming that you will never tell anyone outside this room where that information came from. I don't care what happens to the particular gentleman we're discussing, but I don't want to find myself down in the mud wrestling around with a hog, at my age. You both get dirty, but the hog likes it."

"I don't mind getting dirty," I said. "But I'll be sure to keep you out of the mud."

"Fine. Then let me start by saying that the newspaper industry imagines that it is populated by gentlemen, which of course it is not. Still, there is a germ of truth to the notion. Taken as a group, publishers are no doubt ethically and morally superior to an equivalent number of time-share salesmen or television executives. But the average publisher would nonetheless skin his first-born son alive for an additional half a percent return on gross."

Laura came in with the coffee, breathing hard from all the walking. The old man took a cautious sip, and set it down to cool.

"Bearing in mind what sort of circles Mr. Boucher moves in, then," Mr. Court went on, "you will be interested to learn that his fellow publishers refer to Thurman Boucher as the Cobra."

"I can see it," I said. "That black hair all slicked down."

"It's not so much what he looks like," Ellsworth Court said. "It's what he acts like. He's the kind of creature that'll crawl into your house in the dark and bite you to death before you even know he's there. I'm speaking metaphorically, of course. It may not be literally true that he bites."

"What does he do instead?"

"You know much about the newspaper business, Tom?"

"Practically nothing."

"Well, then, you should understand that most communities large enough to support a daily paper have exactly that. One daily paper. And that includes some mighty big communities. For example Atlanta, Kansas City, New Orleans, Minneapolis, Newark, Memphis, St. Louis, Cleveland. Most of your other major cities are essentially single-paper towns, too. And practically all of your smaller communities are.

"That fact right there, that's what makes owning a newspaper one of the most profitable businesses a man can get into. The Gannett chain's paper in Burlington, Vermont, returns fifty percent on gross. It's in a classic clean market, which is what we call a market without any competition to speak of. Give a small-town monopoly paper to a cocker spaniel of ordinary intelligence and the poor, dumb brute could show a profit of twenty cents or more on every dollar that comes in. The only game in Las Vegas where the house keeps that much of the sucker's money is keno.

"Now I'm giving you the quick tour, Tom, so I'm simplifying a little bit, but what it shakes down to is that just about every little tiny rinky-dink daily in just about every little rinky-dink town in America is worth a million anyway, and generally a lot more. A whole lot more. A whole, whole lot more.

"You ever hear of Ordinary, Iowa? Well, it's between Cedar Rapids and Des Moines. Which is to say it's not exactly a major market area.

"Nonetheless, the paper there, the *Tribune*, went last year for eighteen million. Probably amazed the local folks, if any of them ever found out about the price. They wouldn't have dreamed it was worth that much. Partly because if the old owner was like a lot of small-town publishers, he probably did most of his banking somewhere else. The idea is to keep your advertisers from finding out how much you're taking out of the community.

"There aren't too many publishers like that fellow in Iowa left. Most of them sold out long ago to chains. There's fifteen hundred or so dailies in the country, fewer every year. Only a small percentage are independently owned. The rest belong to chains you most likely never heard of. You ever hear of Harte-Hanks Communications, for instance?"

"No."

"The Donrey Media Group? Freedom Newspapers? Howard Publications? Park Communications?"

"No."

"No reason you would have. They operate out of places like Ithaca, Fort Smith, Santa Ana, Campbell Hall—"

"Campbell Hall?"

"It's in upstate New York. Headquarters of the Ottaway Newspapers. They sold out to Dow Jones a few years back, if you can call it selling out. They wound up with forty-nine percent of Dow Jones and Co. Which already owned the biggest daily in the country. You know which one that is?"

"I know Dow Jones puts out the *Wall Street Journal*," I said. "It's the biggest one, is it?"

"Yes indeed, getting close to two million. But when it came time for that great big old fellow to hitch up to some little lady nobody ever heard of in Campbell Hall, New York, damned if it didn't turn out that each of them had to bring just about the same dowry to the wedding. Makes you think, doesn't it?"

"Yes, it does." And it did. It always seemed to me that anything that looked as cheap and shabby as most small-town papers must be just barely getting by.

"Now when a newspaper does come on the market," the broker went on, "it's generally two ways. The publisher passes the paper down to the next generation, and they all hate each other. So everybody cashes out and splits up the take. Or the second way is the paper winds up with the publisher's widow."

"Mrs. Cushing," I said.

"Yes, indeed, and the Mrs. Cushings are an endangered species. Since there's not very many independent papers left, there aren't very many widows, either. So a man that's real good at acquisitions, he's got to be real good at romancing widows, too."

"Still figuratively speaking?" I said.

"Most times. Generally it takes the form of telling her what a wonderful man her late husband was, and what a wonderful paper he ran, and how much it must have meant to the community, and what a tragedy it would be to have a legacy like that fall into insensitive, callous hands. Now, I wouldn't want to say a word against any of these other fellows that are trying to buy this wonderful paper, Miz Jones, but if what you want is continuity of management . . . Well, you see how it goes."

"Presumably Miz Jones will get those promises in writing, though," I said. "Mrs. Cushing did, anyway."

Felicia had got hold of the sales agreement for me, and the promises to keep Jonathan Paul on were perfectly plain.

"Spoken or written, a promise is no better than the man who makes it," Court said. "That's the big advantage a man like Boucher has. 'Without some dissimulation no business can be carried on at all.' The Earl of Chesterfield said that two hundred and fifty years ago, and it's still true. But you notice he said 'some dissimulation.' Even in business, most folks figure that a man who tells them a thing flat out or makes them a flat promise, the fellow probably sort of means it. Might not mean exactly what you thought he meant, might not mean every bit of what he said, might be holding something back, might change his mind someday. But he probably means at least something sort of like what he said, or anyway the man *believes* he means it.

"Not the Cobra, though. Boucher is a kind of animal that most people aren't ready for. He'll swear right to your face on the grave of his mother that black is white. He won't tell you it's gray, or it's going to turn white pretty quick. He'll tell you it's white right now, always has been and always will be, even though he knows it's black as the hinges of hell. And you're likely to believe it, too, because you're used to dealing with human beings in one form or another. You've never sat across the table from a cobra before."

"Certainly Mrs. Cushing never had," I said. "Boucher put it in writing that the managing editor would stay, and practically the first thing he did was fire the guy."

"I'm not surprised. Back in the silver-mining days in Colorado, whenever one of the miners was raised up to be pit boss he'd fire all the miners he used to work with and hire new ones. He didn't want anybody around that owed his job to somebody else. They called it 'weeding the mine.' Of course, contracts didn't enter into it in those days."

"Seems like they don't today, either," I said. "Boucher told the editor to see a lawyer if he didn't like it. He said any contract could be broken."

"Boucher's right, unless both sides have deep pockets that they want to dip into. Even then a contract doesn't mean a thing except what a judge says it means. And judges don't get onto the bench by way of Jacob's ladder, like angels of God descending from heaven to light the way for us poor heathen. A judge isn't a thing in the world but a lawyer that knew a governor."

Ellsworth Court remembered that there was a lawyer in the room and said, "Meaning no disrespect to your profession, my dear."

"Oh, I've known where judges come from for a long time," Hope said.

I said, "The editor that got fired was a guy named Jonathan Paul. He thought Boucher overpaid for the *Banner*."

"Very likely he did. He generally does."

"Why would he do that?"

"To be sure of getting the paper. More papers mean more power and prestige."

"Also mean more debt, wouldn't they? Particularly if you overpaid?"

"Debt doesn't mean anything to a man like him. He won't pay it back unless he has to. And if the whole house of cards ever collapses, he'll just walk away from it. Debt is only a promise, like any other promise. And his promises are worthless, as he in effect told your friend Mr. Paul."

"But then where would all that power and prestige be? He doesn't want the house of cards to fall down, does he?"

"No, and he doesn't believe it will. He believes he knows more about running a newspaper than the rest of humanity does. He believes he's able to take more money out of a property than anybody else could. Consequently what would be overpaying for you and me isn't overpaying for Thurman Boucher. Under his management genius, the paper will pay back its cost over time, no matter what lesser mortals may think."

"Will it?"

"Possibly, if the economy in general doesn't trip him up. He'll fire everybody he can and cut the wages of everybody else. He'll cut expenses to the bone, make the reporters use scrap paper instead of notebooks, make people turn in the old pencil stub if they want a new one . . ."

"Speaking figuratively, of course."

"Speaking literally. He's done both those things. Then he'll raise the price of the paper and bump up ad rates, preferably in ways that the customers won't notice."

"How could they not notice?"

"A lot of ways. You make your rate card so complicated that it looks like the advertiser is getting more for his money but he's actually getting less. You go from eight to nine columns on a page, say, but you still charge the same price per column inch. Or you shave a little off the size of the page itself. Or you run a big circulation drive and jack up your ad rates because now you're delivering to more homes."

"Well, aren't you?"

"For the moment, sure. But most of those people won't subscribe when the trial period is over."

"The advertisers are businessmen themselves, though. Wouldn't they catch on?"

"Some do, some don't. They're businessmen, but their business isn't newspapers. Besides, where could they go to sell their goods?"

"They could go to this fellow Jonathan Paul. He started a shopper on a shoestring."

"There's your problem right there, that shoestring. He might make Boucher bleed a little, but he won't kill him. You need to be solidly capitalized to take on an existing daily and win. Even then, you'll probably lose eventually."

"Why is that? Everybody in town calls the *Banner* the *Bummer*. I never heard a kind word for it in all the years I've lived in Cambridge. If somebody came along with something better, why wouldn't the readers and advertisers jump at it?"

"They might, for a while. Then what the established paper will do is set up its own shopper, which it can do a lot cheaper because it's got its own presses and circulation department and ad salesmen already. Then they drop ad rates below cost and drive the competition out of business."

"What about the antitrust laws?"

"An antitrust violation is what a prosecutor says it is, and then later what a judge says it is. To get before that judge takes a lot of time and a lot of money. Mr. Paul presumably doesn't have much of either. Mr. Boucher, on the other hand, does."

"Realistically, then," I said, "there's no way to hurt Boucher badly enough so he'd sell off his paper in Cambridge?"

"No way I can think of. An established daily is kind of like a headless nail. Once it's driven in, you can't pull it out."

We wanted to take Ellsworth Court to dinner at the Inn in Little Washington, but it's just about impossible to get out of your obligations as a guest to an old-line Virginian. The only way would have been to tie him up and gag him, and so he wound up taking us. Sure enough, they didn't have coconut cream pie. The closest they could come was *flan*, which is the French word for custard without enough sugar in it.

"How's your *flan?*" Hope asked over their coffee and my tea.

"It's great," I said. "Just great."

"I know how fond you are of it," she said.

Later, in the motel room we found in Luray, I said, "You've got kind of a rotten streak in you, don't you?"

"No, I don't think so."

"Oh, yeah, there's no question about it. How else could you ask about my frog custard in front of the guy that bought it for me?"

"I knew you'd tell the truth regardless."

"I'll tell the truth now. They didn't use enough egg yolks

and they put a lot of burned sugar on the top of it. I can make better custard in my microwave.''

"You should have brought it, then. You clod.''

"Clod, huh? How would you like it if I ripped that towel off you?''

"I guess it would be okay.''

Later yet, we just lay there side by side, talking about this and that, killing time, regrouping.

"You must be excited,'' Hope said. "This will be your first real job since the 1980 campaign.''

"Not true. I worked for the Markham campaign in '88.''

"That wasn't a real job.''

"Sure it was. I made five thousand a week while it lasted.''

"Real jobs have bennies.''

"Then I still don't have one. Boucher's paying me a consulting fee in cash every Friday.''

"Why cash? You're more or less legitimate these days. You have a bank account.''

"I don't want him to think of me as legitimate. He gets off on having a pit bull taking orders from him. That's why he kept Terry Dineen around. We had an ambassador in Laos like that. Asshole used to carry a gun and hang around the CIA guys at Long Cheng.''

"How long are *you* going to hang around *your* CIA guy?''

As usual she was a step ahead of me. Of course that was what I was doing—hanging around with made guys from what was the underworld. To me.

"Long as it takes? Till I get tired? I really don't know. It could be a long time.''

"Exactly what will you do for him?''

"I'll be his personal cop and bodyguard . . .''

"Don't forget chauffeur.''

"Think of me as a personal transportation consultant, okay? Apart from that, it'll probably be sort of like what I did for Carter during the 1980 campaign. Espionage, maybe sabotage. I'll push him and see what he does."

"I don't know about sabotage. You be careful."

"I always am. Hey, it's true. What are you sticking your tongue out for? No, no, leave it out. We'll think of something to do with it."

5

I DROVE BACK FROM VIRGINIA SUNDAY, and showed up at Boucher's house Monday morning at nine. It was off Brattle, on a street I had never been down. The house was bigger than the president of Harvard's and in fact was bigger than any I had ever seen in Cambridge except for the Longfellow House. And the Longfellow House was a museum.

I walked right up to the big front door just like the quality, and rang. Himself came to the door himself, carrying a thousand-dollar briefcase.

"Good morning, Tom," he said.

"Good morning, Thurman," I said.

He digested that for an instant, then said, "Mr. Boucher, I think. Or Mr. T."

"Can't do it."

"Really?" he said. He didn't seem offended, just interested. "Suppose I said I couldn't do it, either?"

"You could always get your prize-fighter back. Depends

whether you want to get somebody to do a job for you or somebody to kiss your ass."

"I imagine I could find somebody willing to do both."

"Sure, if driving is the only job you need done. Which I don't think it is."

"What do you think I need done?"

"Security work. Executive protection. Plant security. Preventive labor relations. Various odd jobs."

"None of which requires being on a first-name basis."

"If it's going to work, I've got to be outside the chain of command. I've got to be seen as close to you, your personal guy. People have to be a little bit unsure about just what my real job is. If I call you mister, I'm just the chauffeur and the hell with me. I call you Thurman and everybody's a little bit scared of me, from the managing editor on down."

Boucher took a moment to think about it, and then said again, "We'll see how it goes."

"Fine. Which way to the garage?"

"Out back. Where's your car?"

"When I need one I borrow one. I don't own a car."

And legally this was true. My 1987 Subaru is in Joey Neary's name, although I pay the taxes and insurance. I also pay the bills from MacKinnon Motors, where Bob MacKinnon and his boys have kept the Subaru going for 140,000 miles so far. As my straw owner, Joey gets to drive the thing on his vacations and on weekends when I don't need it. The point of all this, like the point of my apartment and my post office box being under the name of Tom Carpenter, is to make me at least a little bit hard to find. So I had taken the bus out to Boucher's and walked the last couple of blocks from the stop. No reason for him to see my tag number, even if it was in Joey's name. The day would come when Boucher and I weren't going to be pals anymore.

The car was as pretty a toy as I remembered. Boucher gave me the keys and walked around the front to get in beside me. Possibly he was a democrat. More likely he was buying, for the time being anyway, my argument that the better I was treated the more useful I would be.

Working along those lines, I had dressed up for my new job in the shoes by Lobb of London that I had bought on my way back from Laos years ago. My Fenn & Feinstein summerweight tan cord suit and Brooks Brothers shirt and tie looked expensive, too. Actually they came pre-owned from Keezer's. Generations of Harvard kids have unloaded their back-to-school clothes at Keezer's when they came up short on keg money.

My Subaru would have got us to the newspaper just as fast, but I could see the point of the Rolls now that I was driving one. The point was that everybody looked at you and wondered who that handsome stranger was behind the wheel. Subarus don't make you handsome.

"Who do I see about an office?" I asked when we had parked in the slot with PUBLISHER painted on the wall in front of it.

"Office?" Boucher said, and smiled. "I'm afraid the corner ones are all taken."

"The plumbers were in the basement of the building next to the White House," I said, not smiling back. "All I need is something with a door I can lock and enough space for a phone and a computer terminal."

"See Alan Fogel. He's sort of the day-to-day publisher, although his title is managing editor."

"My title should be nothing. I'm just somebody who's helping you out with this and that, various projects."

"The less people know, the more they'll assume?" Boucher said. "Is that the idea?"

"That's the idea."

"How about me? Am I one of the people who won't know?"

"You're the boss. You'll know everything I do."

"I'd better."

I got out and he got out, not waiting for me to come around and open the door. So far, so good, but it didn't mean he had fallen in love with me. It just meant he thought I might be making sense. And the things I had asked for wouldn't cost him any money to speak of.

The editorial department was on the second floor. Boucher turned me over to Alan Fogel and went on into his own office. It was the only one that had real walls. There were other offices along the same side of the big, open newsroom that filled most of the floor, but they were glassed-in cubicles. The people who didn't rate cubicles had little stalls. It looked something like the language lab Harvard has in the basement of Boylston Hall, except that there were computer terminals in these stalls instead of audio gear. I know about Boylston Hall because I use the men's room there. It's handy to my open-air office on the terrace of Au Bon Pain, which has no public facilities.

When I told the acting publisher what I needed for an office, he said, "Privacy is a little tough, as you can see. You might wind up without windows."

"Long as I can lock it," I said.

He picked up the phone and got somebody to work on the problem. Fogel was five foot six or seven and slightly built. Judging just by the face he was in his early thirties, but an advanced case of male pattern baldness made him look ten years older. His manner was mild and polite, almost shy, and he hadn't asked any questions when Boucher gave him a vague explanation of what I'd be doing. He seemed like a passive man who would conscientiously do everything and anything he was told. Still, he must have known how to use his elbows and knees. Maybe he had just been following orders, but it hadn't taken him long to push Jonathan Paul out the door. I wanted Fogel on my side.

"Do you use Alan or Al?" I asked, knowing it would be Alan.

"Alan."

"I don't have a choice," I said. "It's not Thomas on my birth certificate, just Tom, and not even a middle name except in the army. Then I had three middle names. You ever in the army?"

"No."

"Well, when you don't have a middle name, the personnel clerk writes down NMI, for no middle initial. So the dummies at roll call, they'd always holler out 'Bethany, Tom, N.M.I.' "

"Who are the dummies?"

"The sergeants. That's what everybody . . ."

And on and on I babbled. Shy guys like it when you take up the conversational slack. In the course of it all, I let him know that I didn't know a thing about newspapers and would be counting on him, and that naturally I'd keep him up-to-date on whatever I was doing, which would be mostly personnel stuff and routine security.

By now we were drinking coffee in his glassed office. I would have preferred tea, but coffee was what he asked his secretary for, and so I asked for it, too. To get along, go along.

"Who knows the most about computers in the office?" I asked Fogel. In every office there's always some guy around who climbed inside the computer system long ago and never came out. He's the one who fields everybody's questions, and often it isn't the person you'd think. This time it was the sports editor, a man named Brad Boyle.

"Mind introducing me to him?" I said to Fogel. "A few other guys, too. The custodial and maintenance guys, and whoever runs the press room."

"Willard Doggett and Pat Sheehan," Fogel said. "Sheehan doesn't come on till later, but Willard's here now. He's the building super, the one I was talking to about getting your office set up, such as it is."

"It'll be fine."

"Let's go down and see it, then."

It had been a storeroom on the first floor, and the supplies that had been in it were still piled in the hall outside. A fat bald white guy with a blue-and-red striped shirt was standing by uselessly while two black guys in coveralls were doing the work. "Not there, for Christ's sake," he was telling one of the guys as we came up. "Don't you ever listen to nothing? I told you over here, didn't I?" He had a clipboard in his hand and a plastic Pocket Protector for all the ballpoints in his shirt pocket, which made him the civilian equivalent of a master sergeant. Fogel introduced us.

"No place to plug in a terminal in there," Doggett said to me straight off. "It's just a storage room. Always been a storage room." Willard Doggett wasn't a happy camper, losing a storage room that way.

"What the hell are you idiots looking at?" he snapped, mad at me and Fogel but taking it out on his two black privates.

"Word with you?" I said to Doggett, and led him off a few steps. I slung an arm around his shoulders in what would look like a friendly gesture, but Willard knew better. My fingers were sunk into his fat shoulder, not deep enough to really hurt but just short of it.

"I'm going to be working on various projects for Mr. Boucher, Willard. You follow me?"

I tightened my grip a tiny bit, to help him. Being bullies, sergeants respond very nicely to bullying.

"Some of them are going to involve you, Willard, so I want us to get along. I know you're going to want to get along, too, Willard. It'd be best for everybody. So just get that fucking line in there, okay? Phone line, too. That way we can start off on the right foot instead of you stepping in shit."

I took my arm away, gave him a couple of friendly claps on the liberated shoulder, smiled at him, and said, "That's great. Thanks a lot, Willard."

"What did you say to him?" Fogel asked as he took me off to meet the sports editor.

"I told him how much I appreciated his work and how I'd appreciate even more of it, and faster."

Fogel smiled just enough so you could notice it, but said nothing. Most likely he had his own problems with Doggett. We went back upstairs to the newsroom to meet the sports editor.

Brad Boyle was a short little guy in his thirties with a blue polka-dot bow tie and a red-and-white striped shirt. He wore his light-brown hair in a crew cut. He had an oval-shaped bald spot on the crown of his head, like a putting green surrounded by fairway. He was clicking away at high speed on his computer keyboard, his back to us.

"Word with you, Brad?" Fogel said, and Brad spun his revolving chair around to face us.

"Hey, Alan," he said. "What's up?"

"Like you to meet Tom Bethany."

"Pleasure, Tom. Brad Boyle."

"Tom's going to be doing special projects for Mr. T. I told him you're the resident computer expert."

"Is this a good time to talk?" I asked. "No hurry. I could come back later."

"Now's fine."

"I'll leave you with Brad, then," Fogel said.

"One time's more or less like another," Brad said when Fogel was gone. "I'm permanently swamped."

"Seriously, I could come back. Or buy you a beer after work."

"No, that's all right. I'm just feeling sorry for myself since they took Terry Dineen away from me."

"Terry Dineen?" I said. It was the first I knew that the retired prize-fighter had been anything but a chauffeur. "Who's he?"

"Used to be he was my one-man staff. You follow the fights?"

"Not recently."

"Terry was a top-ranked middleweight. He might have had a real shot at the title, till he killed a man in the ring. Poor bastard felt so guilty he quit."

"First time I ever heard of a fighter turning sportswriter."

"Terry had three semesters at Bunker Hill Community College before he turned pro. Guy wasn't any Hemingway, but mostly he got the facts straight. And of course he knew boxing cold, not that we give it that much coverage."

"Why would you hire a fighter, then? Couldn't you find lots of experienced people who could get the facts straight?"

"There aren't as many as you might think. But you're right, normally I would have hired some kid with a journalism degree. Only Terry was Mike's hire."

"Mike being?"

"Mike Cushing, the former publisher. He was a major boxing fan. Mike was ringside the night Terry killed Boom-Boom Greer. Well, actually, it wasn't till the next day that the hospital pulled the plug on him."

"What made Cushing think of some boxer as a sportswriter?"

"Well, Mike used to try his hand at a sports column occasionally. The only writing he ever did for the paper. He interviewed Terry after the accident and found out the poor guy had a kid who was severely autistic, along with other problems. Terry's purses were just starting to get big enough so that he could handle the bills and suddenly, bang, no more purses. When Mike heard that, he hired him so he could go on the paper's medical."

"Pretty decent thing to do."

"Mike was a pretty decent guy."

"What did you mean when you said they took Terry away from you?"

"Well, there was a big downsizing when the Boucher Group took over. Terry was on the list, and he went to Alan, but Alan said there was nothing he could do. So the poor guy was desperate on account of the kid, and he went straight to Mr. T. The way I got it from Terry, Mr. T said there was nothing he could do, either, until Terry told him the whole story of how he got hired and the kid and all, and Mr. T finally said he could stay on as his driver."

The Cobra was notably short on pity by all accounts. Sick kid stories wouldn't get very far with him. But it's different when you learn you've got somebody on the payroll who beat a man to death with his fists. You hate to let a guy like that go.

"It's a comedown for Terry, of course," the sports editor said. "But at least now his little guy's medical bills are covered."

Apparently word hadn't got around yet that Dineen had been fired again, which might mean that nobody except Boucher had seen our scuffle in the parking lot. Presumably it was just a matter of time, though. Dineen would talk about it, and after that it wouldn't be hard to figure out that the new guy driving the boss around was the mysterious stranger. Then my only friends on the paper would be Boucher himself, and possibly Alan Fogel. So much the better. Those were the only friends I needed.

"Well, what can I tell you about our computer system?" Brad Boyle said. "The real experts are the consultants who do the training and the trouble-shooting, but it's a fairly standard newspaper setup. You're probably familiar with a lot of it already."

"This is my first newspaper job," I said.

"Oh, really?"

"Yeah, mostly I've done security consulting in the industrial relations field."

Whatever that meant, but he didn't ask.

In half an hour, he had given me a general picture of the system. Bookkeeping, billing, and the rest of the paper's financial functions were computerized. So was the entire writing and composing process, from typing out the story all the way through its transformation into camera-ready newspaper pages. The reporters wrote on computers linked by Ethernet cables to a central server. Editors just called the stories up on their screens, edited them, put headlines on top, and sent them along electronically. Most of the stuff that wasn't written by the staff got to the paper via a satellite dish on the roof, or over dedicated telephone lines. Boyle showed me what he called the rack, a board where the satellite feed came in and was channeled into modems that served the computers. The central computer room wasn't much bigger than a storage closet, one full of hundreds of wires.

"What's the security setup?" I asked him.

"Basically there isn't any security. Pretty much anybody could walk in here. Of course we've got everything backed up, so you could always put things back together again in case of accidents."

"I wasn't thinking about accidents," I said.

"What were you thinking about?"

"This and that," I said. "But not accidents."

"Sabotage?"

"It's been known to happen."

* * *

Pat Sheehan, the head of the pressroom, was a man in love with his toy, and it was some toy. Electronic machines like computers and TVs do most of their business invisibly. So does a car, really. Open the hood of the Rolls and the only thing you'd see moving would be the fan. But a newspaper press is laid out in front of you naked, like those old machines in the Smithsonian's Museum of Science and Technology that have belts and pulleys and pistons and cranks moving all over the place.

The *Banner*'s press took up most of a very big room, from roof to ceiling and from wall to wall. The moving parts were oiled and gleaming. The structural parts were shiny and spotless, painted cream-colored with red detailing. Sheehan was tracing one of the red stripes with his fingers as we talked. Like a new bridegroom, he couldn't keep his big, pale, freckled hands off his sweetie.

"Looks sharp," I said.

"One of my guys used to customize vans," the foreman said. "He done the striping."

"So the paper moves through in one huge, long sheet, huh?"

"Lots of sheets at once. Webs is what we call them. You never saw a press run?"

"Only in the movies," I said. "This is my first job on a newspaper." He looked as surprised as Brad Boyle had.

"Oh, yeah?" he said. "Watch this."

He touched a button and the whole huge machine came to life briefly. The webs of paper moved a few feet over the complex maze of rollers. "You want to see something, come down and watch a run someday."

"When do you start?"

"Different times, depending when jobs are ready to go. Main run for the paper itself is usually after midnight."

"How come so late?"

"Can't run 'em till the last sports scores come in from

California. Come by some night, check it out. It's something to see, if you never seen it before."

"Count on it. Does the web ever break?"

"Hey, shit happens."

"Then what?"

"No big deal normally. See these things here? They're like big knives, got them all over the press. If the web breaks somewhere, they come up and cut it into sections so it won't roll up like spaghetti on a fork. Otherwise you got what you call a wrap, which it can take you an hour to dig the jammed-up paper out. A real serious wrap, you can blow up the unit."

"What makes the knives come up?"

"They're electronically controlled. The web loses tension, up those babies come."

If they were electronically decontrolled, of course, those babies would stay just where they were, and maybe the whole unit would blow. As Pat Sheehan's tour continued, more vulnerabilities showed up. In fact the whole pressroom was one giant vulnerability, with machinery running at such high speeds and close tolerances that a few grains of sand in the right place would be crippling. And at the end of the process was a machine called the folder. It was a single choke point where all the webs came together to be cut up into pages and folded. A breakdown there would disable the entire operation.

Driving Thurman Boucher home that night, I asked what would happen if the paper missed a day's publication.

"It's a nightmare," he said. "It happened once up in Middlebury, when the snow built up and collapsed the roof. By the second day we arranged to have the paper printed in another shop, but we did miss one day. The phones were jammed with thousands of subscribers."

"What happens with the ads? You have to refund everybody's money?"

"Normally you just run the ad an extra day. Mainly it's a question of losing face, if you want to put it that way. Papers come out on holidays, weekends, rain or shine. Every day. That's what they do. And if they don't, people won't listen to any excuses. What brings this up?"

"Just walking through the plant, I found a half dozen ways I could shut the whole operation down. Particularly in the pressroom."

"That's why you've got to keep your eye on the pressmen. They can really screw you if they're organized. When I was just out of college, my dad took me to a meeting of the American Newspaper Publishers Association. It was after all that Watergate nonsense and Nixon being hounded from office.

"Kay Graham of the *Washington Post* walked into the banquet hall and everybody jumped up and started to cheer. Just went on and on, never heard anything like it. Finally we all sat down and I said to the publisher next to me, 'What a wonderful tribute to Mrs. Graham for the great job her paper did on Watergate.' Something dumb along those lines, anyway.

"This publisher looked at me like I just got off the boat, and said, 'Watergate, bullshit. She broke the pressmen's union.'"

This was the spot for me to laugh, so I did. "Oh, yeah?" I said. "She broke the union?" I knew she had, actually, but I didn't want to look well informed.

"Absolutely," Boucher said. "Kay Graham sent all her executives off to this secret training camp to learn how to run the presses, and then she smashed the goddamned union. Made her a legend in the industry. Before that the goddamned pressmen had you at their mercy."

"They still have you at their mercy, it looked like to me,"

I said. "Anybody in that pressroom could shut you down in thirty seconds and nobody could prove a thing. You don't even have any surveillance cameras in there."

"Is that right?" Boucher said. "I haven't even got around to thinking about plant security yet."

"I asked around a little. Apparently this guy Cushing didn't like plant surveillance. Thought it was bad for morale."

"Fuck morale," the Cobra explained. "Where are they going to go if they don't like it here? That's the nice thing about a tight job market. It's eat shit or die."

"You got that right," I sucked up. "Besides, they've got cameras now that fit into fake exit signs and smoke detectors. You don't even know they're there."

"Plant maintenance would know they were there."

"Not if you got an outside contractor in."

"You know people who do that?"

"Sure. They wear uniforms that say Acme Electric or something, but they're really security guys." I didn't know if this was true or not, but I could put something together easily enough.

"Look into it, will you? See what it costs."

"You got it."

I was just pulling up to the front of the house, where I'd let him off before putting the car away. With his hand on the door, Boucher said, "That thing you did to Terry Dineen?"

I nodded.

"You think you could teach it to me?"

"Sure, but learning just one thing wouldn't do you much good."

"Teach me a lot of things, then."

"To do it right you need a place to practice. You've got to set aside regular blocks of time, make a real commitment."

"Couldn't you just teach me a few holds?"

"Sure, but I wouldn't. It'd be like you went to Terry Dineen and said teach me how to do that right hook you killed the guy with. Real wrestling isn't just a few holds. It's a whole system. Conditioning, drills, practice, practice, practice. You need a gym.''

"There's a room upstairs where we were planning to put the NordicTrack and the Concept II.''

He took me inside and showed me what had probably been a maid's room once. It was a little cramped for the home gym I had always wanted. Well, what the hell. Go for broke.

"We'd need more space if we're going to get serious about this," I said.

"There's an unused apartment over the garage," he said. "Let's take a look at that.''

The apartment had plenty of room, and it also had plumbing. Maybe I could talk him into a sauna.

"This could do it," I said. "You want me to cost it out?''

"Go ahead.''

"How much do you want to put into it?''

"You tell me.''

"I don't really know. I've used the stuff all my life but I never priced it.''

"Then just put together a list of what you'll need, and we'll see what it comes to.''

"You got it," I said again.

As I was driving the Rolls around back, feeling good about my new job, the cellular phone rang. I knew in theory how to handle the problem, since I had watched Boucher do it often enough. But rather than do something dumb, like run over a flowerbed, I stopped the car. The phone had rung twice more by the time I figured out how to open the compartment and answer it. Nobody seemed to be on the line, and I thought maybe I had hit the wrong button. "Hello?" I said again.

"Hey, how you doing, Bethany?" a man said. "Watch

your back at all times, shit-for-brains, because you're fuck-ing dead."

"Who is this?" I asked.

"Yeah, right. Like I'm going to tell you."

There was a click, and then the dial tone.

I put the cellular phone back in its cradle and watched it a moment, as if it might tell me something. The man's accent had been generic Boston. I didn't recognize the voice.

6

TUESDAY MORNING A DESK AND TWO chairs and a filing cabinet were in the storage room that Willard Doggett was decorating for me. A working phone was on my desk and a Macintosh LC III. This was plenty of computer for me, since I wouldn't be doing much with it except cruising through other people's files. Its main purpose was to show that I was important.

Doggett came in while I was down on my knees, looking under the desk for a place to plug in the thing. "I couldn't get an electrician in till this morning to hook it up," he said. "He's supposed to be in at ten."

He was doing his best to sound ingratiating, so my earlier threats had worked. Petty tyrants react well to threat displays, since that's what they use themselves.

"He'd better be," I said. "Now why aren't there any office supplies in here, for Christ's sake?"

By the time the electrician showed up, I had my file drawers all stocked up with hanging files and little tabs on each one waiting for its name. In my new desk were paper clips, a stapler, pens and pencils, message pads, file cards, yellow legal pads, and stacks of stationery with *Cambridge Daily Banner* on it. Now I was ready to prioritize. This was my list:

1. Home gym.
2. Surveillance.
3. Keys.
4. Records.
5. Phones.
6. Copier.
7. Suspicious incident.

Home gym was first because I had always wanted to have one. Suspicious incident probably should have been higher on the list, but I couldn't see that it made much difference. It was only a list, and I didn't plan to begin at the beginning and not move on to the next item till the last one was finished. Several or all of them would be cooking away at once, probably, in the confused fashion of life itself.

"You want me to do everything, then?" the guy from Beautiful Bathrooms said. We were in the apartment over the Bouchers' garage. "Contract the whole job?"

"Yeah, I don't want to fool around with plumbers, permits, electric, all that shit. Give me a package price for the whole works, installed, painted, everything nice, and we'll see what we can do."

"You mind my asking, is anybody else bidding on this job?"

"I don't see where we need to get anybody else in on it. We'll probably be able to work something out where we both get a good taste, you follow me?"

"Hey, I hear you talking, Tom."

Off he went to pad his estimate, the Beautiful Bathrooms

guy. I had my own padding to think about. I stood in the middle of the empty room, seeing how it would be. The Resilite mat, four inches of Rubatex foam wall-to-wall. If they made it that thick. If not, maybe I could special-order. And of course the walls themselves would have to be padded, too. Six feet high? No, eight would be safer and more expensive. The Resilite bill alone would probably get us close to five figures. Plus we were going to need a Universal machine with all possible stations. Chromed, top of the line. And a brand-new set of doctor's office scales with sliding weights. Or maybe I could find some fancy electronic scales that would cost even more. Sauna and showers in the space where the kitchen was now.

And of course we'd want all those little touches that made a gym a home. Terry cloth robes, full-body towels, a laundry hamper, built-in lockers, shampoo and body lotion dispensers for the shower, Cliff Keen wrestling shoes, Lycra singlets, headguards, neoprene kneepads. I was in gym rat heaven as I went on downstairs and outside, thinking about vinyl conditioning suits, coated nylon workout sets. Shorties or full length? Hey, why not both?

Alison Boucher, wearing a yellow running suit with green piping, came jogging down the street and turned into the drive. Her light brown hair was in a ponytail held by a green ribbon that matched the piping. She looked terrific.

"We meet at last," she said, pulling up in front of me. Before now I had only seen her over her husband's shoulder when I picked him up one morning. She was still breathy from her run, but she wasn't sweating hardly at all. The day was in the eighties. I would have been wet clear through.

"You're Tom Bethany and I'm Alison Boucher."

"Pleased to meet you, Mrs. Boucher."

"Alison, for God's sake. You're all Thurman talks about

these days. You're his new discovery. Is it true you're a mystery man?"

"Is that what he says?"

"I'm fascinated. What about that truck I saw coming out of the driveway? Are we going to have beautiful bathrooms? Beautiful bathrooms fascinate me, too."

"He's going to put in a sauna and shower for the new wrestling room."

"The famous wrestling room. Will I still be able to use my lovely NordicTrack and rowing machine?"

"They could stay in the house, or we could put them out here in the old bedroom that's next to the wrestling room. Up to you folks."

"What do you wrestle in? Sweat suits? Or those kind of jackety things with belts?"

"The things with the belts are for that martial arts stuff where you grab hold of the jackets. Wrestling you're not allowed to grab hold of clothing. You just wear shorts and shoes and tank tops, sometimes tights under your shorts."

"I'd think it would be more fun with sweat suits. I love the feel of sweat suits, don't you? Everything kind of sliding around inside. What are you smiling at?"

"It just made me think of a thing they used to have in the Bangkok massage parlors during the war. You ever hear of the B-course?"

"No, but you've got me breathless."

"You'd be in this thing on the floor like a big rubber wading pool, except the bottom was inflated the same as the sides. Like an air mattress. The girl would run an inch or two of warm water in, and then slick her and you both up with soap, and then she'd wriggle and squirm all over with her whole body, but no hands. It's kind of hard to describe."

"Maybe you could show me sometime, Tom Bethany."

"Maybe if I ever get tired of my job."

"You think Thurman would mind? You might be surprised about Thurman. He can be very open-minded."

She smiled and turned and walked toward the house. She walked with the same kind of twitch to her butt that Marilyn Monroe had.

I hadn't written a memo since the Carter campaign in 1980, and never really missed the exercise at all. But my reentry into the memo world was more fun than I would have thought. It went:

CONFIDENTIAL
(Draft)

TO: Thurman Boucher, Alan Fogel
FROM: Tom Bethany
SUBJECT: Unauthorized Use

1. Preliminary investigation indicates that widespread misuse of the telephones and copying facilities of the *Banner* is occurring. Estimates of the cost of such use to the paper are approximately $260 a month in unauthorized phone calls and $80 a month in free copying done by employees for personal use. Annual cost to the paper is estimated at $4,080, which will probably turn out to be low once further investigation can be carried out.

2. Due to accessibility most of such use is occurring in the editorial and business and circulation departments, although random checks of phone billings reveal misuse by production department personnel as well. In short, all departments of the paper are involved.

3. Incontrovertible evidence exists proving unauthorized use by six employees of the editorial department, three in business, and three in circulation. Evidence against several others is incomplete or questionable, although interrogation would probably reveal their addi-

tional involvement. If you desire, such interrogation and further investigation can be carried out.

4. The activities covered include duplication of personal correspondence, government and credit application forms, college application material, articles from this newspaper and others for personal use, chain letters, résumés, and many other items. Unauthorized phone calls include many intrastate calls and many interstate calls, some lasting more than thirty minutes. Lists of the numbers called are available, as well as the family or personal relationship to staff members of the person or persons listed at those numbers. The employees involved can be terminated with little fear of legal complications if judged necessary, but a more desirable course of action is outlined in paragraph (5) below.

5. As several of the unauthorized users are senior personnel it might be preferred to announce a new and more rational and economical policy on use of the phones and copying facilities. This would involve personal code numbers for users, so that the appropriation of each use can be verified if necessary. A policy of random checks should be announced and carried out to insure compliance with this new *Banner* policy.

6. Subject to your concurrence, implementation steps will be taken immediately.

I looked it over and made two changes: *incontravertible* instead of *incontrovertible* and *accessability* for *accessibility*. A couple of minor spelling errors would add the human touch. Then I crumpled the memo up so it would look like something from the wastebasket.

At breakfast the next day, I got Joey Neary to scrawl "CAN YOU BELIEVE THIS SHIT!" all over the unsigned memo, and address a *Banner* envelope for me.

"We're even," Joey said. "From now on you get your fucking toast any way I want it."

Later that morning I slipped the envelope into the box of the copy editor, a gossipy guy named Ed Salisbury.

"Shit, I never thought of that," I said to the guy from Secure Surveillance Systems.

"Oh, yeah," he said. "System's no good unless you got someplace to watch it. If I put the monitors and VTRs in here, wouldn't be no room for anything else."

"I just got this office and now I've outgrown it. Well, hell, I'll just have to get another one. What's a VTR, anyway?"

"Video timer recorder. You'd want a split screen, so you can watch four cameras at once. One monitor for each VTR."

"Can you set it up so people who come in the office wouldn't see the screen and start to wonder?"

"Sure, we can build it in. Same way you can hide TV screens behind panels in your living room."

"Because I want to have the option, whether to let the staff know they're under surveillance camera or whether not to."

"Let me suggest something to you, then. A lot of businesses, they put surveillance in the rest rooms because of drug activity. Also on the grounds outside for trespassers and what have you. People kind of take those locations for granted. So we could put those types of cameras right out in the open, and that would explain why you got screens in your office at all. Turn off the other monitors and nobody has to know they're hitched up to concealed units, you see what I mean?"

"I still need a new office, though. Right?"

"I could probably jam everything in here."

"No, I want a bigger office."

"On second thought," the man from Secure Surveillance Systems said, "I'm not so sure everything *would* fit in here."

*   *   *

Everybody who was familiar with the paper used one of the rear doors handy to the parking lot, but visitors who didn't know any better generally went around to the front door. During the day a woman who also took classified ads sat at a receptionist's desk in the small lobby, but she went off duty at five and locked the entrance. This meant nobody had any legitimate reason to go to the front lobby after that. Just after six I gathered my equipment and set out for the deserted entrance. I hung around the lobby for a few minutes, looking at the vanity wall full of plaques and photos and trophies that Michael Cushing had put up. Nobody was around, and nobody had seen me coming.

I took my can of spray paint and wrote my message in yard-high letters all over the wall and the picture frames on it. Then it occurred to me that whoever unlocked the entrance next morning might make the message unreadable by taking down the frames and plaques. Only sections would be left, and they would just look like a chopped-up red worm. So I repeated the job on the opposite wall, which was bare. It was also some kind of fake stone finish that would be practically impossible to clean.

Now it read KILL COBRAS on both walls. The paint had run here and there, so the letters seemed to be bleeding. I hadn't planned the drips, but the effect worked for me. I wiped my fingerprints off the spray can and went to put it in the storage room where Willard Doggett's people kept cleaning materials.

A woman named Annie Corbett handled personnel, what there was of it. The heads of each department mostly did their own hiring, and then just sent the new guy along to Annie in the business office to fill in the forms for tax withholding and medical and whatnot.

"This is where you keep them?" I asked her. "Just like this, in a filing cabinet?"

"Well, where else would you keep them? They're files."

"People like to think their personnel files are confidential, not just in open files."

"I keep them locked."

"They were open just now."

"Well, I'm right here. I'm in and out of the files all day. I lock them when I go home."

"I'll see about getting you a bar lock with a CONFIDENTIAL sign on it."

"You mean I'd have to take the bar off every time I needed somebody's folder?"

"No, just take the bar off in the morning and do like you do now. It's more psychological than anything else. Makes people think their private information is safe."

"It *is* safe."

"Anne, I know it and you know it. But do *they* know it? They take a look at this setup and they think, whoa, my résumé is in there. My recommendations, salary information, disciplinary actions, evaluations. Nobody's around, jeez. Anybody could take a look."

"*I'm* around."

"You're never off on an errand? In the powder room?"

"I lock the files."

"Every time?"

"Well, not if it's just for a second."

"There you go. Look, let me just start with what, *A* to *D* of the current employees? How many folders would that be? Fine, that looks good for now."

"What's this in support of?" Annie asked. "I mean, I'm in from *A* to *D*."

"You talked to Mr. Fogel, right?"

"Right."

"So you know it's okay."

"I didn't mean it wasn't okay. I just wondered."

"Strictly routine. Just routine familiarization."

Off and on through the day, I brought an armload of personnel records back to Annie Corbett and grabbed another to take down to my office. My too-small office. I didn't try to hide what I was doing. I wanted it to get around that I was rooting through everybody's files. And if nobody happened to notice what I was carrying, I figured I had made Annie Corbett mad enough so that she'd get out the word.

"Take a look at this," I said to Thurman Boucher once he had settled into the front seat of the Rolls and opened his briefcase on his lap. We were just setting out for home.

"What the hell is this?" he said.

"It's a mouse. From a Macintosh."

"I know that. Why are you giving it to me?"

"It's yours. I stole it from the ad department twenty minutes ago. They're worth about a hundred bucks. I could have stolen the computer, too. Put it in a cardboard box and carried it on out. Nobody to stop me."

"What are you saying?"

"The paper is wide open. Look at that 'Kill Cobras' business the other day in the lobby. I checked with this guy I know at the cops. They never heard of a gang called the Cobras."

"You didn't know? Well, I suppose there's no reason you would."

"Know what?"

"There are people in the business who call me the Cobra."

"Shit."

"What do you mean, 'shit'?"

"I thought it was just a prank. I didn't know Cobra meant you. Somebody puts something on the wall about killing you and I have to take it seriously. Who do you think would have done it?"

"Probably somebody from the news staff."

"Oh, yeah? I wouldn't have thought reporters would be the type to pull shit like that."

"Actually it's about on their level," Boucher said. "Reporters are ignorant, sentimental fools. They think they're working for some kind of religious movement instead of a business. On the one hand, that means you can hire them like preachers, for peanuts. On the other, they can turn very nasty when they discover it's a business after all."

"Like when they get fired."

"Like that."

"How many people did you have to let go?"

"From editorial? Nine so far."

"With more coming?"

"In all probability. We're not where we want to be yet, not by a long shot."

"So we could see more of this nastiness out of them. Probably will."

"Time they learned the golden rule," Boucher said. "Them that has the gold, rules."

"Have there been any other death threats?" I asked.

"Not really."

"What does that mean, not really?"

"You often get threats in a labor situation, but it's nothing to worry about."

"Nothing for you to worry about, maybe. How about if I worry about it, though? What kind of threats?"

"Only one. Some idiot called and said I'd better watch it, something like that."

"How did he get past the switchboard? Or did he call at home?"

"He called on the cellular, actually."

"Just once?"

"Just once. I was driving into Boston with Alison the other evening."

"Do you remember his exact words?"

"It was over before I really registered what was going on."

"Was it anything like, 'Hey, how you doing, Boucher?

Watch your back at all times, shit-for-brains, because you're fucking dead'?"

"He definitely said 'shit-for-brains,' now that you mention it. How did you know that?"

"Because he called me on the car phone, too. It was Terry Dineen."

"No, it wasn't. I know Terry's voice."

"Maybe he had somebody call for him, but Dineen had to be behind it. He knew the phone number in the car."

"The number isn't that much of a secret."

"He called me by name, so he recognized my voice. The other guys you fired, none of them knew my voice."

"If it was Terry," the Cobra said, "I doubt if either of us has much to worry about. Terry's physically tough, but not mentally. Getting drunk and shooting his mouth off, that would be about it for our Terry."

"Drive a guy to the wall, Thurman, and you never know what he might do. I think we ought to take him seriously."

"By all means take him seriously then. Do whatever you think is advisable, as long as you don't tell me about it."

I turned the key, and the Rolls-Royce's huge engine came to life instantly. You could hardly hear it, but you could feel a sort of smooth, strong vibration in the frame.

"Terry's got friends on the paper," I said. "Everybody you fired has got friends on the paper. Probably one of them vandalized the walls. They're liable to start stealing more than usual, too, now that they can justify it to themselves as guerrilla warfare. It could get serious. For instance that hundred-dollar mouse I walked off with. Turn it over, there's a serial number on the bottom. Only there's no record of that serial number anywhere at the *Banner*. No way to prove it belongs to you instead of me. At least the serial numbers of the computers themselves are on the original purchase orders, if anybody was to go to the trouble to dig them out."

"Which evidently you did, I take it?"

"I've been checking around, yeah. Nobody keeps serial numbers on the phones, either. Vacuum cleaners, floor buffers, power tools, TVs. Nothing. The police could catch some son of a bitch walking out of the building with that Sony from your office and they'd have to let him go. They couldn't prove it wasn't his."

"Get somebody from each department to make up a list."

"I'm already on it, but the real problem isn't the serial numbers. It's the physical security setup, which basically it doesn't exist. Nobody can even remember the last time they changed the locks. Nobody keeps track of keys. There must be hundreds of them floating around. Every one of those guys you let go, they've still got keys."

"You want to change the locks, go ahead."

"I got a locksmith company lined up already."

"Good for you, Tom. Feel like you can whip me tonight?"

"It wouldn't surprise me."

"Me either, but let's go make sure."

The sauna wasn't hitched up yet, but the new wrestling room was usable. We had already had a couple of after-work sessions. Boucher wasn't bad, for a total beginner. He was strong and aggressive. He had good balance and reflexes.

"Stretches first," I said when we were changed and ready. "Then bridging."

"Jesus, I hate those bridges."

"Everybody hates them. Let's go."

"Willard," I said to the building super next morning, "we got to establish key discipline here."

"What do you mean by 'key discipline'?"

Willard was sitting in my little office. In my office that was even littler than the little one he had next to the stock room. He was trying to keep the hostility out of his voice because he wasn't quite sure yet who I was and where I ranked. So he was about three-quarters obsequious and one-quarter attitude.

"What it means is that keys are getting up on their legs and walking all over this goddamned building, Willard."

"That keyboard's right in my office, locked up."

"What's locked? The keyboard or the office?"

"Both."

"Show me this keyboard."

"You want to see it, come on and see it. Ain't no secret."

"You got an ass and a half there, Willard," I said as I followed him to his office. Partly I was riding the building supervisor because I wanted to get control of the whole physical plant. But mostly it was because I had been watching the way he handled his staff. He bullied them the way dumb lifers bullied me for three years in the army.

Doggett tried to pretend I was only kidding, the way a sergeant will when a captain makes a crack about his uniform getting too tight. "You can't drive a spike with a tack hammer," he said.

Willard Doggett's office was not only bigger than mine, it also had a small window in it so that you could tell if it was day or night without even leaving the room. The keyboard was in a little cabinet on the wall. Doggett opened it to show me, and sure enough there were lots of keys in it, tagged and hanging on hooks.

"You notice something, Willard? The door to your office was open and so was the door to the key cabinet."

"This is my private office. Nobody comes in without I say so."

"Way it looks to me, anybody who wants to, they can walk right in."

"Everybody knows this is private."

"Jesus, Willard, give me a break. Grab the key to the storage room next door and let's have a look."

"It's probably open."

"It probably is, but let's look."

It was open, as I already knew from having checked twenty minutes before. "My guys are in and out all day," Doggett said.

"Them and anybody else. What's that over there?"

"That's the shelf where we keep the paint."

"Bring that can of red over here, will you?"

Doggett reached up for the empty can of spray paint I had stashed there the night before. I had a handkerchief ready when he handed it to me, and I made a show of keeping my fingers off the can as I slipped it, wrapped, into my pocket.

"The hell are you doing?"

"Fingerprints. This looks like the same color red somebody used in the main entrance. I'm going to have it checked."

"Fingerprints? My fingerprints are on the damned thing now."

"I wouldn't be surprised."

"You saw me put them there."

"Take it easy, Willard. If there's somebody else's prints on the thing, you're in the clear."

"What the hell are you trying to do here?"

"My job. Come on back to my office." The home court advantage is supposed to be important in these bureaucratic games.

"Now let's forget about that spray paint for a minute," I said once I was settled behind my desk in the power seat and he was out front where the peons sit. "See that wastebasket there? How come it's empty?"

"It's emptied every night."

"By your guys?"

"Certainly by my guys."

"Never by you?"

"I'm the building supervisor."

"I left the door locked. How do your guys get in?"

"They have keys. They have to, to do their jobs."

"Nobody else has keys to this office?"

"Certainly not."

"So if I tossed something in this wastebasket, the only people who would be able to get their hands on it would be you or your guys?"

"That's right."

"Reason I ask, I wrote a draft memo a while ago about misuse of the phones and the copying machines. Then I changed my mind and decided not to send it, so I chucked it. Next thing I find out, copies of it are circulating all over the office. How do you explain that?"

"Maybe somebody dug it out of the Dumpster outside."

"That's it? That's your explanation?"

"Look, if you don't trust me, just say so."

"I don't trust you."

Willard just sat there, surprised speechless, so I went on.

"First thing, you're taking kickbacks on supplies," I said. Actually I didn't know that, but the odds were heavy that he was. He opened his mouth to say something, but I didn't bother with it.

"Shut up, Willard. I can prove it, and I will if I have to. The legal term for what you've been doing is uttering forged invoices. It's a class C felony, only I'm hoping we can avoid the police on this thing. Now we got a case of defacing private property with death threats—"

"I didn't have nothing to do with that, and you know it."

"No, I don't know it. I don't care, either. The point isn't whether you did it, it's whether Mr. Boucher and Mr. Fogel will think you did it. Whether they're going to believe me or some asshole that's been ripping them off. Think about it, Willard. If I start going through your desk and your files, exactly what am I going to find?"

Plenty, from the way he was moving around on his chair and avoiding my eyes.

"You still know how to cut meat, don't you?" I asked.

"How do you know I'm a meat cutter?"

"Your personnel records, Willard."

"You got no right."

"Complain to Mr. T, then."

"What do you want?"

"You still got your meat cutter's card?"

"Sure I got it."

"I want you to cut meat."

"You're firing me?"

"Actually I'm trying not to fire you. I'm trying to let you quit right now, today, with nobody but us two knowing why. Otherwise this whole mess will end up down at Central Square, Western Avenue."

That was Cambridge police headquarters.

Doggett's shoulders sagged, and he looked down at his hands where they rested on his huge thighs.

"Who do I see?" he asked.

"Go to Annie Corbett in the business office and tell her you're quitting for personal reasons," I said. "She'll tell you what the paperwork is."

I didn't really know myself. I had never downsized anybody before.

7

"I HEARD YOU LOST YOUR BUILDING super," I said to Boucher on the way home the next evening. "Going to replace him?"

"I imagine so. Alan Fogel's looking into it."

"Those are going to be pretty easy shoes to fill."

"No doubt. But somebody's got to fill them."

"Why don't I do it? That way you'll save Doggett's salary."

"You've got plenty of things on your plate, and there might be more before long. I don't want you tied down with purchase orders for light bulbs and cleaning supplies."

"I wasn't planning on doing the actual work. I figured one of Doggett's guys ought to be able to do that. He'd be the building supervisor, but he'd be under me."

"Then I'd be paying Doggett's salary to him, and he'd need another man to do his old job, and we're right back where we started."

"Let me look into it. I may be able to figure a way to drop Doggett's whole salary to the bottom line."

"More power to you. If you come up with anything, run it past Alan."

I knew Doggett's salary because the personnel files had payroll data in them. By now I knew everybody's salary. The salary figures had made the pattern clear: fire most of the old-timers who had been creeping up the salary scale for years, and replace them with younger, cheaper people. Those who weren't replaced took salary cuts.

The one who had taken the deepest cut was the former boxer, Terry Dineen. He hadn't been making much as a sportswriter, but he dropped down by a third after he was fired and rehired as Boucher's chauffeur. Now he was down to nothing, or at best an unemployment check that would run out soon. There wouldn't be much work around for a ruined middle-aged middleweight, and unless he found a job with a big company he wouldn't be able to get insurance for his son's preexisting condition.

I felt guilty even though there hadn't been anything I could do about it. Boucher had made it clear that Dineen was finished the moment I put him down, whether or not I agreed to take his job. And Dineen had thrown the first punch. But I still felt guilty. The only hope of getting Dineen on the payroll again was to get the *Banner* back into Jonathan Paul's hands. And the only way to do that, as far as I could see, was for Boucher to decide that his new toy was more headaches than it was worth.

My basic plan was to turn the *Banner* into a manager's nightmare, with Boucher paranoid about his entire staff and his entire staff paranoid about him. My model was the Trickster's second term, with me playing Kissinger to Boucher's Nixon. Bringing out the worst in Boucher, which shouldn't be hard. Egging him on to more and more suspicion, secrecy, and cruelty. If I could goad the Cobra into enough of a frenzy, maybe he'd bite himself to death the way Nixon did.

* * *

By the middle of the morning, Doggett's two black guys had moved me into his old office. One was named Rosey Punderson and the other was William Wells. As I knew from the files, they both made seven bucks an hour.

"Hang around a second, will you, Rosey," I said when they had got me all squared away. When William Wells was gone, I asked Rosey Punderson if he could find me a bar lock to go on Doggett's former filing cabinet.

"One of them things that goes through the handles and you padlock it on top?" he said.

"Right."

"We ain't got nothing like that around."

"Where do you suppose we'd go to find one?"

"I ain't got the slightest idea."

"Well, maybe I'll see one in a catalog."

An hour later I ran across Wells in the men's room and asked him the same thing.

"Bar lock, huh?" he said, and I nodded.

"Bar lock," he repeated. "Okay, I'll get you one."

"Hey, William," I said just as he was about to go out the door. "You know what a bar lock is?"

"I ain't got any idea," he said. "But if there's one out there, I'll find it."

I told him to hold on a second, and we'd walk down to my new office together.

"Sit down," I said when we were there. I had two visitors' chairs in this office, instead of the one I had had back in the old office, before my coup.

"How would you like to be the new super?" I said.

"Moving into this office, I thought *you* was the new super."

"No, I got other stuff to keep me busy."

"You'd be my boss, though?"

"How do you figure that?"

"The man that gives you the job, he's the boss."

"I'd be the boss, yeah. Let me tell you the deal, William. It's kind of a weird deal, but see what you think. First off, it looked to me like Doggett sat around on his ass most of the time while you guys did the work."

"You got that right."

"So it shouldn't take much of your time to do at least as good a job as him."

"I don't know about the paperwork. I never done that kind of work."

"That's part of the deal. I worked in an office for a while in the army, so I can help you figure it out. How hard can it be if Doggett did it?"

"I guess not too hard, you look at it that way."

"The only hard part is being responsible. Staying on top of things, making sure they get done."

"I'm the one mostly does that anyway."

"I figured. Now here's the weird part. I can make you building supervisor, but I can't give you a raise."

"You saying I be super on top of my old job and I don't get nothing extra for it?"

"You only get three things extra. You get to learn how to do paperwork from me. You get the title. And you get to write your own recommendation when you leave. You tell me what to put down, I'll put it down and sign it."

"Why I want to leave?"

"You'll be a qualified and experienced building supervisor then. Why would you want to hang around for the shit money we're paying you?"

"Why would the next guy offer me any more than I'm making?"

"Because I'd say on your recommendation that you were making however much you wanted to get out of the next guy."

"What if I just keep on doing what I do?"

"Well, we'll probably have to hire some other asshole like Doggett to do the paperwork."

"So all's that's happening here is you want to look good with the big bosses?"

"You got it, William."

"Well, okay. I'll give you a hand if you give me one. We see how it goes. Now tell me something, since we done cut the bullshit. What the hell is a bar lock and where do I get one?"

"So your total here comes to eight thousand, six hundred and twenty," the Beautiful Bathrooms guy said. We were sitting on the bench of the sauna he had just put in over Boucher's garage. It was the only place to sit, now that the floor mat was down in my new little gym. The heat in the sauna was off, and we were going over the Beautiful Bathrooms bill.

"Which means eight hundred and sixty-two for my sick cousin," I said.

"Right. I brought it in cash."

"I been thinking. I think he needs a thousand."

"Hey, hey, what is this? We had a deal. Ten percent."

"Yeah, but I been thinking how many times am I going to buy a sauna from you guys, you know? This is a one-shot for both of us."

"A deal is a deal."

"A better deal is a better deal. Rewrite that thing and bump it up a hundred and thirty-eight to make up the thousand and we're both happy."

"All the cash I brought was the eight sixty-two we agreed on."

"Take the extra out of your own pocket. You'll get it back when Mr. Boucher's check clears."

On the way back to the *Banner*, I dropped by the post office and mailed the money anonymously to Terry Dineen. It amounted to more than three weeks of the salary he wasn't getting anymore. At least for a while I'd be able to keep him going from kickbacks on my various special projects. The surveillance system was going to give the boxer a particularly good payday.

That night I went by Jonathan Paul's place after supper. He lived just off Mass. Ave. on the way from my building toward Central Square. His small house was stuffed full of furniture that mostly dated from the thirties and forties. Probably he had moved into his parents' place when they died and left everything as it was.

"Want a beer?" he asked. "Bud all right?"

"That's okay," I said. "Nothing for me."

Bud, Miller's, Coors, all the television beers taste like beer on the rocks.

"How goes the battle?" Jonathan asked.

"Not bad. This is the first job I ever liked."

"You sound like you mean it."

"I do. The few jobs I've had, I'd always felt like an outsider. So naturally I'd feel like an outsider to the insiders, too, and we mistrusted each other. This time my job is to pretend to be an insider, and it seems to come natural. I'm the boss's fair-haired boy. Does that make sense?"

"I'm not sure."

"Doesn't to me, either, but that's the way it's working out. Maybe it's like one of those actors that's shy except when he's onstage. Anyway, it turns out I can't actually *be* an insider but I can do a hell of an imitation of one. I even fired my first guy."

"Who was that?"

"Willard Doggett."

"Good choice. He would've never been hired in the first place, except his uncle was the Cushings' family butcher. Who's taking his place?"

"William Wells."

"I would have never thought of him, but it's probably another good choice. What are you doing hiring and firing in maintenance, though?"

"I figured it would give me access to the whole building, so I did a hostile takeover. I'm having all the keys changed and keeping the spares in my office. I'm having hidden cameras put up. Monitors in my office, of course."

"Hidden cameras? What the hell for?"

"So people will get pissed off at Boucher when they eventually find out about them. Which of course they will."

"I was going to say."

"If they're too slow finding out that they're all on 'Candid Camera,' I might even leak it myself. I don't want any happy campers around."

"Neither does Boucher. He rules by fear."

"That's fine up to a certain point. But if you push things far enough, sooner or later you get mutiny."

"Later, probably. It's a tough job market out there unless you like flipping burgers."

"Oh, I've got a lot of ideas to speed things up. Ideas to mess up Boucher's head, too. For instance, the other day he was complaining about people stealing all the papers out of a bunch of the *Banner*'s coin boxes on Mass. Ave. You wouldn't know anything about that, would you?"

"No."

"Of course not. I'm the one that's been doing it. It got a nice reaction, though. The Cobra's convinced it was you . . ."

"Jesus, Tom."

"Hey, business is a contact sport. Boucher says that all the time. Anyway, stealing all those papers got me to wondering if you guys really were doing any dirty tricks like that. I mean, you're on your home turf and he's not. There must be a lot of shit you could pull."

"Nothing like stealing papers. Just more or less routine stuff. Rack position, things like that."

"What's rack position?"

"Well, suppose a friend of yours runs a corner store. He's going to put your paper right up there where it can be seen, isn't he? Maybe make your competitor's paper a little hard to spot? Or suppose you happen to play poker with a guy that manages a big apartment complex and it just so happens he doesn't let the other guy's newsboys inside his buildings."

"You play poker with guys like that, do you?"

"Some, but mostly my circulation manager's the one who does. He worked thirty-one years for the *Banner* till one day he wakes up and finds Fogel just gave his job to his twenty-seven-year-old assistant."

"Ask your circulation manager for a few specifics, will you? Particular stores and buildings, whatever he's doing and exactly where."

"What for?"

"So I can give Boucher name, rank, and serial number."

"Why would we tell him our business?"

"What could he do about it if he knew?"

"Nothing."

"Fine. So let's piss him off."

Paul gave it a little thought and then nodded. "What the hell, why not?" he said.

"Another thing," I said. "How would you like a bright young woman to do your books or something."

"We contract out the bookkeeping."

"Couldn't hurt to do it in-house. There's somebody I have to talk to first, and then I'll get back to you on this. Now that I'm an executive, I get back to people on things."

"Are you really an executive?"

"In my mind I am. I've got a staff of two, now that I took over Willard's empire. I'm ordering all kinds of expensive shit for the paper. The surveillance system, stuff like that. I built Boucher a gym."

"A gym?"

"Sure, a wrestling room over his garage. Three evenings a week I teach him how to wrestle. He had to learn after he saw me put down Terry Dineen."

"Poor Terry. I loaned him a hundred last week, and you could see it tore the heart out of him to ask."

"I couldn't help it," I said unnecessarily. I had already told Jonathan Paul that I tried to talk Boucher into keeping the prize-fighter on, which was true. But I still felt guilty. After all, I could have just walked away from Terry Dineen. Or I could have turned down Boucher's offer. Maybe he would have changed his mind and stuck with the boxer.

"I'm not saying it was your fault," Paul said.

"Partly it was. Anyway, I feel shitty about it. I'm assuming I can count on you to hire him back on the sports desk if Boucher sells the paper to Serena Cushing."

"Absolutely, but it's a big if. Meanwhile, they're going to cut off the medical insurance for Terry's kid before long, and his unemployment checks won't last forever. All he's got to fall back on is the cash value of his life insurance policy."

"Maybe he can hold out for a while."

"Hard to see how."

"Let me tell you something entirely between us, okay?"

"I guess."

" 'I guess' is no good. I don't want anybody else to know under any circumstances, particularly Dineen. Okay?"

"Okay."

"I'm stealing from the paper. I sent Dineen a thousand bucks just today."

"Jesus, Tom, that's crazy."

"It's kickbacks. No way the suppliers would turn me in, because they're getting a piece of it."

"It's crazy anyway."

"Probably. But maybe it'll tide the poor bastard over till we can get him back on a payroll."

"Nice thought, but it's still crazy."

"I'm not asking you whether it's crazy. I'm just telling you what I'm doing."

"Hey, hey, simmer down. There's good crazy and bad crazy."

"I'm sorry. I just feel kind of touchy about the whole thing. The poor dumb bastard. I should have just let him hit me and walked off. The hell with it. We've talked about it enough. Tell me about Brad Boyle. How come a guy with his seniority survived the massacre?"

"Well, it helped that he's the unofficial computer guru . . ."

So we talked about other stuff, mainly the people at the *Banner.* Paul filled me in on all the holdovers from the Cushing days, and I told him whatever I could about the new people—mostly just the bare facts from the personnel files.

What with one thing and another, I was on my way out before I remembered to ask Jonathan Paul what kind of car he drove.

"Just your basic transportation," he said. "An '88 Plymouth Colt."

"I'll ask you the same thing Boucher asked me after he fired Dineen. Ever drive a Rolls, Jonathan?"

"Nope."

"Like to?"

"Boucher's?"

"No, but one just like it. The Cushing estate wants to lease it for you."

"Loosen up," I told Boucher, and his fingers eased on my left arm.

"If you were sure you wanted that arm, then you'd want a good grab on it, all right," I said. "But you can never be sure. Supposing you decide to go for something else. Before you can make your own move, you've got to let go of my arm. Slows you by a fraction of a second. Gives that fraction of a second to me."

I dropped my own hand from Boucher's arm and dove for his knee. The idea is to grab the toe of the forward foot with one hand, and the heel with the other, and force him to the mat by leaning into the inside of his knee with your left shoulder. But Boucher was just quick enough so that I missed my hold on his foot and had to settle for immobilizing it with my left hand. The instant he moved his free foot to regain his balance, I grabbed that ankle with my own free hand and dumped him face forward onto the mat.

In the real world I would have been on top of him the instant he hit, but I jumped to my feet instead and waited for him to get up.

"Shit," he said, lying there.

"You did good," I said. "You spoiled my knee dive."

"Yeah, but I should have thought you'd go for the other leg."

"We watch too much football. Guy only manages to get one leg, so he holds on for dear life. He'll practically never think of going for the other. Stupid game."

"You ever play?"

"Only in high school."

"Where was that?"

"In New York."

"City or state?"

"State."

Boucher smiled. By now he knew he'd never get much personal information out of me, but he didn't push it. He probably liked the thought that I had plenty to hide. He hired me because he thought I was mysterious and sinister, so I didn't want to spoil things by pulling out my baby pictures and high school yearbook.

He was on his feet now and took up position in front of me. "Let's work through that again, slow," he said. "Show me this knee dive that I supposedly spoiled before you dumped me on my face."

So I choreographed it for him in slow motion, stopping when I had my left shoulder properly positioned on the inside of his left leg just below the knee. "All I've got to do is shove, now that I've got your foot trapped," I said. I shoved enough so that he'd get the idea but not actually go down. "You don't want to shove too hard, though."

"Why not?"

"You'd blow the guy's knee for good. Lateral hits like that are what turns running backs into car salesmen."

"How hard is too hard?"

"Full force is too hard. You're just trying to get the guy on the ground, not lose the match for unnecessary roughness."

"In real life they don't call unnecessary roughness," Boucher said.

What perked him up was punishing holds. Whenever I mentioned that something was illegal, he'd wanted to play the maneuver over and over again until he got it down—or figured he had it down.

"Go ahead," I said. "Break my knee."

"Go full force?"

"Give it your best shot."

Boucher dove, and I let him get a good hold on my leading foot. Before he could ram his shoulder into my knee, though, there was nothing there to ram. I was already halfway to the mat and when I got there I wrapped him up immediately.

"Try it again," I said when I had let him up.

I gave him a couple more shots at crippling me, making him look foolish each time.

"Okay, enough," I said. "The point here is that you're not going to make good progress if you get hung up on particular moves. You could practice the knee dive for six months and I'd still get away."

"You're an experienced wrestler, though."

"Other people might get away, too. Maybe by accident,

because of the way they were standing or the way they shifted their weight. Maybe they're stronger, or quicker, or they've got a wooden leg. Who knows? What you ought to be learning isn't a collection of moves. It's a whole process."

"Okay."

"Specialize and a good man will kick the shit out of you every time. It's like if a pitcher could only throw low and inside."

All this was a regular riff that I used on the Harvard wrestlers, although Boucher didn't know about me and the Harvard wrestlers.

"Look, Thurman, I understand that you're not interested in competition wrestling. What should we call what you want to learn? Combat wrestling maybe?"

"Sounds close enough."

"Fine. So we don't have to pay a whole lot of attention to pinning holds, for instance. You don't want to just pin somebody, I mean, what would be the point? So he wouldn't run away while you talked to him?"

Boucher smiled. No, of course that wasn't the point. Boucher was a Wall Street killer, a rich boy for the cover of *Forbes*.

"But we've got to work through the basics first," I said. "Position. Balance. Flexibility. Taking your man down. Going behind. Hold-downs. Escapes. Even pinning holds. Plenty of pinning holds will break bones if you apply a little more pressure."

"You're the boss. What's next?"

"Bridges. Down on your back."

Not many nonwrestlers can do a good bridge, and Boucher was no exception.

"Up, up, up," I said. "Watch."

From lying flat on my back I went up into a high bridge, with most of my body weight supported on the top of my head and the rest on the bottoms of my feet. Bridges were a literal pain to do in the old days of canvas mats, but at least our fancy new foam rubber mat didn't grind your scalp.

"Now you try it," I said, letting myself back down.

Boucher wobbled and strained, the veins standing out in his neck. I let him rest a minute, and then had him try again. And again. And again.

Then we did spinners and jumping jacks and leg raises and pull-ups on the fancy Universal machine I had bought. Then we went back to drills and more drills until he was pretty near the end of his string. It had taken longer to wear him down than it would with most beginners. Boucher had promise. He was strong and quick and aggressive, and he stuck to it without complaint.

"Jesus, what a workout," he said once he had collapsed onto a bench in our fancy new sauna.

"Another month and you'll be used to it."

"I don't understand why I'm not used to it already. I thought I kept in pretty good shape, but I'm sore all over anyway."

"The weights and the machines don't give you the same range of movement. You're using hundreds of muscles now that you haven't used since you were a little kid. Two-year-olds and wrestlers are about the only ones who twist around enough to give all the machinery a workout. Well, maybe gymnasts do too."

Boucher nodded and closed his eyes. I closed mine, too, and let the heat seep into me. After a while I started to talk.

"I was in the Bow and Arrow a couple nights back, heard some guys talking about the *Banner*. Over I go, naturally, and pretty soon I'm buying them beers and they're buying me beers, mostly me buying, you know. One of them lives in the Edgemere Apartments, you familiar with the building? Over by Kendall Square? The rest of them all live out by Porter, though. One of them's got a little mom-and-pop out there.

"Anyway, the Edgemere guy says his super is tight with some guy that used to deliver the *Banner* in the neighborhood, but now he works for the *Cambridge Trader* and so he got the super to keep the *Banner* newsboys out of the building. They got to leave the papers in a pile in the lobby, you ever hear of that? Can supers do that?"

I opened my eyes and saw that now Boucher had his eyes open, too.

So I told him about the racks in the mom-and-pop store, too, and one or two other scams that Jonathan Paul had found out about for me.

"The thing is," I said when I had emptied my bag, "there's only so much you can find out from the outside of an organization. This guy Paul works out of the back of a drugstore, you imagine? I wish I was a fly on the wall there."

"Or a bug, huh?" Boucher said.

"Bugs are a possibility. I'll think about it."

"I wonder why I don't know about these circulation problems already," Boucher said. "Kennealy's got to know."

Gerry Kennealy was the *Banner*'s circulation manager, the twenty-seven-year-old who had replaced the old manager.

"Nobody likes to bring bad news to the boss," I said. "Maybe Kennealy's waiting till he's got the problem solved before he tells you about it. Or maybe he doesn't want you to know."

"Why wouldn't he want me to know?"

"Maybe he doesn't want the problem solved. New ownership and everything, it's hard to tell who's on your side and who's stabbing you in the back."

8

GERRY KENNEALY MAY HAVE BEEN only twenty-seven, but he had been working in the paper's circulation department one way or another for sixteen years. He started out as a carrier at the age of eleven, and then helped out on the trucks part-time while he was going to junior college. Once he had his degree as an associate of arts, he was qualified to work full-time at the job he had been doing part-time all along. But the A.A. only got him to the bottom level of the American mandarinate, and the footing was slippery down there, and Kennealy was looking worried.

As he should have.

For one thing, not only was he in front of the big boss himself, but Alan Fogel and I were there to add to the intimidation.

For another, Thurman Boucher hadn't asked him to sit down. So he had to stand in front of Boucher's big, bare desk like a schoolboy called in by the principal, only this was far worse than the principal. This was an American prince of the blood, a man able to make the world believe, whatever the truth was, that his net worth was well into nine digits.

"Tom here was able to pick it up in a neighborhood bar," Boucher said with a mildness that wasn't deceptive at all. Cobras don't have to holler to kill you. "How come you didn't know about it, Gerry? You're supposed to be my circulation manager."

"I knew about it."

"Tom here knew about it, too, only he was kind enough to share it with me. He thought I might be interested, since I'm the publisher. Didn't you think I might be interested?"

"Yes, sir, I knew you'd be interested, Mr. Boucher, only the only thing was I didn't want to bother you with it till I was on top of the situation."

"Just how did you intend to do that?"

"Well, sir, Mr. Boucher, actually there are a couple of things. Three or four things . . ."

"Which means you haven't got a clue, doesn't it? Did it occur to you that *I* might have a clue? I've been in this business nearly as long as you've been alive, after all."

Gerry Kennealy had been in it since the age of eleven himself, but naturally he didn't bring that up. "Yes, sir, I should have done that, sir. I see that now. Next time I will, Mr. Boucher."

"This time is what we're worrying about. How many locations is this happening?"

"A dozen or so. Well, maybe twenty, twenty-five."

Boucher turned to me. "Well, what about it, Tom? We've got a situation developing here. What would you do?"

"Make the drop."

"There you go, Gerry."

"Make the drop?" Kennealy asked.

"Pay the sons of bitches," Boucher said.

"Pay them? I don't understand. How?"

"Ask Alan later. He'll tell you how we did it in Salisbury.

We expect much better things from you in the future, Gerry. Now you can go."

"Yes, sir," the circulation manager said, and practically ran for it.

"What a moron," Boucher said when Kennealy was gone. "Well, at least he works cheap."

"What did you do in Salisbury?" I asked Fogel.

"Special sales bonuses in the locations where we were having difficulty."

"When you're only getting thirty-five cents a copy, how much of a bonus can you afford to give?"

"We were driving a competitor out of business," Fogel said.

"You can afford whatever it takes in cases like that," Boucher explained. "You'll get it back later, once you've killed off the competition and reestablished a clean market."

"Can we kill off this guy?" I said. "Jonathan Paul?"

"Oh, absolutely," Boucher said. "If he ever becomes really bothersome."

"He's picking up a lot of our insert business," Fogel said. "That's the trouble with shoppers."

"How do you mean?" I asked. "In fact, what are inserts, as long as I'm asking dumb questions?"

"Advertising inserts," Fogel said. "The things from Star Markets and Lechmere that are stuffed into the paper. Newspapers can deliver them cheaper than the post office can."

"And a shopper can deliver them even cheaper," Boucher said. "Costs are lower for the shopper."

"Why?"

"For one reason, because the shopper has little or no editorial costs. It probably just runs free handouts and boilerplate, or it may run no news at all. But if you just want your inserts delivered, you're not going to care if nobody reads what they're wrapped in."

"You are going to care about household penetration, though," Fogel said. "Newspapers with paid circulation never reach every household. You're lucky to have fifty percent penetration."

"To be precise," Boucher said, "the *Banner* had forty-three point two percent household penetration in Cambridge itself last week. Less in Somerville and Belmont and so on."

"Whereas a shopper isn't limited to just subscribers, so it can theoretically have a hundred percent penetration," Fogel said.

"Do we know what the *Trader* in fact does have, Alan?" his boss asked.

"Maybe in the sixties, but that'd be a guess. When we get things squared away here in our own shop, we'll start tracking Mr. Paul's little effort."

"One just like yours," I told Boucher. We were coming up on a stoplight on Mt. Auburn Street, next day on the way home from work.

"So it is," he said. Actually it was newer than Boucher's, although Rolls-Royces changed so little that you couldn't really tell. But it was a Silver Spur III as opposed to our Silver Spur II. Two days ago, it had been painted Storm Grey just like ours. Fortunately it already had the Silverstone Grey interior with the slate piping. That would have been a major expense to change, since Rolls-Royce uses only unscarred and unscored hides from Denmark. They're unscarred because Danish cows are dehorned, and the Danes use electric fences instead of barbed wire. Also Denmark doesn't have the warble fly problem you've got to contend with in England, where the grubs dig their way out and leave little holes in the hide all along the backbone. I knew these things from the Rolls-Royce literature in Boucher's garage.

The enemy Rolls was one lane over from us and a couple cars ahead. The light changed and the line started to move.

"Look at that," Boucher said. "He's got some kind of

bumper sticker on it. Can you imagine putting a bumper sticker on a Rolls?"

"Guy's got to be a total asshole," I said.

"Wait a minute," Boucher said, all of a sudden excited. "There's something about . . . Catch up to him!"

So I rammed it to the fire wall, just like peeling out of the high school parking lot only better. When you're used to an '87 Subaru, a three-ton toy with a fuel-injected 412 cubic inch V-8 engine brings a whole new world of motoring pleasure to children of all ages. The acceleration pressed us back into our seats as I swung to the right lane so I could blow past the three cars ahead of me in the left lane and get a little running room.

"Pull even so I can see him," Boucher said, not quite hollering but sounding urgent.

No trouble. The other Rolls was rolling along at a good clip but nothing special. The driver didn't even seem to know that a couple of superheroes were closing in on him. He didn't even turn to look when I pulled even. He and I had talked that over a lot, whether to flash a finger or be cool, and cool won.

"That son of a bitch," Boucher said. "Okay, you can drop back now."

"Guy you know?"

"That's Jonathan Paul."

"Guy that puts out the shopper?"

Boucher nodded.

"You don't mind my asking, what does a car like that cost?"

"They list at a hundred and ninety. I imagine you could jew the dealer down by at least twenty thousand."

"First time I ever saw TV in a car."

"TV?" Boucher said.

"What it looked like. Some kind of little screens anyway,

on the back of the headrests. Both sides. You suppose you could get different channels on each one?"

"I wouldn't know."

"Probably those TVs cost as much as a lot of people's whole car. How could a guy like him afford a car like that?"

"Good question."

"Maybe he borrowed it," I said.

"Who would loan him a Rolls-Royce?"

"Yeah, you're right. Can you rent them? Maybe that's what it said on the bumper sticker, some agency name."

"You didn't see what it said?"

"Too busy driving."

"It said 'My other car is a Cadillac.' "

Felicia Lamport could eat a couple of pints of ice cream at a sitting, no problem. So we were at Herrell's, which used to be a bank before it turned into an ice cream shop, sitting inside what used to be the vault. Now it was painted to look like a very bad artist's idea of an undersea grotto. The grotto smelled like the milk room in a dairy.

Felicia had rocky road and vanilla bean. I had butter pecan and vanilla bean. All four pints were hand-packed, of course. Our experience on previous dates had been that the second half of the first pint and the first half of the second pint were the best. At the beginning it would be a little too hard and at the end it would be getting soft. But as the fellow says in another connection, there ain't no such thing as bad ice cream.

"What do you think?" I said at last. "Want to split a fifth one?"

"Two's my limit these days," Felicia said. "I'm afraid the years are creeping up on me. You may get me a cup of black coffee, however. And then you can tell me how you're coming along with the revolting Mr. Boucher."

"Mr. Boucher isn't revolting," I said when I got back with her coffee and my tea. "Not to his inner circle, like me."

"I don't think of you as inner circle material, Tom."

"Oh, yeah, he lets me sit in on all kinds of stuff. I think he's grooming me."

"Grooming you? You don't mean the sort of grooming monkeys do, do you?"

"Certainly not. He's grooming me for higher things. The other day he asked me what I thought of our op-ed page."

"What did you tell him?"

"I told him I'd rather read the back of a cereal box."

"Did you really?"

"I really did. He laughed, so I asked him if he actually paid money for that stuff. He said unfortunately he did."

"Who do they run? I must say I never noticed. Pat Buchanan and people like that?"

"The *Globe* has every columnist you ever heard of tied up, including the neo-Nazis. Turns out that's normal. Big papers buy up columns and comics they never even use. The idea is to keep them out of other papers in the area."

"That sounds vaguely unconstitutional to me."

"Me, too, but Boucher straightened me out. Buchanan is just a commodity, like a brand of beer. You buy a franchise to distribute him in a certain area. Editorial material is just product. Grow up, Felicia."

"I'm growing fast. Do you suppose your revolting friend would like free product, Tom?"

"No question about it."

"Why doesn't he fill up his op-ed page with the musings of Harvard professors?"

"Do they work free?"

"Don't tell Mr. Boucher, but some of them would pay him."

"Did you happen to see this, Thurman?" I asked my revolting friend the next morning. We were on our way to the office, and I was holding out a folded copy of yesterday's *Cambridge Trader*. I had highlighted an item in the help-wanted column.

"Bookkeeper," it said. "Get in on the ground floor with a small but growing publishing firm. We are seeking an experienced person to keep books and manage our office. Grow with us in both responsibility and salary! Call 681-8181 for an interview."

"So?" Boucher said once he had glanced at the ad.

"I noticed it because it was so long. They didn't leave out the little words to save money, the way most people would. I checked the number for the hell of it and it's the number of the paper."

"Stupid to hire a bookkeeper," Boucher said. "They should contract that out. But maybe most of the job is running the office."

"Alan was saying someday we're going to start tracking what the *Banner* is up to. Why not now?"

"What are you suggesting?"

"Why don't we send him a bookkeeper?"

"That'd be fun, wouldn't it? But he'd know anybody we sent over."

"I know a girl who could do it."

"What would we have to pay her?"

"Not much if she got the job. Jonathan Paul would be paying her a salary, and we'd just sweeten it up a little. Maybe promise her a job at the *Banner* for helping us get rid of the *Trader*."

Boucher turned it over in his mind. "This person," he said. "Is she somebody you can trust?"

"I've known her for years. Why don't I at least tell her to call up for an interview? If they make her an offer, I'll bring her in so you can meet her."

"Sure, send her over to the son of a bitch. Bumper sticker on a Rolls. I can't get over that."

"Guy's a total loser. No class at all."

"I was telling Alison about those TVs in the headrests, and she said she wasn't even aware they had such a thing available. Which I have to say I wasn't aware of either. Long and short of it is she thinks they might be kind of fun to have on long trips. Can you look into it?"

"I'll get on it. Something else I was thinking of, too. I still can't believe a loser like that owns a Rolls. Got to belong to his rich uncle, something like that. If you won't need me till lunch, I'll go downtown to Motor Vehicles and check it out."

"You know somebody there?"

"I'll manage."

No reason to tell him that in Massachusetts any citizen can just stand in line, pay five bucks, and get all the information listed on any other citizen's vehicle registration. And in fact I didn't even need to go that far. I just drove over to Felicia's house and sat around in her kitchen for an hour while we talked over the possibilities. "I think Tingley, Davis is the firm you want," she said. "I've known George Tingley since he was six. I can't imagine him knowing Mr. Boucher socially, and he certainly wouldn't do business with him. I'm sure he'd rather eat off the sidewalk."

So at lunchtime I told Boucher that title to the Silver Spur III had been transferred to Jonathan Paul from somebody called Tingley, Davis only ten days before.

"What the hell is Jonathan Paul doing driving a car that used to belong to Tingley, Davis?" Boucher asked.

"Who's this Tingley guy?"

"It's not a man. It's an investment banking firm. Bunch of goddamned hidebound Boston Brahmins who still do business exactly the way their grandfathers did."

"Maybe they sold him the car."

"Why would they have it to sell?" Boucher asked. "Tingley, Davis is the kind of place where the senior partners drive old Buicks. What the hell connection could there be between Jonathan Paul and Tingley, Davis?"

"Would they be fronting the guy money for his paper, maybe? Is that the kind of business they do?"

"It would be totally out of character," Boucher said. "What the hell is going on, anyway?"

"Maybe my girl can find out," I said. "If she gets the job."

"Is that what she is? Your girl?"

"Just a manner of speaking. If I want a girl I hire one."

"I'm sure it's cheaper that way."

"Plus hookers don't want to spend the night. I don't like anybody around me when I'm asleep."

In fact I didn't mind it a bit. When you come from a litter of eight, you're used to sleeping all jumbled up like puppies. But I was afraid Alison Boucher would eventually come on to me again. It wasn't clear whether she had been hinting at a twosome or a threesome, but neither one sounded like a very strong career move. So I wanted to plant the idea that there was something odd about my sex life. Preferably that I didn't really have one, which had the added virtue of being, most of the time, true.

Gladys Williams hadn't always been a medical student. When I first met her, she was a lab technician for the Cambridge police. Before that she had worked for Mass. General and in Harvard's biology department, all the time taking courses at Lesley College. None of the courses had been in bookkeeping or accounting.

"I've never worked in a real business," Gladys said. "I couldn't even keep the books in this dump." By which she meant The Tasty, where we were breakfasting.

"I said you'd be the bookkeeper, I didn't say you'd have to keep the books."

"The columns add themselves up, is that it? Forget it, Bethany. I'm busy at the hospital. I haven't got time."

"You don't need time, either. This is a no-show."

"How's the money?"

"It's a no-money, too. Well, not strictly. The *Trader* won't be paying you anything. But Boucher will be slipping you a hundred bucks a week off the books."

"I've got to say I'm warming up to this, Bethany. You sure there's no work involved?"

"You get a chance to meet the Cobra, if you call that work. He wants to scope you out."

"Hey, I want to scope him out, too. Maybe he'll pay off my student loans."

"Probably he will. That's how he got so rich, giving away money."

"Do I report to him? I mean, if I do, that's work."

"We'll see if he wants you to."

"How do I know what to report?"

"You and me will sit down with Jonathan Paul and make up stuff to mind-fuck him with."

"That's work, too."

"Come on, Gladys. You and Felicia ganged up to get me into this thing in the first place."

"Actually that's true. Well, shit. Okay."

"The fact of the matter is that most people don't read the op-ed page, and practically nobody reads the editorial page," Boucher said. "A lot of my papers don't even have editorials, and no one has ever even noticed, let alone complained."

"How come anybody has them, then?" I asked.

"Two reasons. One is to make the owner feel important . . ."

". . . Which a man like you certainly doesn't need," I finished. Flattery will get you everywhere. In real jobs I had never been able to slather it on, but now that I had a fake job, my nose seemed to brown right up.

"The second reason is to make the editor feel important," Boucher said. "That's why I seldom interfere with editorial policy. It doesn't cost a cent to let editors and reporters run loose in their playpens, up to a point. Their pathetic little egos mean more to them than their paychecks, thank God. Let them write their editorials. Since nobody reads them, after all, and since they cost me practically nothing."

"But you do pay something for the syndicated columns, though?"

"A little. Probably shouldn't."

"Reason I ask, I had an idea about getting Harvard professors to write columns for nothing."

"Christ, professors are even worse writers than reporters and columnists."

"You say nobody reads the stuff anyway, so what's the difference?"

"Not much, I suppose."

"I know some people who know some people on the faculty. You mind if I talk with Alan about trying to round some stuff up for him? Or is he one of those guys who likes to feel important?"

"I raised Alan by hand. He understands that the difference between a good paper and a bad paper isn't the words. It's the numbers."

When I was at Iowa, wrestling and going to the occasional class, there was a kid in my dorm from South America. I never bothered to find out where in South America, but it was someplace with mountains because that's where Diego went to shoot peasants. Maybe he was lying, but if so he was a hell of a liar. "In movies everybody hold himself and do like this," he told me once, staggering around. "Never happen like this. Fall down only, that's all. Good shot, they never move no more. Not so good shot, do like this." He got down on the floor and acted out a man trying to drag himself to shelter, or a man in spasms. I saw a man die from a bullet wound once, and he went into the exact same kind of spasms. But I never saw them in a movie, and I don't think Diego did either.

Anyway the point is that this was a guy so rich that he once lost a new station wagon and didn't even know what state it was in. He and his friends were driving back from Aspen drunk when the car started acting up late at night in a snowstorm. They made it to a farmhouse where the farmer let them leave it in a barn while they hitchhiked for help. All three of them fell asleep in the car that stopped for them, and the driver didn't wake them up till he dropped them off in Council Bluffs. Nobody thought to ask him where he had picked them up. It had to be Kansas or Nebraska, though, or possibly eastern Colorado. So that was it for the station wagon and Diego had to buy another.

And that isn't the point either. The point is that Diego had never been skiing before that trip to Aspen. Apparently all he had done in the mountains back home was shoot Indians. When he sobered up back at college he had fallen in love with the sport. So he subscribed to everything and talked to everybody and went out and bought three pairs of the most expensive skis on the market, and a closetful of the kind of space suits and Darth Vader helmets that the Olympic downhillers wear, and boots in enough different colors so that his outfits would always be coordinated. He jetted out to the Rockies every weekend, and Diego's weekends ran four or five days. He and his personal instructor were the first up the mountain every morning and the last off it every night. Diego was a pretty good athlete to begin with, and he worked at this new thing, drunk, hung over, or sober, until he got to be a hell of a skier.

Boucher was like that about wrestling. He had me buy him every book on wrestling that was in print, which wasn't very many. So then I plugged my Mac into the Hollis system at Widener Library and got used-book dealers to search the market for the few wrestling books that Harvard had in its collection. Then I had the dealers search for whatever was listed in the bibliographies of the books they came up with, although wrestling books aren't much on bibliographies.

I was even getting into the art world. When I came across a photo of a wrestling painting by Degas, Boucher set me to work finding out if any preliminary sketches for it existed. The painting showed naked Spartan girls challenging naked Spartan boys to a match. It was hanging in the National Gallery in London, out of even Boucher's grasp. But its existence gave him ideas, and now I was supposed to be poking around galleries and museums for leads on art with a wrestling theme.

It was fun, of course. There I was, being paid a salary to realize all my boyhood dreams with somebody else's money. I didn't think of it as his private gym, his private collection of wrestling books and art. I thought of it as mine. What right did he have to it? I was the one who picked it out. I was the wrestler, not him.

Although to be fair, he was getting pretty good. We had been at it hard for only six weeks now, and already he could have made the squad at a small college that didn't take wrestling too seriously. That wasn't bad for a novice in his forties, not bad at all. Amazing performance, really. Either that, or I was a hell of a coach.

The real reason, though, was rage. Boucher didn't show it most of the time, but he was like a membrane bloated with anger and about to burst. I knew all about that kind of thing, because the anger was in me, too, under just as much pressure. So when he let his aggression out, mine came right out to meet it. And to contain it, balk it, thwart it, because I was a little faster and a lot more skilled.

We were down on the mat in the starting position with me underneath, which gave him the advantage. To give him more advantage, I told him to holler go. As I figured he would, he started his move an instant before he hollered. I let him get me down on my stomach before I began my escape and reversal. "Shit," he snarled when I had him on his back, and then he smiled a good-sport smile to take the edge off of the snarl. I smiled back. Neither of us was fooled.

"Let's do it again," I said.

We did it four times running, and I managed an escape and a reversal each time. "See what I did?" I asked after the fourth time.

"Seemed different each time."

"That's the point. Never be predictable."

"The way I was, huh?"

"Now you got it. You started with the same move four times in a row. Okay, eyes closed."

I kept my eyes open, while he wrestled blind. The point is to develop balance based on feel alone. Wrestling is one of the few sports the blind can excel at.

This time I slacked off so that Boucher and I were wrestling more or less evenly. He wouldn't be doing his balance much good if I kept him down all the time. He knew I was slacking off, naturally. It was well established in every bone and muscle of his body that I was dominant. It drove him crazy, which in this case took the form of beating his head against a stone wall. Instead of going with the flow, learning the moves at fifty percent power, he went flat out every minute. Flat out meant that pretty quickly he was completely exhausted.

"Takes it right out of you, doesn't it?" I said. Boucher was lying on his back, his chest heaving.

"You're still going strong," he managed to get out.

"I've been at it a long time, so I'm more efficient. The more you know, the less you work. You'll get there."

I could have told him he'd learn more if he'd take it easy, but it wasn't advice that he'd be able to take. The Cobra was irritable by nature. Besides, it would have been bad advice anyway. His kind of savage, relentless aggression was one of the most valuable qualities a wrestler could have. No one reaches the top without it.

Boucher was in good shape, so it didn't take long for his breathing to slow down and his strength to come back. Now it was his turn to win, or at least seem to. I ended each session with some new trick that he could practice on me. Generally a rotten trick, which was the kind he preferred.

We stood facing each other, both of us in a slight crouch, balanced and easy. He knew how to fall without hurting himself by now, so there wouldn't be much risk in what I was about to show him.

"If you can get a guy to shake hands with you, his ass is yours," I said. "Go ahead, shake."

As I expected, he landed well, breaking his fall with his feet so his back and head wouldn't smack the floor too hard. And the four-inch mat soaked up a lot of the shock, so he was more surprised than hurt.

"See?" I said. "You can't do anything about it even if you know it's coming. Well, actually there are countermoves, and we'll get to them eventually. For now, let's learn the move itself."

We walked through it slowly half a dozen times until he began to get the feel of it.

"Okay," I said when he was ready, "let's do it for real."

I varied the problem slightly for him each time, shifting balance or direction so he had to compensate. Once he botched it completely, but for the most part he sent me flying spectacularly to the mat on my back. I was about to roll over and hop up after my sixth or seventh fall when I heard hands clapping.

It was Alison Boucher. In her simple pale yellow dress with little white sandals on her little tanned feet and a green ribbon in her hair, she looked like a picture from the kind of catalogs you get if you live in an outlying suburb with a Republican ZIP code.

"I'm impressed, Thurman," she said.

"Don't be. He's letting me do it."

"I'm still impressed. I'm impressed he's willing to let you do it, too."

"It's not dangerous with a mat," I said. "You just have to know how to fall."

"Well, you fall beautifully, Tom. And you throw beautifully, too, Thurman, if that's the word."

She went over to Boucher, who was bare chested and running with sweat, and she in her pretty pastel dress took him in her arms and kissed him. When the kiss ended, he caressed her cheek with the backs of his fingers. His sweat had made dark patches on her frock. She leaned forward, stopping short of a kiss, and put her tongue out till it just touched his lips.

She didn't look at me, but she knew I was looking at her. The message might have been "See how very much in love we are?" Or maybe "Come on in, the water's fine." Or something else, or nothing. But it certainly wasn't hostile.

"Well, I'll leave you boys to your fun," she said and headed toward the door. Just before she got there, she spun around.

"Lord, in all the excitement I almost forgot what I came over for," she said to Boucher. "Robbie Haseltine called to make sure we were still coming to Canton."

"Why wouldn't we? We told him we were."

"I know. What he really wanted to say was that we were welcome to stay at their house and they would have some local people over that he wanted us to meet, and yatata, yatata. He's such a total twit."

"You won't have to put up with him much longer, Lissy." It was the first time I had heard the nickname; he had always referred to her as Alison before.

"Thank God for small favors," she said. "Robbie's good-looking enough in his way, but he's not exactly Mr. Excitement."

"Ask him if they've got room for three," Boucher said.

"All right. Who else is coming?"

"I thought I'd bring Tom along."

"Hmm," she said, looking at me. "Good idea."

When she had gone, I asked Boucher who Robbie Haseltine was.

"He's the editor of the *Canton Times-Dispatch*. The publisher is his mother-in-law, Christina."

"You're buying the paper, are you?"

"It's looking good so far."

"What use would I be?"

"I just wanted to give you a look at the process. I have a feeling you might be good at acquisitions."

"I don't know anything about financing, contracts, that kind of stuff."

"It's not about that. It's about making people do what you want them to do. Wrestling no hands, if you can imagine such a thing."

Sure I could. I had been doing it with him since my first day on the job.

9

THE FOLLOWING TUESDAY BOUCHER'S
secretary, Louise, told me that Mr. T's three o'clock appointment had canceled, and I asked her to slip me into the slot
instead. I wanted him to meet Gladys Williams.

So she was sitting with me in the outer office, wearing a
disguise. "Jesus, Gladys, where did you get that dress?" I
whispered so Louise couldn't hear. "You look like Debbie
Reynolds."

"Debbie Reynolds was before my time, you superannuated
old fart."

"I notice you heard of her, though. You think that's what
a bookkeeper is supposed to look like? Debbie Reynolds?"

"*A*, Bethany, Debbie Reynolds never wore anything like
this. *B*, you're probably mixing her up with Audrey Hepburn
in *Sabrina*. *C*, Audrey Hepburn never wore anything like this,
either. You're thinking of demure, Bethany. A quality, not
a person. What I got on here, asshole, it's demure."

"Somehow you don't sound demure."

"When it's time for demure, you will find me totally demure."

"Mr. Boucher will see-you now," Louise said.

I went in alone. I wanted Gladys on tap, but I didn't know if Boucher would want to meet her face-to-face. He might want to keep his hands clean.

"Sit down, Tom," he said when I went in. "What do you have that can't wait?"

"Only one thing, really. But I thought I'd run through a couple of other things while they're on my mind. Alan said to go ahead and give it a shot with the Harvard professors, so I got a couple of yeses and a maybe. Alan says the stuff they came up with is pretty bad, but that's not the point."

"The point being it's free, huh?"

"Well, that. But mostly it's community relations. All this *Bummer* stuff? What I was figuring with Alan, once we start running crap from these professors, what are they going to say to each other at the faculty club? Did you see my piece in the *Bummer*, Professor? I don't think so. We're buying dignity here."

"I suppose the stuff is completely unreadable as written?"

"Sure, but it's key to run it as is. My friend who gave me the idea, she says professors are like politicians. They all think they can write. If we started changing the stuff into English, they wouldn't send it in. Look, Harvard is the key to respect in Cambridge."

"Not M.I.T.?"

"M.I.T. is about brains. Who cares, you know what I mean? But Harvard is about money. She has, this is my friend who knows Harvard I'm talking about, she has another idea, too. She says we can buy our way in by printing the *Lampoon* for nothing."

The *Lampoon* was Harvard's humor magazine. Its clubhouse was a funky little castle sitting on a sliver of land between Bow Street and Mass. Ave. Judging from the piles of empties that were always out back, its main function was parties.

"The *Lampoon* has millions of dollars in the bank from the movies and parody issues," Boucher said. "It doesn't need free printing."

"No, but it'll take it. We get the professors on board by printing their garbage, and we get the kids on board by printing the *Lampoon*'s garbage. If you couldn't do it for free, maybe you could do it at cost. At least think about it."

"All right."

"Okay, next thing is the surveillance cameras. The system's mostly up and working, the visible ones in the rest rooms and parking lot plus the hidden ones everywhere else. The monitors are in my office."

"What have you picked up so far?"

"Some drinking on the job. A couple transactions that could have been drugs but no way to prove it. It's only been a week or so."

"What are we going to do about the drugs and the drinking?"

"Nothing. We just keep it in the bank. What we want to do is get tape of as many people fucking up as we can. Suppose we get labor problems down the road? Well, if we've got something on practically everybody, we can use it to squeeze them. Suppose you want to fire somebody that's basically just fucking off, but you can't prove cause. You come to me and I got him on tape. Now you're not firing him because he's a fuck-off or a union red hot. You're firing him because he deals pot or he rips off office supplies or whatever. Anyway the system is up and running is all I wanted to tell you. Any really good stuff that comes up, I'll let you and Alan know about it."

"Just me," Boucher said. "How are you coming with that business over at the *Trader*?"

"That was the main thing I wanted to talk to you about. She got the job."

"Good for her."

"I didn't know if you'd want to meet her or not, but she's outside if you do."

"Bring her on in, sure."

I went out and got Gladys, wearing her "Lawrence Welk Show" disguise. For all the time I've known her, she's never had fewer than two men on the string at once. She lets them know about each other, on the theory that she'll get better performance out of them that way. She likes them shy and inexperienced, on the theory that they won't have any bad habits to break, and she can train them up right. Whenever she has a stall vacant in her stable she goes looking for the guys who stand around at the edges of parties. If they strike her as smart and trainable after a few minutes of conversation, she just says to them, basically, let's fuck. I've seen her do it. Case the crowd, move in, and she's out of there with her catch in ten minutes, max. Once when I was a kid I saw a red-tailed hawk blast through the leaves of an old oak tree, nail a squirrel off his branch, and carry the poor bastard away without even slowing down. That was Gladys, too.

"What do you do with them when you get them home?" I asked her once.

"I hustle them straight into the shower," she said. "You want to make sure they're cleaned off good. Besides, we're not talking Warren Beatty here. My kind of guys, they get overstimulated unless you gentle them down at first, get them used to the human touch."

So there she was, Gladys dressed up as Miss Goody Two-Shoes, doing a groupie act for the captain of industry himself.

"Gosh, Mr. Boucher," Gladys said, adoration winning out over her natural awe and shyness, "this is a really wonderful opportunity for me. I've been reading about you for years, only of course I got to say you look a lot younger than your picture, but all they ever run in the *Wall Street Journal* is those little drawing things instead of real pictures and you never know whether they really look like the real person or not."

She was babbling, poor thing. I bet the pope hears a lot of that, too, during his audiences.

"You read the *Wall Street Journal*, do you?" Boucher asked.

"Oh, absolutely. My first accounting professor said a person with business ambitions should read it every day."

"You have business ambitions, I take it?"

"Please don't laugh at me, Mr. Boucher, but I do." Now she was the young Judy Garland, singing her heart out to Mr. Gable.

"I'm not laughing at you," the Cobra said. "I have been accused of having business ambitions myself."

"I'll just bet you have, Mr. Boucher. May I say something, Mr. Boucher? May I say that I'd give anything to work for you?"

"Consider it done, Gladys. Tom will take care of the details."

"No, I meant directly for you, someday. Really for you. Is there a chance that if I do well on this special assignment that maybe you would . . . ? I mean if something might open up, of course."

"Something always opens up, for the right person. Just demonstrate that you're the right person, and you'll see."

"I'll be the right person. I'll do anything I humanly can. You know what it would be like for me, working for a man like you, Mr. Boucher? It would be like being accepted to a great university. Like Harvard, only even better."

"Well, we don't give out degrees at the Boucher Group, but there can be other rewards. For real producers."

"I'll be a real producer. Just tell me what information you want, and I'll get it for you."

"Let's wait for a few days at least, until we see what your job gives you access to. Then we can decide what to focus in on. Tom, you keep me in touch. And Gladys, we'll talk again before long."

"Thank you, sir, Mr. Boucher. Thank you so much."

"Hang on for a minute, will you, Tom?" Boucher said as Gladys headed for the door.

"I'll be right out," I told her.

When she had gone, Boucher said, "Homely little thing, but I think she's just right for the job."

"You don't have to keep her on afterward, you know," I said. "That wasn't part of the deal."

"I just might, though. That naked desire to please can be very useful."

"Wouldn't it be a tip-off to Jonathan Paul if she quit his paper and went straight to work for the *Banner?*"

"Oh, I'd start her out somewhere else. Sometimes the hardest thing is to find out what's going on at your own papers. Be a good way for her to learn the business, actually. Maybe someday I could make her a publisher."

"From a bookkeeper? I thought you had to be an editor or something."

"People from the news side tend to make poor publishers. They don't have the intelligence for it, or the temperament. My best publishers come up through the business side, or from the advertising or circulation departments. You don't have to know anything about the news side to run a paper. No reason you couldn't do it yourself."

"Apart from not knowing a thing about the business."

"Would you like to learn?"

"Why not?"

"Why not, indeed. I could move you around for a few years, various papers, various departments. You'd pick it up fast.

Christ, it's not rocket science, its manufacturing and merchandising and distributing a product. And that product, contrary to what most people assume, is not news. It's advertising."

"When you put it like that, I see what you mean."

"You might make a terrific publisher."

"I'll be damned. I never even thought about it."

"Well, think about it. It's partly why I thought it would be good for you to come along on the Canton trip. Be a fly on the wall. You might pick up a few things."

Gladys was waiting for me in the outer office, and I walked her back to her car.

"Personally I wanted to puke, but the Cobra loved it," I told her. "Greed groupies turn him on."

"Sure they do. Deep down, everybody wants to have groupies."

"He wants to make us publishers."

"Us? Me I can understand, but you, too?"

"What he more or less said is any asshole can be a newspaper publisher."

"Speaking as a newspaper reader, that sounds about right to me."

"Only thing is, Gladys, you got to make your bones. I already know you're mean enough for the job, but you've got to convince Boucher."

"What do I got to do?"

"You go over to Jonathan Paul and he tells you what he wants you to tell Boucher, and then you go to Boucher and tell him that this, that, and the other are the types of things you can find out, and Boucher says go do it, and so then you go whack up corpses for a few days with Serena, or whatever you guys do in medical school. Then you go back to Boucher and pump him full of all the bullshit Jonathan gave you. Like a good girl."

"That's me all over."

* * *

KILL STORY

In the early primaries of 1980 I worked for Teddy Kennedy, and then I jumped over to the Carter campaign when Kennedy flamed out at the convention in Madison Square Garden. A campaign is a high-pressure, big-money operation that balloons up from nothing and then collapses, all in the space of less than a year. It's like being fast-forwarded through the whole life cycle of a bureaucracy. You can learn a lot about what's wrong with the world by watching how the scum beats the cream to the top.

Actually the rules are so simple that you'd think anybody could become a campaign manager, or at least secretary of labor or ambassador to Morocco. But only a lucky few are born entirely without shame.

In the past I've had a problem with shame myself, I'm ashamed to say. But now, in my role as future publisher, it no longer bothered me. Free at last, I could sit in my office and plot my rise just like any other corporate striver.

The first rule was to plant yourself in the boss's line of vision, which I had lucked into by decking Terry Dineen. This put me into the front seat of a Rolls-Royce with Boucher at least twice a day. And of course I had him all to myself three or four times a week in our new gym.

The other rules were equally standard and obvious stuff, like taking credit for your subordinates' good ideas and blaming them for your bad ones, keeping anybody below you from contact with anybody above you, kissing the asses above you on the ladder and kicking the ones below. None of it required any particular brains. You just had to be willing to do it.

And now at last, after all the wasted, foolish years, I was willing. And so now, at last, I was in the fast lane. What should I do, here in the fast lane? Fire somebody? Steal an idea? Sabotage somebody else's idea? The hell with it. I'd just watch my surveillance monitors for a while, see what was going down in the rest rooms.

I locked the door so nobody would wander in, and I opened the closet door that hid my array of switchers, splitters, and monitors. The sixteen-inch monitor showed four pictures at once, in this case the men's and the women's rooms, the pressroom, and the loading dock. Nothing was doing except for a couple of smokers outside on the dock, feeding their lung cancers. I was about to switch cameras when the phone rang.

"Is this Mr. Bethany?" said a woman's voice. "Tom Bethany?"

"Speaking."

"This is Mary Dineen, you don't know me. Terry's wife. Please don't hang up."

"Hang up? Why would I hang up?" But she was right. I wanted to.

"They just hang up in Mr. Boucher's office, and Mr. Fogel never calls back and I don't know where else to try. I have to talk to somebody and nobody else would so I thought maybe you."

"Sure, Mrs. Dineen, go ahead."

"It's about Terry, what he might do. I'm afraid. Can I talk to you?"

"Go ahead."

"Not just a voice over the phone, Mr. Bethany. My family's all passed away and Terry's always down to Garvey's drunk and I can't leave Kevin so I'm here alone all day long going crazy, all I got anymore is the TV. Can you come out? Please, okay? Please."

"Where is it you live?" I asked.

When she had told me, I checked with Louise on Boucher's lunch plans. When she said he was working straight through, the way he often did, I told her I'd be back in an hour. Then I called a cab.

The Dineens lived in a ground-floor apartment in the rear of one of the box-shaped three-story clapboard houses that make up the neighborhoods just south of Central Square. The porch outside the apartment had been painted battleship gray, but now it was mostly the darker gray of the weathered wood underneath. Most of the paint was also gone from the screen door that led into the kitchen. Mrs. Dineen was in the shadows on the other side of the door, looking cute. What can I say, that's how she looked. Cute.

It was the screen and the shadows, though. When she opened the door and I could see her up close, she just looked tiny and worn out. A peppy little girl after the pep had all gone, and the clear, smooth skin loosened into a map of tiny wrinkles, and the tight blond curls turned to gray. She wore a cotton housecoat or wrapper, whatever they call them, with a blurred and faded pattern of flowers. When a woman expecting a visitor doesn't bother to change out of a thing like that, she's given up completely.

"You want a beer?" she said. "I keep a couple cans in the refrigerator in case his royal highness drops by to leave off his laundry."

"No, thanks."

"I keep a jar of Kool-Aid in the fridge for Kevin. You like Kool-Aid?"

"Kool-Aid's fine."

"Well, sit down at least. We still got the furniture."

I sat in a chair that had a bedspread over it. My mother used to do the same thing, to hide the worn and torn upholstery in our Goodwill armchairs. A noise came from the next room. It wasn't speech but it was a human sound. Through the doorway I saw a kid of ten or eleven wearing only shorts. He was hunkered down on his heels, busy with something on the floor.

"That's Kevin," Mary Dineen said.

"Hi, Kevin."

"Don't bother," his mother said, not bitter but just explaining. "He understands what you say but he won't answer.

It's like he was born inside a big bottle, that's what one of the doctors told me. Anything that gets inside the bottle hurts him. He doesn't like it when even words get inside the bottle, God forbid you should actually touch him. Poor thing."

"But he knows how to talk?"

"Oh, yeah. He can even write out the alphabet, make out words. It's just he wants to be alone inside that bottle and not be hurt. So he won't answer you, doesn't make any difference whether he understands you or not. Won't say anything straight at another person, either, even though he could."

Raising her voice, she said, "How about some nice Kool-Aid, Kevin?" and then her voice went back to conversational level. "He wants it, but he won't tell me so. After a while he'll be looking out the window, anywhere except at me, and he'll say, 'Kool-Aid.' "

"What's he got in there?"

"Old magazines. St. Bridget's gives me the leftovers from the rummage sales. He likes *National Geographic*s best."

"Does he read them?"

"Just looks at the pictures, all day long. That's his whole life. He cuts out whatever catches his eye. Then he puts them in folders, piles and piles of folders, and never looks at them again."

Kevin took after his father, but his features and his limbs didn't fit together quite right. Or maybe it was the way he moved, or held himself. It wasn't a thing you could explain or describe. You just knew right off that something was wrong with him.

"Who knows?" I said. "Maybe it's nice inside the bottle."

"That's what you try to hope," she said. "But I don't believe it. Maybe it hurts less inside, but he acts like it still hurts."

I didn't say anything, having nothing intelligent or helpful to say. Mary Dineen looked down at her hands as they lay in her lap. She held up the fingers of her left hand with her right hand, as if she were examining the nails. After a moment, still looking down, she began to talk.

"I don't blame you for what happened," she said. "Terry does, but the truth is he would have lost his job anyway. Mr. Boucher already spoke to him twice about liquor on his breath. He started in hard with the booze after they fired him from sportswriting."

"Kool-Aid," Kevin said. It didn't sound like he was calling out a request. His voice was neutral, a kid talking to himself in the next room. Mrs. Dineen got him a glass of the stuff and set it down on the floor beside him. He didn't look at her, or at the glass. She came back, sat down in exactly the same position as before, and started talking again.

"The drinking is worse, now that Terry's got no job to go to. He lives on the unemployment, which he used to say he'd never take, unemployment was for the coloreds. But what else can he do? Nobody wants him and I can't go to work, not with Kevin.

"Now his friends from the office are taking up collections for him, and of course that makes him feel even more useless. He went to Brad Boyle and tried to give the money back, but Brad said he didn't know who to give it back to, he didn't know anything about it."

"How did the money get to Terry?" I asked, afraid I already knew the answer.

"It comes through the mail in cash," she said. "No letter with it, no return address. Every time one comes it makes him feel worse. He takes a couple hundred and he's down to Garvey's and I don't see him for two or three days."

So much for playing Santa Claus. What's more, I had mailed another eight hundred dollars just that morning, a kickback from the contractor who put in the surveillance equipment at the *Banner*.

"Mr. Bethany, Terry's killing himself with the drink and

it seems like there's just nothing I can do about it. He didn't drink so bad when he was fighting, back when we were happy. That's all he's ever been really good at, the boxing. You knew he killed a man in the ring?"

"I heard about it, yes."

"That was when he started up with the really heavy drinking. It helped some that Mr. Cushing gave him a job, God rest his soul, but the truth is the job was beyond Terry. He was always stretching to be something he didn't really have the head for, poor man. But losing the job was even worse than having it. He's crawled all the way into the bottle this time. Same as poor Kevin, you could say."

"Some women would leave him," I said. "I always wished my own mother would have left my father."

"We don't do that. He's my husband for better or for worse, and worse it is. Besides, my own family is gone, and he's all we've got, me and Kevin. For the boy's sake I've got to try everything."

"So you called me. I don't know that there's much I can do, Mrs. Dineen."

"Maybe not, but I'm begging you to try. Look, from what Terry and Brad tell me, driving is only like part-time for you. They say you've got the maintenance job now and something to do with personnel, security, something like that. Nobody seems to know exactly."

"It's various areas, yeah. Whatever the boss tells me."

"What I'm asking, Mr. Bethany, is if you could say a word to Mr. T for Terry. You're busy with bigger things, after all, you don't want to fool with the driving. Let Terry do it again, he don't mind what he makes. Minimum wage even, just so we get back on the medical for Kevin. It's not just he's autistic, Mr. Bethany. He's sick all the time. Whatever's going around, he gets a double dose of it. His kidneys are bad, he's got liver trouble, his heartbeat isn't right."

"I can talk to Mr. Boucher, Mrs. Dineen, but I have to tell you I don't think it'll do any good."

"But you'll say a word? Tell him you're not mad Terry decked you? If you're not mad, why would Mr. T be mad, right?"

"I don't know. There's no telling with Mr. T."

"Terry's too quick with his fists, I know that. He knows that now. He understands he can't go around knocking people out. Like Mr. T told him, he's a prize-fighter, his fists are deadly weapons. Thank God at least he didn't hurt you too bad. He said you were only out a minute or two. You're all right now, aren't you?"

"Sure, I was just a little sore the next day." The poor bastard hadn't been able to admit how he got fired, even to his wife. Or maybe especially to his wife.

"So if you was to tell Mr. T there's no hard feelings as far as you're concerned, I don't know why he wouldn't give Terry another chance, do you? I guarantee he'll stay off the booze."

"Nobody can guarantee that."

"The first time Mr. T catches even a whiff on his breath, he can fire him and no harm done. Will you at least try? It's not for Terry or me, Mr. Bethany. It's for the boy."

"I'll try, like I say. But once Mr. T gets down on somebody, he doesn't change his mind. I don't want to sound negative here, Mrs. Dineen, but don't get your hopes up."

"I won't, but God bless you for at least trying after what he did to you. You're a big man to forgive him, Mr. Bethany."

"One more thing before I go," I said. "If any more of that money comes in the mail, I'd hide it from Terry."

"Terry always handled the money, but you're right. You think more will come?"

"I don't know. I'm just saying if."

"So there I was, feeling like the poor woman's Secret Santa because I knew the check was in the mail," I said to

Hope Edwards. I had called her at home that evening, to lean my head on her shoulder. "Suddenly it turns out all I've been doing is making her husband feel even shittier than usual."

"I know how you enjoy flogging your unworthy self, Bethany, but most of the money in fact seems to have gotten through to that poor woman and her child."

"Them and Garvey's."

"What *is* Garvey's, anyway?"

"Just another neighborhood gin mill with a collection box for the IRA. Full of a bunch of pathetic losers pretending they're Wild Irish Boys."

"Sounds harmless."

"Well, it's not. You couldn't find a single healthy liver in the place, not even if you put them all together. Not too many functioning brain cells, either. I'm an expert on saloons."

"So's Terry Dineen, and it started way before he had a Secret Santa."

"Come on, Hope. Can't you at least let me feel a *little* bit like a shit?"

"Hey, whatever turns you on."

"I kept wanting to tell Mrs. Dineen what I was really up to at the paper. At least it would have given her some hope the poor bastard might get his job back eventually."

"Why didn't you tell her, then?"

"I didn't dare. She's desperate, and Terry's drinking himself to death. What if they talked to some friend at the paper and Boucher heard about it?"

"Are you really going to ask Boucher to rehire Terry?"

"No. I'd be stepping out of character and it would be hopeless anyway."

"Why don't you get him a job on Jonathan Paul's little paper, then?"

"I doubt if they have medical insurance."

"Still, it would be a chance for him to get some dignity back."

"Paul's paper is barely getting by as it is. I doubt if they can afford another person."

"Go to Felicia and what's-her-name, the daughter . . ."

"Serena."

"Serena, yes. They ought to be willing to underwrite a new sportswriter for the opposition paper."

"Why didn't I think of that?"

"Because you were having too much fun thinking about how evil and worthless and stupid you are."

"Assuming you're right, and I don't concede it for a second, did you ever stop to think that people who are always right can be a major pain in the ass?"

"We're underappreciated all right, I'll grant you that. Now call Felicia."

Sure enough, Felicia Lamport turned out to be perfectly willing. I called her right after I had talked to Hope. When I told her about Hope's suggestion, she came up with a scheme of her own for the Dineens to move out of their dump and into the vacant Cushing house. "It needs a caretaker anyway," Felicia said. "I don't see why the estate couldn't buy a health insurance policy for the family in exchange for that. I'll talk to Serena tomorrow, and then talk to Jonathan Paul about some way we can make it possible for him to give Mr. Dineen something useful to do. God knows the money is there. In fact it's amazing how much money is there. I've never been an executrix before, but I'm taking to it very nicely."

10

MY NEW BUILDING SUPERVISOR, William Wells, was installed in the former storeroom that had been my office for the first few days of my corporate career. I spent the next morning in there with him, passing along some of the administrative expertise I had picked up in the army. I had been a sort of clerk, really, in the office of ARMA, our army attaché in Laos. At the time the Kingdom of Laos was a wholly owned subsidiary of the United States except for the portion that was a wholly owned subsidiary of the People's Republic of Vietnam. The U.S. Army's role in this was pretty small, compared to the U.S. Air Force and what was locally called CAS, which was the Central Intelligence Agency. ARMA's main job was to supply and pay the Royal Lao Army, which was made up almost entirely of conscientious objectors.

"William," I was saying, "don't sweat the small stuff. File it under the company name or the salesman's name, doesn't matter as long as you can find it. In fact, the harder it is for

144

anybody else to use your files, the better off you are. You don't want 'em in your files. You want to be the indispensable man, the only man who can find anything around this damned place. You follow me?"

"I follow you."

"Good. Now let me tell you about the whole point of paperwork. Way before they assigned me to Laos, we used to have an ambassador who was some kind of fat commando. Everybody had to be thin. So the army attaché back then set up a monthly overweight report on fat soldiers, how much weight they gained or lost the month before, okay? So there was this one warrant officer and he was kind of a porker, so he was our overweight guy. When they were breaking me in as clerk I say to the old clerk, What do we do about Chief Warrant Officer Faria for the overweight report, we put him on the scales every month or what?

"This guy I'm replacing, he says you gotta be nuts, Bethany. Faria would go apeshit if he knew he was on the report. What you do, you just give him a couple of pounds one month, knock off a pound or so the next month. Like that.

"I go, Listen, this Mickey Mouse report was set up by assholes that rotated back to the world maybe two, three years ago, right? Now nobody gives a shit. So what about if I just don't send the thing in to MACV next month? The guy goes, You do that and it's your ass, not mine. I told you to send it to Saigon. What you do after that is your business.

"So I didn't send it to Saigon, William, and you know what happened?"

"Nothing?"

"Oh, no. MACV comes right back at me, some major's name on the bottom, asking me where's the monthly overweight report. You see what I'm saying here? That's what the whole point of paperwork is, William. Not because it makes sense. The point is to keep the major from firing a rocket up your ass."

"I see what you mean, boss."

The phone rang, and William answered. "Yes, ma'am, he's here," he said, and passed the phone to me. It was Terry Dineen's wife, sounding very bad.

"Hold on," I said. "Let me get back to my office."

In my office, I picked up and said, "Thanks, William, I got it."

Mrs. Dineen said something that went by me too fast to sort out.

"Slow down, Mrs. Dineen," I said. "Who's going to do something stupid?"

"He found out you were here."

"Found out?"

"Kevin said your name, just out of the blue like he does. He was just cutting out pictures and it popped into his head."

"You sound funny, Mrs. Dineen. Are you all right?"

"It's nothing. He hit me is all."

"Terry?"

"He never did that before."

"Did he hurt you?"

"My mouth is cut inside and my face is swollen up some. I'll be okay. It's Terry."

"Start with when the boy said my name. Tell me everything."

"Well, Terry jumped right on it, said, 'Where did you hear that name, Kevin?' and of course Kevin doesn't answer. 'Where did he hear it, Mary?' he hollers. 'Was that prick here?' Pardon my French."

"Don't worry about it. Just say what he said."

"Well, that's what he said. I said no, you wasn't here, I must have just mentioned the name talking to myself, which tell the truth I do a lot of, Mr. Bethany. But he went on and on how he didn't believe me, I was a lying bitch. He don't usually use that language with me but he's feeling bad, you understand? He's out all night God knows where, and God forbid I should ask him, and he rolls in drunk in the middle of the morning and he's feeling guilty so he had to make out it was my fault. So he kept after me and after me, and finally I admitted it, yes, you were there. So then it's what was he doing here, what did he want, and I couldn't think of nothing to say so I told him the truth, that I asked you to come.

" 'You asked him to come?' he says, by now he's shouting so all the neighbors can hear. 'It's not bad enough the prick takes my job, now he's got my wife, too.' And I tell him no, it's nothing like that. 'So what is it, then? You tell me.'

"By now poor Kevin is screaming, not words, just like an animal howl, and Terry is pissed like I never seen him, so I should have kept my big mouth shut, but like an idiot I told him."

"Told him what?"

"That you were going to try and get his job back for him."

"Oh, Jesus."

"Yeah. That's when he went totally berserk. He's tearing the covers off the bed. He's pulling the drawers out of the dresser, throwing them on the floor. Long story short, he comes up with this envelope.

"I totally forgot it's in there, but it's another one of those letters full of money, come just this morning and I hid it with my underwear and stuff where he never goes, and now he's screaming like a man possessed, whore this, bitch that, and the money goes all over the place and he starts hitting me and I go down on the floor and then he stops all of a sudden and just stands there.

"He's got his hands over his eyes so nobody should see he's crying and he's saying like I'm sorry, I'm sorry, I never meant to do it, I'm no good to anybody, I'm better off dead. Then when he says that he goes running out the door leaving the money all over the floor and me crying and Kevin howling and that was only just now. So I'm calling you, I didn't know who else to tell. I think he meant it, Mr. Bethany."

"Did he ever talk about it before?"

"He talked about how a person could do it."

"How?"

As soon as she told me, I hung up in a hurry. I thought about the way the Red Line trains leave the underground Kendall Square station and get up enough speed so that even though you know what's coming, it startles you every time when the train roars suddenly up out of the dark tunnel and into bright day. It takes a few seconds for your eyes to get used to it, and then you see the white sails of dozens of boats, up the river and down it to the Museum of Science and the Charles Street dam beyond.

I didn't take the time to call Boucher's office and tell Louise I was going to be out of the office for a while. I didn't take the time to call a cab. I headed straight out to the parking lot, half-running, and jumped into the Rolls.

Kendall Square wasn't far from the *Banner* plant. I got out of the side streets in a big hurry, but traffic on Broadway slowed me down a little. At Kendall Square I picked up Main Street and headed toward the Longfellow Bridge, where the trains came up from underground. A concrete roof covered the railroad cut that ran down the middle of Main, dividing the two eastbound lanes from the westbound traffic. I got over to the right so I could turn off onto Memorial Drive before the bridge and look for a place to park.

Just before the turn I saw Terry Dineen. He was sitting on a low guardrail, looking across two lanes of traffic at the mouth of the tunnel. I couldn't tell if he spotted the Rolls. I was too busy making the turn onto Memorial to check the rearview mirror, and then I was around the corner. There was no place to park, naturally. I couldn't even find an illegal spot until I was a hundred yards or so down the drive.

I pulled in front of the fire plug and ran for it, not even bothering to lock the car doors.

Terry must have spotted me, all right, since by the time I got there he had left his perch on the guardrail. He had made it across the road and onto a narrow strip of weeds and sand. Between this narrow curb and the tracks was nothing but waist-high iron railings, buckled from years of sideswipes. A sign on the railing said DANGER, THIRD RAIL ALIVE, NO TRESPASSING, in white letters almost illegible against a faded red background.

Dineen's back was to me. His head was cocked, as if he was expecting to hear something, and then we both heard it. The rumble of a train in the tunnel, still faint but growing. No breaks appeared in the traffic. The noise from the tunnel grew louder.

"Hey!" I shouted, trying to watch both the traffic and Terry Dineen, who was gripping a section of bent-over railing, ready to vault. "Hey!"

The roar of the train was growing, but he heard me. He turned around, and then turned back to the tunnel.

I saw daylight in the oncoming traffic and ran for it.

"Hey!" I shouted again as I dodged cars. "What the hell are you doing?"

"Let me alone," he hollered over his shoulder. "Fuck you, Jack!"

I was on his side of the roadway now.

I grabbed for him, not thinking to protect myself, and he suckered me just the way he did the only other time we met. This time it was a left hook that caught me in the side of the neck and almost put me down. But I kept my grip on his right wrist and tried to pull him away from the Braintree train I saw over his shoulder, about to roar out of the tunnel. We were both shouting, but the noise of the train swallowed everything up.

I had lost my footing from the punch, and when he turned

and surged toward the tracks he carried me with him. Just as he dove over the iron railing fence, I let go and fell to my knees in the safety of the weeds. The roar and the rush of hot wind and the clatter of steel on steel made my eyes shut, and when I forced them back open all I could see was legs and hips, and after that only the iron wheels screaming along the rails.

I got to my feet, trapped between the train and the stream of traffic. The oncoming drivers didn't know what had just happened, but the motorman did. The brakes were squealing and the noise of the train was changing pitch. I spotted another hole in the traffic and ran for it. I didn't look back till I had reached the Rolls-Royce.

Then I saw that the train was stopped on the Longfellow Bridge, and a couple of men were walking back along the right-of-way toward the tunnel. The motorman might have seen two figures beside the track, but it would be a moment before he learned that one of them had disappeared. By then it would be an excellent idea if I really had disappeared.

Not that I thought the thing through that way. My system was already in full flight mode, my heart pounding from the fear and the running. After my glance at the train, I jumped into the car because it was the fastest way to keep on fleeing. I was down by M.I.T. before I noticed the parking ticket stuck under the wiper. I lowered the window but couldn't quite reach it, so I turned on the wipers. This left me steering with my left hand for a second, and during that second the ticket swept across the windshield and kept right on going, tugged loose from the wiper by the airstream.

The little speck of white fluttered around in my rearview mirror, getting smaller until it disappeared too.

WHEN I GOT BACK TO THE *BANNER*, the newsroom receptionist said, "Oh, Mr. Bethany, there you are. Mr. Boucher has been trying to reach you. You better call him."

"Thanks, Janice."

The words came out in a croak, surprising both of us.

"Sore throat," I said.

It probably wouldn't occur to Janice that what I had caught wasn't a cold but a punch in the throat. Back in the office, I called to see what Boucher had on his mind.

"What's wrong with your voice?" he asked.

"Just a cold. Twenty-four-hour thing. I'm getting over it."

"Those summer colds can be mean."

"I don't want to pass it on," I said. "Probably we should be on the safe side and skip wrestling practice tonight."

The last thing I wanted to do was wrestle, after seeing a man cut in half because of me. Maybe that was overstating it, but the poor guy would still be in one piece if I had never showed up in his life.

"Did you happen to see the editorial page today?" Boucher asked.

"Glanced at it. You mean the thing by the Harvard guy?" Felicia had convinced one of her buddies from the English department to send in a thousand words of sludge that he hadn't been able to get anybody else to publish. She had showed a copy to me first, as an example of what was wrong with American education.

"Professor Grigsby, yeah," Boucher said. "Let me read you the first sentence."

"Shoot."

" 'No one who thinks at all seriously about what, it is quaint to recall, was once known as the Republic of Letters can have failed to note in the latter half of the twentieth century that the extraordinary flowering of superb criticism from the textual compost heap of what has unfortunately come to pass for literature in what will one day no doubt come to be known as the Post-Joycean Period far surpasses in ingenuity, creativity, intelligence, and just sheer *fun* the far-too-often graceless, obvious, and pedestrian material upon which it is forced, *faute de mieux*, to comment.' "

Thurman Boucher gave me a second or two to digest that, and then said, "Well?"

"Well what?" I said.

"What the hell does it mean?"

"It means English professors are better than writers."

Boucher thought about that for a few seconds and then said, "I guess it does at that. How did you know?"

"Same way as you. I asked."

"You asked the professor?"

"No, I asked my friend. The one who knows all the Harvard people. She's got those guys figured out. That's how she knew we could get them for free."

"Somehow I doubt if Professor Grigsby is going to get his meaning across to the guys down at the Legion Hall."

"Doesn't matter what it means, does it? What does George Will mean, you come right down to it. The idea is just to add a little phony class."

"You're a man of surprises, Tom. Do you read George Will's column?"

"No, but I look at the picture they run with it. The dorky glasses and dorky bow tie, you know he's class. Same way with Buckley's made-up accent."

"The messenger is the message."

"Whatever," I said, hoping we'd get off the subject. Stop me before I slip out of character again.

Boucher obliged by getting to the purpose of the call, which was that he had run across a picture in a magazine of a French nineteenth-century bronze that showed two men wrestling, and would I track the thing down?

After he hung up, I got to thinking that it was a sin for a Catholic, which a Boston Irishman like Dineen almost certainly was, to go over the wall before serving out his full sentence here below. Would the church refuse to give a suicide a proper burial? It seemed to me that they went in for some final cruelty along those lines.

Boucher liked to glance through the paper on the way to the office in the mornings, estimating the ad lineage and counting the number of stories. His theory was that papers should have a lot of little stories, as opposed to stories long enough to actually tell you something. He kept a story count, the same way General Westmoreland used to keep a body count. Reporters had to meet quotas, so many stories a week. Naturally they gravitated to the short story, rather than, say, the informative or the useful story. Still, as I could see by glancing over at Boucher's paper, Terry Dineen's death had gotten eight inches or so of coverage, as much as the ho-hum Red Sox loss to the Yankees that was on the same page of the sports section.

"You read this about Terry Dineen?" Boucher asked.

"Not yet. Just the headline, that a train ran over him."

"Jumped or was pushed, the police are saying."

"More likely jumped."

"Why?"

"Guy's out of a job, gets to thinking and drinking. It happens."

"I doubt it in this case. The motorman said two men were struggling beside the tracks when he came out of the tunnel. Time he got the train stopped and walked back, Dineen was the only one there. Cut in two at the waist."

"Jesus."

"That would be something to see, a man cut in half. You ever see anything like that?"

"Never did."

"A few years ago we had labor trouble at one of our Maryland papers. One of the picketers was lying down in front of the gate and got his head run over. The TV cameras got it on film, but it was too gruesome to go on the air with."

"I can imagine."

"They didn't think it was too gruesome when Terry killed Boom-Boom Greer. I remember seeing it on TV at the time."

"I guess it looked like any other knockout."

"Not really," Thurman said. "The knockout came at the end of a sustained beating. Very bloody business, as I recall."

"The ref probably kept it going because of the TV. I knew a guy once with NBC news, he told me the rule for nightly news. Simple rule—'If it bleeds, it leads.' "

Boucher smiled.

"You ever run across Terry except that one time in the parking lot?" he asked me.

"No, I never saw him before."

"I meant after."

"After? No. He had somebody call me that time, that's all. Same as he did to you."

"He's not going to be making any more threatening calls, is he?"

"No, that's it for the calls."

"He never waited for you after work or anything?" the Cobra asked.

"No, I only saw him the one time."

"Mmmh," Boucher said. It didn't sound skeptical—just registering what I had said, as if it was just about the answer he had expected. He unfolded the *Boston Herald*, which was also delivered to his house, along with the *Globe*.

"Son of a bitch!" he said, holding the tabloid up. "You see this?"

BISECTED! the headline shouted. Under it was a photo of ambulance attendants, four of them, carrying two stretchers. You could tell from the bulges under the sheets that each stretcher only carried half a body.

"Take a look at that," Boucher said. "Rupert would have been proud." This was Rupert Murdoch, the Australian smut peddler who used to own the *Herald*. When I was doing research on Boucher I came across a *New York* magazine profile where he told the interviewer that Murdoch was the greatest newspaper publisher since William Randolph Hearst.

"What does the story say?" I asked.

"Piss on the story. Look what the picture says. What a fantastically great picture! How the hell did our guy miss a shot like that?"

Normally Boucher injected his venom into subordinates quietly, but today the shouting began as soon as he hit the city room. It continued as he marched Alan Fogel and the city editor and the assistant city editor and the photographer into his office. I could still hear it through the closed door as I left for my own little office downstairs.

I got the answering machine when I called Gladys Williams, but her voice gave me another number to try. A man answered that one, sounding hostile. Presumably he was a member of Gladys's string, thinking I was one of his rivals.

"Got a minute, Gladys?" I said when she came on the line.

"Yeah, right."

"Hey, you left your number on the machine."

"That was in case the hospital called, asshole. I'm on standby."

"I bet you are, you lovely thing."

"Come on, what is it, Bethany? Christ, it's not even ten o'clock."

When I first met Gladys she was a lab technician for the Cambridge police, working the scenes of crimes and accidents. Now she was seeing the other end, patching up victims in the emergency room. So nobody knew more about emergency medical procedures than Gladys. I told her about the photo on the front page of the *Herald*.

"Is this normal?" I asked her.

"No, it's total bullshit. No way would you use two stretchers."

"You still know people you can talk to down at police?"

"Sure."

Gladys was back to me within ten minutes, and two minutes later I was up in the newsroom. Alan Fogel was in his glassed-in office with MANAGING EDITOR on the door.

"Spare me a minute, Alan?" I asked.

"Come on in."

"I never heard him like that before," I said, pointing my thumb at Boucher's office.

"If there's one thing Mister T hates it's being beaten on his own story," Fogel said. "After he got it all off his chest he fired Whitney for missing the shot."

Dale Whitney was the photographer I had seen in the publisher's office earlier.

"What did Whitney say?"

"He got there late, that's all. The ambulance had gone."

"Pretty tough on the kid," I said. "The *Herald* got there late, too."

"How could the *Herald* get there late? They had the picture."

"The shot's a phony. I thought so when I saw it, so I called a friend of mine on the cops. What happened, the *Herald* guy shows up just as they're buttoning up the ambulance. He hears the guy's cut in half, so he follows the ambulance to the hospital. Then he tells the EMTs if they'll round up another couple guys from inside the hospital, they can all get their picture in the paper."

"Wait a minute, Tom. You're telling me that they took half of poor Terry's body off the stretcher and put it on another stretcher, just to make a better picture?"

"Yeah. Too bad our guy didn't think of it."

"Who's your source?"

"I promised him I wouldn't use his name."

Fogel looked like I had just snatched away his big new Teddy bear.

"But I got the names of the four ambulance attendants right here."

Fogel looked like I just gave him back his Teddy bear, along with a book of tickets for all the rides. He took the list of names from me and went charging off toward the city desk. After listening long enough to grasp the story, the city editor shouted out the names of a couple of reporters, and they joined the two men at the city desk. Then Fogel headed for Boucher's office.

Modestly, I left.

I showed up at the plant early next morning and grabbed a paper, so I could read it before going to pick up Boucher.

For a little newspaper, the *Banner* did a hell of a job on the story I had given Fogel. Terry Dineen, who had been kissed off in a few paragraphs by the *Banner* only a day before, had been transformed overnight into a major celebrity and something of a secular saint. His early amateur years in the C.Y.O. and the Golden Gloves were covered in detail. So were his years as a professional, and the tragedy that ended his boxing career, and his remarkable rebirth as one of Cambridge's most beloved sports commentators.

Boxing experts were interviewed. So were former opponents, who praised his skills and sportsmanship. So were relatives, and former newspaper colleagues, and schoolteachers and junior college instructors and neighbors and high school classmates. You would never have learned from the *Banner* that the valued and beloved sportswriter had been fired from the paper, rehired as a chauffeur, and then fired again. The only tragedy in his life was the unfortunate death of Boom-Boom Greer.

Terry Dineen was never the same after that tragedy, his widow said. It was hard for him to concentrate and he sometimes seemed to have lost his will to live. He struggled for years to forget, but the nightmare would not leave him. He had bad dreams, night sweats, a drinking problem. Mrs. Dineen wondered if it might not be something like the Vietnam vets had. Post-traumatic stress disorder as a result of Boom-Boom's death.

Terry accepted a less stressful position at the paper, but even that was more than he could handle. Finally he decided to resign from the *Banner* and seek professional help while he devoted himself to the care of his invalid son. But before he could find that help, his demons overcame him.

All this was secondary to the big story of the day, though: DINEEN DEATH PHOTO FAKED. One of the ambulance attendants had talked, and then the others had confirmed it. Efforts to reach the *Herald*'s editors for comment on its unethical behavior had naturally failed, which was no surprise. Newspaper executives practically never talk to reporters, for the same reason Pat Robertson wouldn't go to a faith healer.

But a whole parade of professors of journalism and of ethics had been willing to go on record with the *Banner*, professors being notorious quote sluts. They were all outraged, of course, but not nearly as much as the *Banner* itself.

Boucher had personally dictated a long editorial, which Fogel tried unsuccessfully to tone down. It accused the *Herald* of "the journalistic equivalent of body snatching." *Cynical, sacrilegious, callous, sensation-seeking, insensitive, cheap, low,* and *despicable* were some of the other words.

When I arrived to pick up Boucher, he had his home-delivered copy of the *Banner* opened to the body-snatching piece he had written. "This is one editorial they'll by God read," he said. "Did you see it yet?"

"On the way out, yeah."

"How'd you like it?"

"Pretty good. You sure tore the *Herald* a new asshole."

"I did, didn't I? It was nearly as much fun as if we had had that damned picture instead of them."

"You were just blowing smoke in the editorial, then?"

"Sure. We got beat on a great picture, so we did the next best thing. We turned the other guy's picture into a great second-day story. Watch and see if the TV doesn't piss all over the *Herald* tonight. They love to stick it to the print press because we stick it to them so often."

"Think the *Herald* photographer will get fired?"

"I wish he would. Then I could hire him."

"After you beat up on him till he got fired?"

"Sure. I'd play it that the guy learned his lesson, we're willing to forgive and forget. Not like those bastards at the *Herald*. It'd be great. Keep the story alive a few more days."

Boucher looked at me closely. "Or maybe you'd rather see the story just die?" he said.

"Me? Why would I mind one way or another?"

"No reason, I guess." He was still inspecting me, but now with a hint of a smile. First there had been the business with Boucher asking me whether I had run across Terry since his firing. Now some more hinting around. It was coming clear what Boucher had in his mind.

Today's Dineen story had backed off a little from the angle that an unknown man might have pushed him under the wheels. Somebody else was on the scene, certainly, because the motorman saw him. Now, though, the motorman was telling police he couldn't say exactly what the two men had been up to. Some kind of a struggle, hard to tell who was doing what. But Boucher himself, judging by his insinuations, wasn't backing off from the unknown assailant angle. I couldn't see any harm in that, as long as he didn't share his thoughts with the police. And I didn't imagine he would.

"You don't think the *Herald* really will fire the photographer, do you?" I said.

"I doubt it. *I* certainly wouldn't."

"Good, because there's another way you could keep the story going and make them look bad."

"What's that?"

"Hire Whitney back."

"Who's Whitney?"

"That kid Dale Whitney. The photographer you fired."

"Oh, Dale. I didn't know his last name."

"See how it would be? He was fired for missing the picture but he didn't miss it at all. There was no picture. Those rotten bastards at the *Herald* faked it."

"Practically ruined the career of an innocent kid," Boucher said. "Yeah, I like it. Make another good editorial, wouldn't it? Maybe do it as a letter from the publisher, front page. Maybe that would be the way to go."

Later that morning I dropped by the sports desk to talk with Brad Boyle. The sports editor hadn't been handling the Dineen stories, but he would presumably know his former reporter better than anybody else in the place would.

"How's Mrs. Dineen getting along?" I said.

"As well as you could expect. Going through the motions and not much more. I've been helping out with the arrangements and all."

"There wasn't anything in the stories about a suicide note. She mention a note?"

"She said the police were asking the same thing."

"So there wasn't any?"

"No note, no. He just rushed out. They were having some kind of ruckus, and he hit her."

"Did he say anything to her about what he was going to do?"

"She says no."

That meant she didn't want people to think it was suicide. Why not? The church? Insurance?

"Did she say who this other guy was? The guy the motorman saw?"

"No, but I've got a theory on that, just between you and me and the bedpost. I figure he didn't want to upset his wife, so he staged his death so he could get a proper church burial."

"Staged it?"

"Sure. That's what he brought that other guy along for. Probably some drinking buddy."

"I don't follow you."

"So it would look like maybe it wasn't a suicide. It's real ironical, too. If Terry had been a good Catholic, he wouldn't have had to go through all that bother."

"Why not?"

"Because years ago the church started treating suicides the same as any other death. Nowadays they give suicides a regular church burial like anybody else, which if Terry was still a good Catholic, he would have known it."

"Poor bastard."

"The other thing was the insurance."

"Life insurance?"

"Yeah. On account of the kid, Terry carried four hundred thousand in term life. They don't pay on suicides."

"Actually that's changed, too," I said. "Nowadays most companies pay unless it's a brand-new policy," I said.

"Maybe Terry didn't know that, either. I doubt if he read the fine print any more than he read the Bible."

Boucher was running around manic all day, rehiring Dale Whitney, making arrangements for our upcoming trip to Canton, bothering everybody, and otherwise playing media mogul.

"What do you think of this?" he said to Alan Fogel at one point. The Cobra read aloud from the publisher's letter he had dictated earlier: "The editors of the *Herald* have apparently not mastered the vital distinction between the hard but clean journalistic competition which is at the heart of a free, democratic press and desecration of a corpse."

It sounded to me like he was saying competition was at the heart of desecrating corpses, but I was just a beginner at the newspaper game. "It's got a lot of punch," Fogel said. "I don't know about *desecration*, though. Strictly speaking, didn't the train do the desecrating?"

I remembered the technique from the days when I used to watch courtiers swarming around the various orifices of political candidates. You told your meal ticket he was basically terrific, and then threw in some minor objection to make it sound like you weren't a total brunser.

"Yeah, but what the hell," Boucher said. "We're not writing for rocket scientists. Once the average newspaper reader gets past two syllables, he's in way over his head."

It's a common view of the public in businesses like publishing, advertising movies, TV, politics, and PR. A friend of mine used to be a sexual whore as opposed to an intellectual one. She tells me a lot of prostitutes look down on johns because they have to patronize prostitutes.

Normally Boucher wasn't too many laughs. In fact before now I had never seen him what you would call happy, and I hated to see him stay in that condition for long. So after lunch I called Jonathan Paul at the *Cambridge Trader*. Jonathan said he was pretty busy, but under the circumstances he could spare a few minutes for me right around Boucher's normal quitting time.

On the way home I spotted Paul's Rolls-Royce in the rearview mirror, coming up fast. It swung out and blew past us, with me careful not to look over at the driver. "Bastard," Boucher said. The other Rolls-Royce pulled away from us and just beat the red light that caught us at the next corner.

"Goddamned son of a bitch," Boucher said.

"Was it that guy Jonathan Paul?"

"Didn't you see his stupid bumper sticker?"

"I wasn't paying attention."

"I think that little shit is purposely trying to bug me."

"Wouldn't surprise me."

"I'm sure he is. He didn't look at me when he went by."

"Why would he look at you?"

"You always look at people in a Rolls. Everybody does."

"Even if you're driving one yourself?"

"Especially then. If he didn't look, it means he knew it was me."

"Maybe he waits on a side street and pulls out when we come by. You think?"

"That lousy bastard. He won't be driving a Rolls when I'm through with him. Be lucky if he can afford to ride the T."

12

THAT WAS MY FUN FOR WEDNESday. Thursday was routine, but on Friday I had a sexual experience with Boucher's wife, and I guess in a weird way with Boucher, too.

Thurman and I were having our usual training session after work and before the late dinner the Bouchers ate when they were home, which was most evenings. They weren't much on going out.

We started off with jumping jacks and stretching, to get loose and warmed up. Then we just messed around for a while, what a boxer would call sparring. Boucher went full out, and I went at about three-quarters—up considerably from my effort level in our early sessions. Boucher was making good progress.

Next we worked on what he called dirty stuff. These were moves that would be barred in regular wrestling. Or they were moves you'd never have occasion to use in a match, like blocking knife strikes or disarming an opponent. We had a routine worked out, eight different maneuvers that we'd practice during each session. I had him repeat each one on me at least half a dozen times, while I varied my responses slightly so he could cope with the unexpected. The idea was to repeat and repeat and repeat the moves until they became as automatic as tying your shoes.

Thurman had just put me on my knees, when a voice said, "You boys look like you're having fun." Alison Boucher was standing by the door, wearing one of her stylish running outfits. This one was robin's-egg blue.

"Hi, Lissy," Boucher said. "Have a nice run?"

"Too hot. You gents have got it easy in here."

Naturally I had seen to it that our little gym was air-conditioned. How else could you cool down after a rough workout, or a long sauna bath?

"Take a break?" Thurman said to me. I was still on my knees, where he had put me just as Alison Boucher showed up. I nodded. He dropped down beside me, and patted the mat for his wife to sit down, too. There were no chairs in the wrestling room, and nothing else that could hurt you if you landed on it. She dropped down easily beside us. She moved like a dancer.

"The way I had Tom by the wrist there?" Boucher said. "That was the move I told you about, the one he used on poor Terry Dineen that time in the parking lot."

"Really? It doesn't look terribly dangerous."

"It isn't, unless you try to get up. Then the other guy breaks your wrist. Here . . . No, let the expert show you. Tom?"

I got up and took her hand. Her little hand. Her pretty little hand. It was a sweaty little hand, too, after her run. I put mild pressure on her wrist, forcing her to her knees in front of me.

She looked up at me, from her submissive position. "What are you going to make me do?" she asked.

"Try to get up."

She tried, but couldn't. So she stayed on her knees. I kept hold of her hand, but loosely, as Boucher started to talk.

"A trained wrestler like Tom can do amazing things. He can make you use your own weight against yourself. You think you're going one way, and suddenly you're going another. You could go under a train, even. Isn't that possible, Tom?"

"Sure it's possible. But it didn't happen."

"I wanted to reach you that afternoon for something or other. Louise tried three times, but you were always out of the building."

"Well, I was. I was chasing down a print in a gallery on Newbury Street."

"A wrestling print?" Boucher was smiling. This was just friendly stuff, not a hostile interrogation.

"Yeah, by this guy Sir Philip Orpington."

"Uh-huh. Being on Newbury Street at the time, naturally you wouldn't have been taking a little stroll near the Longfellow Bridge."

"No, naturally not." I was smiling, too.

"Just wanted to get that straight," he said. "Tom's something, isn't he, Lissy?"

"Yes, he is." Alison Boucher said. She was looking at me as if she really believed I was.

The more I denied having anything to do with Dineen's death, I knew, the more convinced they would be that I had killed him.

"Whether I'm something or not," I said, "I've only seen Terry Dineen one time in my life."

"Have it your way," Boucher said.

"He had somebody call me that one time, but aside from that I had nothing against him. He never followed up. Never even told anybody about that business in the parking lot, as far as I can tell. Which is natural. If you're supposed to be a tough guy and somebody puts you down on the ground, you don't go around telling people about it."

"Of course not."

"I'm not getting much of anywhere, am I? Because of course if I did clip the guy, I'd be saying the exact same thing as if I didn't."

"Of course."

"Well, I'll say it straight out, then, and let it go at that. I didn't throw anybody under any train."

That much was true, anyway, although I didn't expect they'd believe it. Hoped they wouldn't, in fact.

"Well, I'll say something straight out myself, then," Boucher said. "Forget about Terry. Did you ever kill anybody else?"

"I was five years in Southeast Asia for the government. It was a live-fire exercise."

"Apart from in a war."

"Thurman, these are personal things you're asking about. I'm uncomfortable with personal things. I do what needs doing, leave it at that."

"Happy to hear it, Tom."

I still had Alison Boucher's hand. She was still on her knees in front of me, looking up with her mouth slightly open. I could hear her breathing, as if she were still out of breath from her run. She hadn't been breathing like that when she came in, though.

"Tom," she said, "would you teach me to wrestle, too?"

"Fine with me, if Thurman doesn't mind you sitting in."

"Show me now. Show me how you start."

I looked over at Boucher. He nodded. I remembered what Alison had said, the first time we met, about how open-minded her husband was. It was pretty open-minded to let some guy roll around on a huge foam mattress with your wife, but he was the boss.

"Okay, get yourself set on all fours."

* * *

"Let me get this straight, Bethany," Hope said over the phone later that evening. "Now you're giving wrestling lessons to the boss's wife?"

"A lesson. Singular. There may not be another."

"This is weird, Bethany."

"You don't know how weird."

"I'm listening."

"Any chance one of the kids might pick up on the extension?" She was at home in Washington, and her children were out of school for the summer.

"That weird, huh? Go ahead, I'm alone in the house."

I told her how things had started out innocently enough, except that under the circumstances I had to watch where I put my hands. Pretty soon I noticed that she wasn't putting her hands anywhere. She wasn't using them at all. At first I didn't understand what was happening. Then, when she had maneuvered herself around so that her breasts were rubbing my groin, I caught on to what she was doing. I explained it to Hope.

"The first time you met this woman, you told her about some Bangkok massage parlor routine?" Hope said. "Didn't that strike you as a little forward?"

"Hey, she started it. She was talking about how things would slip all around if you wrestled in a sweat suit."

"So at that point you naturally didn't have any choice. You were forced to tell her about this B-plus routine you used to get in Bangkok."

"B-course."

"Why did they call it that?"

"Shit, I don't know. They're inscrutable."

"But not Mrs. Boucher. She sounds definitely scrutable."

"That was my impression when she was giving me that tit job."

"How did it work out?"

"Not so good. I'm too shy."

"Yeah, that's what everybody says about you."

"Jesus, Hope, her husband had a ringside seat."

"Didn't you do orgies in Bangkok?"

"Actually, no. This was as close as I ever got. I looked over at Thurman and he had this friendly little smile on his face. Seeing that smile was like getting a jock full of ice cubes."

"What a colorful concept."

"It's not just a concept. It's what they do in rugby after a guy gets kicked in the balls."

"You're about to tell me war stories about when you played rugby with Prince Panya's team in Laos, aren't you? That won't work, Bethany. Let's get back to your boob-wrestling session with this Boucher slut."

"Well, she could feel she wasn't getting anywhere, I guess. So next thing I knew she took a scissors grip on my thigh and started taking care of herself."

"I hope it worked out better for her than it did for you."

"Oh, yeah. Practically immediately."

All the wriggling around had raised her to a considerable pitch even before she grabbed my leg between hers and started to squeeze. I had enough sense to spare Hope the details of Alison Boucher's performance, but it was impressive. She worked her way up the scale from moans to a final scream in less than a minute and then came back down slowly as I watched the red flush fade from her face and throat. Thurman watched, too, still with the same little smile.

"She's some comer, isn't she?" Thurman said.

It was a social situation that Miss Manners hadn't prepared me for. "What the hell was I supposed to say?" I asked Hope. "I just nodded and let it go at that."

"It had to have been at least a little bit exciting," Hope said.

"It was too weird to be exciting," I lied. It had been so exciting that Alison Boucher couldn't help noticing.

"Is she attractive?" Hope asked.

"She's a good-looking woman in a standard kind of way. Looks a little like Christie Brinkley."

"I meant was she attractive to you."

"Just the opposite, actually. I was disgusted."

This was what the circumstances called for, a flat-out, total lie. The fact was that Mrs. Boucher made me feel like one of the poor, lust-craved slobs that James M. Cain used to write about. If she had said, "Rip me, Frankie," I might have torn her clothes off on the spot and given her husband the show he wanted. I almost did it anyway.

"You're a pretty hard man to disgust, Bethany," Hope said.

"Tell you the truth, she scared the shit out of me. It would have been like jumping a tiger." This time I was telling the truth. That's what it would have been like all right, and it would have been scary. And I would have done it in the blink of an eye if it hadn't been for Hope.

"Hell hath no fury like a tiger scorned," Hope said.

"I know," I said. "Fortunately I had been thinking about how to handle that very problem ever since she came on to me that first day."

"This I'd like to hear."

"You're not gay, are you?" Alison Boucher had said once the flush had faded and her breathing had calmed down. She still held my leg between hers, but loosely. She was looking right into my eyes, checking for the lie.

"Don't tell me you're gay, because I felt different."

"I'm not gay. It's not that."

"He could just be bashful," Thurman said, surprising me. It was the first time he had spoken since my session with his wife had started. "Why don't I go back to the house and leave you two alone?"

"It's something else," I said. "It's a rule I have."

"If it's married women," she said, "we're all friends here."

"What it is, I only go with whores."

"For God's sake, why?"

"I don't ever like to lose control."

"Restraint games? Thurman likes that sometimes, too, don't you, darling?"

"Control of myself, I mean. I don't like to be out of control when anybody else is around."

"Aren't whores anybody?"

"They're paid, so you're in control."

"Do you understand this, Thurman?"

"I think maybe I do. You're talking about the actual orgasm, right?"

"That's right."

"Where you're kind of exposed in front of the other person?"

"Right. At their mercy."

"Do you feel exposed and at my mercy with me, Thurman?" his wife asked.

"Sure, but personally I can handle it. I can see where somebody might not be able to, though."

"Nobody's completely out of control when they come," she said.

Thurman and I both smiled.

"I am?" she asked. "Well, maybe. But it's only for a little while."

"A little while is too long," I said. "I just don't like anybody looking at me when I'm not there. I can't even sleep if anybody else is in the room. Well, I can. I had to in basic training. But otherwise I won't."

"You drink, don't you?" Thurman asked.

"Not much. Not to the point where I lose it. Drugs I don't mess with at all. You can never tell about the dosage."

"Pray you never need surgery," Alison said.

"I don't know about major surgery, but I had a bullet cut out of me once with nothing."

"What happened?" Thurman said.

"It hurt."

"See what I told you?" he said to his wife. "Be easier to get a bullet out of old Tom than personal information."

When I finished telling Hope that the Bouchers seemed to have swallowed my control freak bullshit, she said, "Sometimes you amaze me, Bethany."

"How do you mean?"

"You have these totally weird flashes of inspiration that would never have occurred to anybody else. How did you guess that Boucher would feel helpless during orgasm?"

"Because I do. That's why we get along so good, on account of we're bent the same way."

"But you cope differently than he does."

"God knows I try."

There was noise in the background on her end, and then Hope said, "Paul and Steven are back home. Keep me posted."

"I will."

"And, Tom?" It was serious when she called me Tom.

"Yes?"

"Promise you'll stay away from tigers."

"I promise."

After she hung up, I leaned back in my La-Z-Boy recliner and considered that promise. In addition to my outright lies, there were things I hadn't told Hope about the strange session with the Bouchers. Hope and I came of age during what one of our generation's now-forgotten holy men called the greening of America. Letting it all hang out was considered wisdom instead of childishness, or that was the general belief. What Hope and I believed, though, not that we ever talked about it, was that plenty of things should go unsaid.

Consequently I hadn't told her about the rest of the business with Lissy. Once Alison had come back to Planet Earth, she said, "Wow, did anybody ever tell you you give great leg, Tom?"

There wasn't much to say to that, since a piano leg would have done the job just as well. But still, manners are manners. "No, but thanks, Alison," I said.

"Call me Lissy."

As far as I knew, nobody but her husband called her Lissy. I looked over at him. He looked friendly, encouraging.

"Lissy," I said.

"You don't have to come, you know," she said. "You do your thing, I'll do mine."

"If you did yours, I might not be able to help doing mine."

"Think about it, though."

"I will."

And I was. It wouldn't change the equation, whatever the hell it was, between Thurman and me. Once a man has watched his wife bring herself off against another man's thigh, a step or two further isn't going to make much difference. And it probably wouldn't change the equation between Hope and me, since I wouldn't be dumb enough to tell her. On the other hand, I would know, and maybe the knowledge would cause some tiny rearrangement of my emotional furniture. And maybe that would take Hope and me in a new direction.

So the best thing would be to stay away from tigers. I hoped I could. Just after my new friend Lissy told me to think about it, she looked deliberately down at the effect she had had on me. Slowly, all of us watching, she extended her forefinger. The nail on it was clear polished, manicured, and medium long. Still slowly, lightly, and just once, she scraped her nail along the taut fabric.

"There," she said. "Now, that didn't hurt, did it?"

I thought that was sort of funny. The fact was that Alison Boucher may have been weird or depraved or whatever, but she was also fearless and funny and self-mocking and bright—and sexy as hell.

Next day was Saturday, but Boucher wanted me to pick him up anyway. He planned on spending the morning in the office. I didn't look forward to the ride in. How he would handle what had happened the previous day in the wrestling room? He was from the age of Aquarius, too. Would he want to share his feelings with me, explore our relationship?

Thank God he didn't. He handled it by not handling it, by acting as if nothing at all had gone on between Alison and me. Maybe nothing had. Maybe that was the feeling he was sharing with me, that what had occurred was nothing out of the ordinary. Take my wife. Please.

"What about your friend Gladys Williams?" he asked during the ride. "Any news from her yet?"

"I'm meeting with her tonight, actually."

"Well, let me know Monday what you find out."

"Will do," I said. I always wanted to say that. It sounded to me like something a Harvard M.B.A. might say.

"You can tell us about it on the way to Canton," Thurman said.

We were flying to Canton Monday on the corporate jet, via Boucher Group headquarters in Brewster, New York. My role was to stand off to one side and watch how a newspaper acquisition was carried out. Alison was coming along, too, which on the rational level I hoped wouldn't turn into a problem. On a more primitive level, of course, I also hoped it would.

I spent the Saturday morning running surveillance tapes in my office, which was turning out to be not nearly as much fun as I had thought it would be. In fact it was not only duller than baseball but even duller than golf. The fastest the tape would run was triple speed, which helped some but not enough. No matter how fast the tape runs, an empty corridor or men's room amounts to watching a still photo. At long intervals a figure would appear, moving herky-jerky on the speeded-up tape.

All I learned in three hours was that one of the receptionists had a good sexual harassment case against an assistant city editor. I marked the number on the tape counter for possible future use. She might complain about him helping himself to her breast, or one of these days I might find it useful to have the assistant city editor in my pocket. After Boucher called down to say he was ready to go home, I stopped on my way upstairs to splash cold water into my eyes. They burned, and I was surprised to see that they didn't look red in the mirror.

That evening Felicia Lamport held a dinner meeting for the co-conspirators—Gladys Williams, Serena Cushing, Jonathan Paul, and me. After the plates were cleared away and the coffee served, Felicia produced a yellow legal pad.

"I have prepared an agenda," she said. "I've never had an agenda before, and as you might imagine I'm terribly proud of it. I may have agendas for everything from now on."

"Whoa," Gladys said. "Just like the White House."

"What a discouraging thought," Felicia said. "On the other hand, we may have a more effective management team. We'll hear from you first, Tom."

"What about?"

"About item number one, but of course you don't know what item number one is. It's the death of Serena's mother. Is there any chance that it wasn't suicide?"

"Not much, but Gladys is the one who used to work for the police department. She looked into it a little."

"They're carrying it as a suicide," Gladys said. "There was no note, but sometimes there isn't."

"She would have left a note," Felicia said. "I insist on that."

"Well, a plastic bag doesn't get over your head by accident, so let's think about murder," Gladys said. "It was theoretically possible for a murderer to have escaped out the window, but lots of things are theoretically possible. The cops couldn't find any marks of a ladder under the only open window. There were no marks on the windowsill, or in the ground under the window. Nothing seems to be missing. Nothing indicates that she resisted. The neighbors didn't see anyone entering or leaving the house. So there's no evidence that it was murder, and a good deal of evidence to suggest it wasn't."

"What do you think?" Felicia asked Gladys.

"I think the cops are probably right, which I know isn't what you want to hear. There was no reason for anybody to kill her. Nothing was stolen from her jewelry box or her purse."

Felicia said, "Another person with connections to Thurman Boucher has showed up dead under ambiguous circumstances. Terry Dineen."

"They weren't ambiguous," I said.

"They were at least a little ambiguous," Jonathan Paul said. "No note this time, either. And a witness who disappeared."

"This isn't for your paper, right?" I said. "It's just for the group?"

"Right."

"I was the witness."

After I told them about it, Serena Cushing said, "I wondered if it might be something like that. I remember Dad saying once that Terry carried more insurance on his life than Dad did himself. The poor man couldn't stand the thought that his child might wind up in a state institution."

"We have to move this meeting along," Felicia said. "It's very important to move meetings along. Item number two is the Rolls-Royce. Is it turning out to be worth the three thousand a month?"

That question was for me. The only dealer who handled Rolls-Royces in the Boston area was out in Natick. Their Rolls experts, a gent appropriately named David W. Thomas III, had laughed when I asked him about renting one. But then he remembered a customer who was about to leave on a three-month round-the-world cruise and might not mind having somebody pick up his installment payments for a while.

"I'd keep the car a little longer," I said. "Every time Jonathan shows up in that thing, it spoils the Cobra's whole day."

"Shouldn't we tell them about Tingley, Davis?" Felicia asked.

Since the others didn't know about my arrangement with Tingley, Davis, I started out to explain that it was this old investment banking house, see . . .

Then Felicia took over and told us she had once been "great friends" with the senior George Tingley. "Tom has informed Mr. Boucher that Jonathan's Rolls was purchased from Tingley, Davis," she said. "I haven't mentioned to George that we took his firm's name in vain, but there was really no reason to tell the poor man. I did sound him out in general about our friend Mr. Boucher, however, and found him to be very contemptuous indeed of the man and his business methods. So perhaps George might help us, in some way that was terribly discreet and didn't cost him any money. George is notoriously discreet and notoriously cheap."

"I'll try to think of something," I said.

Jonathan Paul and Gladys settled on the general types of phony data that she ought to feed the Cobra, and Jonathan said he'd cook up precise figures while I was out of town with the Bouchers.

"How about if some mysterious visitors show up one day and inspect the *Trader*'s operation?" I said. "Some guys who look like investment bankers."

"That doesn't sound very discreet to me," Felicia said.

"Nobody would actually show up, Felicia," I said. "What does Boucher know? Gladys tells him they showed up, they showed up. All your banker buddy would have to do is refuse to talk to the Cobra if he ever called to ask who the guys were."

"I'm sure he'd have no trouble refusing to talk to the revolting Mr. Boucher. But what would the point be of all this?"

"I'd like Boucher to think that there's major money behind the *Cambridge Trader*, and not Serena's money."

Once Felicia had got our reports and distributed assignments to everybody, she had me deliver an overall status report.

"Doesn't look too bad," I said. "All the snooping I'm doing has people pretty much on edge. Everybody is afraid of me expect Boucher and his hatchet man, Fogel. Everybody is afraid of them, too, so the three of us are pals. I'm getting a little dirt here, a little dirt there, on people in the various departments. Like the assistant city editor I told you about, the one who groped the receptionist. I know everybody's salaries and I've got total physical access to the whole plant. Once things start to go wrong, I'll be able to get everybody accusing everybody else of sabotage. It'll turn into a real snake pit."

"What kinds of sabotage?" Serena asked. "You don't mean causing actual damage, do you? These are people who worked for Dad and Mom. I don't want them charged with arson or destroying property or something."

"Nothing like that," I said. "Most of it will be corrupting or losing information. The computer network is unbelievably vulnerable. The whole system is run like an honor box."

"What's all this sabotage going to lead to?" Jonathan Paul asked.

"I can't really predict it. I'm just tossing as much sand in the gears as I can, and we'll see what happens. If the *Banner* gets to be too much of a pain in the neck, maybe Boucher will look for a buyer. If that happens, he won't be able to get his money back, at least if the newspaper broker was right. Boucher way overpaid for it, so he'll be looking at a big loss. And then Serena rides up. With her it isn't a business judgment, it's sentimental. She's willing to pay the same price he paid her mother for it. He gets out of a lousy situation by selling her a dog at no loss to himself. What do you think? Sound logical?"

"Well, maybe," Paul said. "I guess it's barely possible."

"Yeah," I said. "Barely is about all you can say at this early stage. But what the hell, it's worth it just to watch his neck turn red every time he thinks about you and the *Trader*. Besides, all it's really costing us is the lease on the Rolls."

"And your time," said Serena.

"Hey, I'm making a good buck, and the boss is teaching me the business."

13

BREWSTER IS ON ROUTE 22, about an hour's drive north of New York City. The Boucher Group's Learjet put down at Danbury Airport, where a stretch limo and driver were waiting for us. The limo was silver with smoked windows, and the back was like a little living room for the three of us. Being a press lord was good duty. There was a phone, and a little foldout rig that held a PowerBook 540C, the top of Apple's new line of portables. Instead of a trackball, it had a little pad. You just moved your finger around on the trackpad, and the cursor moved around on the screen. I would have jumped up and down and hollered, Hey, mister, can I try it? except I was being cool. We lean, mean killing machines, we run very cool.

Headquarters turned out to be a three-story Victorian house on an elm-shaded street of other big houses on other big lots. A small sign in front said BOUCHER GROUP in gilt letters carved into white-painted wood. Out back was a carriage house. The main building rose to a copper-sheathed dome, with a lightning rod on top of it. Smaller lightning rods stuck up from the many gables and at both ends of the ridgeline. The house was painted grayish purple with red trim, bright as a toy.

"Those were the original colors," Boucher said. "We found traces of them buried under a half inch or so of paint when we stripped the building. Lissy's decorator got them matched."

"He said it was common back then to paint homes in fantasy colors," Alison Boucher said. "It gave me a whole new view of my great-grandfather, building himself a huge dollhouse to live in."

"This is your house?" I asked.

"Now it belongs to the Boucher Group. They made me a fabulous offer for it, didn't you, darling?"

Which meant Thurman had drained off company money for himself by overpaying his wife for her house. The purchase price would have been written off as a business expense.

"Looked a little different in those days, didn't it?" Boucher said.

"You can't *imagine* how dreary it was, Tom. Daddy was probably the last of the classic old general practitioners in America. He had this dreary office on the ground floor, filled with yellow oak mission-style furniture. Glass-fronted bookcases with instruments inside them. It was just immensely, immensely dreary growing up an only child in that house."

"Her father was drinking himself to death downstairs and her grandfather was doing the same thing up on the third floor," Boucher said.

"Poor things," Alison said. "They had both succeeded by the time Thurman showed up to rescue me."

"My first newspaper job was here," Thurman said. "I got sick of Yale my sophomore year and wangled myself a job as a reporter for the local weekly."

From my research into Boucher's meteoric rise I knew that Yale had tossed him out for plagiarism. And landing the job hadn't taken much wangling, since the local paper was part of his father's small chain.

But my research hadn't turned up much about Mr. Boucher. "Was your great-grandfather a doctor, too?" I asked. "The one who built the house?"

"No, he was on Wall Street. I've never been clear just what he did, but he apparently did it very well. Grandfather went to medical school, but he never had to practice, and so he didn't bother. Daddy didn't have to practice either, and in fact he pretty much stopped seeing patients after Mother died. At which point I was six. You can imagine what sort of a life I had, rattling around in that old house. I went away to boarding school when I was eleven, and I used to look forward to school the way the other kids looked forward to vacation."

After that, I would have thought she'd set out to create the largest possible family. Coming from the opposite situation, anyway, I had left the litter first chance I got, and later left my wife and my own little daughter. But maybe the Bouchers couldn't have kids, or maybe she figured kids would cramp her style. Or she just didn't want to inflict childhood on somebody else.

"I'm not good with children," she said, as if I had spoken my thoughts out loud. "Some women just aren't made to be mothers."

"Lots of women," I said. "But most of them don't know it."

"I know it," Alison said. "I'm a man's woman."

Her husband didn't appear to be listening. I felt like somebody in an unfamiliar and unwholesome church, unsure of how to behave. I didn't know the rules of the Boucher marriage. I didn't understand what my role was supposed to be.

Inside headquarters the decorator had created an interior

to match the playful exterior. Victorian furniture that had once been heavy and dark was now bleached or painted in pastels. Paintings were hung with maroon velvet ropes from the ceiling molding, but they were light and bright paintings. The floor was covered with off-white carpeting. Oriental rugs that probably dated back to great-grandfather's day had been placed here and there. On a wood floor they would have seemed dark, but on the white carpeting they seemed colorful.

Fourteen people worked at Boucher Group headquarters, I knew, so the second floor had to be used for offices, too, and maybe the third as well. Nobody looked cramped, from the glances I got through open doors as we passed. The offices weren't as expensively decorated as the large entrance room, but they were all done in the same general mix of Victorian and modern.

Boucher's office, though, was totally different. It looked a lot like his office back at the *Banner*. "Louise," Boucher said to his secretary, "this is Tom Bethany."

"A pleasure to meet you, Mr. Bethany," Louise said.

"Nice to meet you, Louise," I said, and then it hit me. His secretary in Cambridge was named Louise, too. This office in Brewster didn't just look a lot like his office at the *Banner*. It was identical, from the dark blue carpet on the floor to the framed hunting prints on the wall. The furniture was the same, and arranged the same way. On Boucher's desk was the same folder of budget projections I had last seen on his desk Saturday morning, in Cambridge.

"Do you have to be named Louise to be Mr. Boucher's secretary?" I asked her.

"Oh, no," she said. "It's just that we keep everything identical. My real name is Mary Ellen."

"Good for you, Tom," Thurman Boucher said. "You'd be amazed how many people are too unperceptive to notice that I have duplicate offices. It's the only way you can run a business efficiently from two places at once."

"Every document in every file folder is the same in both offices," Louise said. "The phone logs and appointment logs are the same. If Louise in Cambridge works overtime, I stay in my office here, too. If Mr. T leaves a paper on his desk up there, he ought to be able to reach out his hand and find the exact same paper here when his plane lands."

"What about Louise in Cambridge? Is she the real Louise?"

"The real Louise is retired," Boucher said. "She was the first secretary I ever had. Not the best, because they just keep getting better. Just the first."

Headquarters Louise smiled, pleased. She was a happy camper. I knew from the Cambridge payroll figures that Boucher understood the first rule of politics, which is to carry your home precinct. Everyone really close to him was paid generously. In Cambridge, that meant Alan Fogel, Louise, and me.

"It's never just the money," Boucher was saying. "By definition, anybody you buy a newspaper from already has plenty of money. The trick in negotiating an acquisition is to find out what the person really wants more than anything else in the world."

We were at 22,000 feet in the Learjet, on our way to Canton. We'd be getting there in time for dinner, which we were having at the house of Christina Haseltine, the owner of the *Times-Dispatch*. She was putting the three of us up, too. Boucher's lawyer was in town already, staying at a hotel.

"Tell Tom about the Rockland paper," Alison Boucher said.

"Best deal I ever made. The Harte-Hanks people were after the paper, and they had already made an offer of twenty-six to the publisher, guy named Cleve Gibbons. Then by accident I found Cleve's hot button."

"It wasn't an accident that you recognized what you had, though," Alison said.

"Well, to that extent it wasn't an accident, no. I just meant that Cleve happened to bring the subject up, that part was an accident. There had been a piece in the *Times* just that day, piece by some doctor who couldn't get the hospital to unplug his father and let him die. Cleve got to talking about that, and there was something about the way he sounded that hit me. This guy, I said to myself, now this is a guy scared shitless. So I poked around a little, kept him talking.

"Turned out his uncle had spent six weeks in intensive care after a stroke and they wouldn't let him die. Cleve didn't believe the doctors when they said you don't feel any pain after a stroke. He kept thinking his poor uncle was lying there for six weeks screaming inside and he couldn't tell anybody. So he had a living will made out and all that, Cleve did, but he got afraid all over again when he read this doctor's story. If a doctor couldn't put his own father out of his misery, what chance did he have?

"So I offered him a million less than Gannett, except I included an absolute guarantee that he wasn't going to die in a coma in the intensive care ward."

"How could you guarantee that?" I asked.

"I told him I'd see that he never got to the hospital in the first place. I agreed to give twenty thousand dollars a year to a local hospice, half of it in escrow and only to be paid if Cleve died in the hospice. I put a doctor on retainer on the same basis. Plus I would refund the million-dollar difference between Gannett's price and mine to his heirs if he was kept alive against his wishes."

"The guy believed all that?"

"You're right. Legally it would turn out to be full of holes, most of them put in by my lawyers, actually. What he was buying was somebody to be on his side, if a bus ever ran

over him and left him a vegetable. Somebody with re-
sources. Somebody tough enough to go in and yank those
tubes out personally if necessary."

"How much has it cost you so far?"

"Ten thousand dollars to the hospice. Cleve died on his
kitchen floor six months after he sold me the paper. Massive
heart attack."

"What about the ten thousand in escrow?"

"They wanted it, of course, but he didn't die in the hospice, did he? Actually they might have won in court, the
way the contract read, but it would have cost them more in
legal fees than the five thousand they stood to gain."

"I thought it was ten."

"Five. Cleve only lived half a year, remember."

"Pretty slick," I said, knowing he'd mistake it for a compliment. In the Cobra's world, you had done a good day's work
if you welshed on a five-thousand-dollar debt to a hospice.

"That's all there is to it," Boucher said. "Just find the
seller's hot button."

"What about the *Times-Dispatch?*" I asked. "Did you find
a hot button there?"

"We think so. The situation is that the majority owner,
eighty percent of the voting stock, is a woman in her late
sixties named Christina Haseltine. She's had her son-in-law
running the paper since her husband died eight years ago.
Robbie Haseltine."

"Her son-in-law's name is Haseltine, too?"

"How could that be, huh?" Boucher said. "Well, that's all
you need to know about Christina Haseltine, right there. Her
daughter met Robbie in college. He was named something
or other, who cares? But it wasn't Haseltine. His old man
was a schoolteacher in Wisconsin, something insignificant
like that, anyway. The kid was majoring in journalism, and
so was the Haseltine girl, Marcia. Eventually she brings him
to meet the folks so he can ask for Marcia's hand. The old

lady has no problem with that, except she points out that Haseltine is a great name locally and she swore to herself the paper would always be run by a Haseltine, and Marcia is the only one left, and to make a long story short, Robbie, how about you move in with Marcia and me when you get back from the fancy honeymoon I'm paying for and then do me one more little favor. Go down to the courthouse and change your name to Haseltine."

"I bet the kid had fun explaining that to his old man back in Wisconsin."

"The schoolteacher? You think he minded? The fact is, most people would sell a lot more than their name for a shot at that kind of money."

I nodded. Not only was he the boss, he happened to be right.

"So Robbie and Marcia still live with Mom," Boucher said, "only now they have three little kids of their own."

"Quite a crowd."

"Only six people, and the place is huge."

"It's the mother-in-law that makes it a crowd."

"Well, there is that. Anyway, that's the human equation we're working with. The daughter is busy raising the kids, out of the picture as far as the paper is concerned. The mother is a sweet old thing who very efficiently castrated her prospective son-in-law even before the marriage. The son-in-law is currently running the paper, and very badly."

"Does the mother know he's running the paper badly?"

"Not really. The fact is that her dear departed husband ran it badly, too, so she has nothing to judge by. She has no idea how much money she ought to be taking out of a marketing area like that."

"What's your hot button, then?"

"You tell me, Tom."

"The dead husband."

"Sure. Obviously. She wants to keep him alive forever, in the form of Robbie."

"But you don't want that?"

"Certainly not. Robbie's a moron."

"How are you going to work it out?"

"You'll have a ringside seat, Tom. Keep your eyes and ears open."

The Haseltine mansion was a huge place, all right, new enough so that the trees hadn't had a chance to grow up to the house yet. It was four or five miles out of town, and close to the road so everybody could admire it—a big three-story cube of white-painted brick. In front there were columns holding up a three-story portico with a big chandelier hanging from its ceiling. In America any boy can grow up to live in a fake White House. And too many do.

We pulled up to it in a rented Cadillac, which Boucher drove. "I want the Haseltines to wonder who the hell you are," he explained. "Why is Thurman Boucher driving this guy around? How does he fit in, anyway?"

"What's the point?"

"Just to keep them off their balance. When we get down to negotiations, now and then I might turn to you and ask something as if I need your approval. Think it over and nod, unless I have my hands clasped. Then think it over and shake your head."

"Okay."

"We'll go over it again tomorrow, before we sit down with the lawyers."

"No need to. I've got it."

The big front door opened, and the Haseltines, old and new, came out. Christina Haseltine was short, with fluffy white hair. She had plump soft cheeks and a little mouth and was built like the Pillsbury doughboy. She didn't look a thing like a dragon lady. Nor did Robbie Haseltine look like a eunuch. In fact he was a six-footer who looked a little like Al Gore, which is to say his profile belonged on a coin. On an actual human, though, features that regular are handsome but dull.

". . . my associate, Tom Bethany," Thurman Boucher was saying, "and of course you remember my wife, Alison."

"Welcome to our humble abode," Mrs. Haseltine said. It was the first time I ever heard those words delivered seriously.

"Pleasure to meet you, Tom," Robbie said. "Great to see you again, Thurman. Alison, these your bags?"

Robbie locked onto the two pastel suitcases he figured must be hers, and stood with them in his hands. He was braced like a dog waiting for permission to cross the street, and as soon as she nodded he was through the door in front of her. Thurman and I wrangled our own luggage, with Christina Haseltine following along behind. We all headed off to the left toward what would have been the east wing, except that this white house had been built on a different axis.

"I'm so sorry you're missing Marcia and the children," Christina Haseltine said, "but every summer I have to give them up for two weeks to visit Robbie's parents in Wisconsin. I know I must sound selfish, since I get to enjoy them the whole rest of the year."

The interior of the house was like Robbie, handsome but dull. The furniture was expensive reproductions, mostly with that tan finish that isn't the color of any wood I've ever seen. It seemed unlikely that the kitchen was carpeted in pale blue, but every other inch of the house was, including the bathrooms and closets. And every window had floor-length drapes.

I didn't see any bookcases anywhere, although when Mrs. Haseltine showed me to my bedroom I found two volumes of *Reader's Digest* condensed books on the bedstand. I always wondered who bought those condensed books. Newspaper publishers, apparently.

I freshened up, as they say, in the bathroom across the hall and went on down to dinner. We had roast beef, corn on the cob, peas, mashed potatoes, and a salad made of iceberg lettuce and sliced tomatoes. The tomatoes were the solid, tough-skinned kind with pale pink flesh and no flavor and practically no juice. They're out of season in the summer, but you can find them if you look hard enough.

The conversation was as exciting as the menu. Although I have an abnormally strong memory, I couldn't even say what we talked about. All I remember is how good Thurman Boucher was at fitting himself to the company. If dull was the flavor of the day, then dull was what he would do. He was right down there with Mrs. Haseltine and Robbie, wallowing around in tedium. The only thing that preserved me from total stupefaction was Alison, who rolled her eyes at me now and then when no one else was watching. Once she slipped a coffee spoon deep into her mouth and pretended to retch. I made a small noise.

"I'm sorry, Tom," Robbie said. "What did you say?"

"Nothing. I got something caught in my throat."

I caught it just in time, too, or it would have come out as a full-blown laugh.

Mrs. Haseltine excused herself and went upstairs at half past ten. We all followed her twenty minutes later. "Big day tomorrow," Thurman said to Robbie, heartily. Hearty wasn't a word you'd normally connect with Thurman, but he did hearty as well as he did dull. In fact the two generally go together, as in Willard Scott.

"Wish I could be with you guys tomorrow," Robbie said, "but I've got to keep an eye on things down at the shop."

"Know what you mean," said Thurman. "No rest for the weary, huh?"

"Well, you got to keep on top of them every minute."

"Isn't that the God's honest truth, though?" Thurman said.

Behind him Alison, with no spoon handy this time, gagged herself with a finger.

My queen-size bed had a quilted coverlet, trimly tailored so there would be nice sharp edges all around the Beautyrest. It looked as comfy as a gurney. I managed to get the coverlet loose around the pillows, and skinned it back enough to let me wedge myself between the taut sheets. I left an arm free of my restraints, so as to be able to read a *Reader's Digest* condensed book.

By eleven-thirty I was in the heart of the Holy Land, where a rabbi's beautiful daughter was about to face the joys and burdens of her heritage—and her own deepest yearnings: " 'Yes, I understand all that!' Chaya Leva insisted, biting the pillow pressed to her chest to keep from screaming in frustration."

In the Holy Land, apparently, human speech could pass miraculously through clenched teeth and pillows.

But the spell was broken by a thump from the hall, not loud but solid sounding, as if something heavy had made it. I heard a woman's voice, and then nothing. I wriggled my way up and out of the bed, pulled on my pants, and stepped to the door. Still no sound.

I switched off the light in my room and looked out. The hallway was empty. A night-light showed in the bathroom across the way, but otherwise the hall was dark. I switched on the ceiling light in my bedroom to see if I could spot what had made the noise. Past the bathroom to my left was a small table against the wall, with a vase full of flowers on it. They didn't seem to have been disturbed, but nothing else around could have fallen. When I went over to check, my bare feet felt wetness on the rug.

I considered the geography. The Bouchers' room was to

the right of mine, at the end of the hall, so the voice had presumably been Alison's. She couldn't have been headed for the bathroom, because they had their own. She couldn't have been headed for my room, because the vase of flowers was to the left, past both my room and the bathroom. She could have been headed downstairs to make herself a sandwich, but there were no lights on in the stairwell.

Past the stair landing the upstairs hall led to the other wing, which wasn't lit, either. I felt my way along the corridor, which must have been what Alison was doing when she knocked over the vase and set it back in place. I was well past the landing when I saw a thread of light escaping from underneath a door to my left. A note seemed to be taped on the door. I eased closer, but it was too dark for me to read what it said.

Since no noise came from behind the door, I drifted back to the stair landing, where I had felt a light switch along the way. What the hell, since the light was on inside the room, they wouldn't notice a light in the hall. I flipped the switch on just long enough to see that all the doors in that wing had signs on them, lettered in a child's hand with Magic Markers. One said MY ROOM, one said CHRISSIE'S ROOM, one said BABY TED'S ROOM, and the last one said DADDY AND MOMMY'S ROOM.

That was the door with the light showing under it. I flipped the switch off and went back to listen. Now I could make out the sounds I was expecting. I could have gone on back to my condensed book at that point, because what else was there to learn? Naturally, though, I stayed. The noises got faster and faster, and at the end were drowned out by noises I had already heard.

My reaction surprised me. It was jealousy. How could Alison possibly get in bed with such a zero? How could the zero get her to make those sounds? Then rationalization kicked in. She was probably faking. Even if she wasn't faking, she had been much louder with me. And then she had nothing but a leg to work with. Besides, who cares? I could have had her but I turned her down already. Thanks, Lissy, but no thanks.

That's what I tried to tell myself anyway as I went back down the hall to my bed and the rabbi's beautiful daughter. A little later I thought I heard Alison passing my door on the way back to her own room. Cheap little whore.

14

THE NEGOTIATIONS WERE THE
next day, in the conference room of the local law firm that
did the *Times-Dispatch*'s legal work. "There's no home court
advantage unless the visiting team thinks there is," Boucher
had explained to me. "If they think meeting on their turf
gives them an advantage, good luck to them. Actually if
anything it gives me an advantage. They start out owing
me."

The other team was also ahead on lawyers. Their lead bull
was a gray-haired man about Christina Haseltine's age, the
Ferguson of Ferguson, Milwright and Hoskins. She called
him Will.

He had two young associates with him, in case there was
any actual work to be done. Ferguson introduced them as
Frank something and Harv something else, and they said
hello around the table, and that was the last we heard from
them. Their only function, apparently, was to take notes and
listen to whispered comments from the senior partner. Not

194

that they wouldn't show up prominently on the bill, of course.

Our only lawyer was a man named Leslie Whitten. We had picked him up at his hotel and driven him to Ferguson, Milwright and Hoskins. He spoke so softly you had to lean forward to hear him, and he looked as if he couldn't be more than a year or two out of law school. "Leslie's function is to look inexperienced," Boucher had said. "In fact he's been representing us for eleven years and he probably knows more about the newspaper business than any lawyer in America."

"Well, I wouldn't say that," Whitten said.

"Of course you wouldn't," Boucher said. "That's my point."

As far as Christina Haseltine and her lawyers knew, the Boucher Group's purchase of the *Times-Dispatch* was a done deal and today's session was just for both sides to congratulate each other and sign on the dotted line.

"Gannett had already offered them fourteen million," Boucher said on the way over. "We're getting the paper for thirteen-five."

"Why didn't she just take Gannett's offer?" I asked.

"Because I brought the old bitch up to speed on what Gannett did in Santa Fe."

"What was that?"

"Back in the seventies they bought the *New Mexican* from Robert McKinney with an ironclad employment agreement that he'd keep on running it. Then they fired his manager and a bunch of his other people. McKinney lost control of his paper."

"Well, he finally got it back," Whitten said.

"Yes, and he had to go to the federal courts to do it," Boucher said. "The point, though, is that Christina and her idiot son-in-law were only vaguely aware of the whole story. Till I put them in contact with some of the people Gannett had fired. Robbie was particularly moved by their stories, which I figured he might be. So Gannett's offer started to look not so good. Then Leslie here had the brilliant idea of going to the court records and digging out the exact wording of the employment agreement Gannett had broken. We pointed out that this must be an absolutely unbreakable contract, since it had been upheld by the United States courts. Then we pointed out the ways that Gannett's proposed agreement with the *Times-Dispatch* was different from their old *New Mexican* agreement. Various little escape hatches they had learned to slip in after their disaster out in Santa Fe. We, on the other hand . . . actually, it's Leslie's idea. Tell him, Leslie."

"Well, it was just sort of a gimmick, really. We said we'd sign the exact same agreement with Mrs. Haseltine that Gannett Newspapers had with McKinney, word for word except for the names. That way she can be sure Robbie Haseltine will have a bulletproof contract."

"Today's going to be just a formality, then?" I asked. "The papers get signed and then everybody goes out to lunch?"

"Not exactly," Thurman said. "It should be interesting to watch."

So there I was, the fly on the wall, waiting for our side to surprise both me and their side. Their lawyer opened the proceedings.

"Where shall we start?" Will Ferguson asked. "Do you folks have any final problems you want to take care of?"

"May I say something?" Thurman said.

"Please do. That's what we're here for."

"What I'd like to say is that I find it very significant that Robbie isn't here with us."

"I don't know why he'd need to be here," Mrs. Haseltine said. "I can look out for his interests."

"I didn't think for a moment you couldn't, Christina," Boucher said. "Or wouldn't. What I thought was so significant was that he chose to put out the paper today instead of wasting time here with us. It's first things first with Robbie. That's what attracted me to the *Times-Dispatch* to start with. Sound management. Your late husband and then you, Christina, and now Robbie, that's what gives the property its worth. That's what I'm buying. Robbie's dedication. The tradition of journalistic service to the community that your late husband established and you carried on, Christina."

This was pretty much what Boucher had said when he took over the *Cambridge Daily Banner*, I remembered. Just prior to firing most of the senior management.

"Well, I'm sure that's all very nice, Thurman," Christina Haseltine said. Whatever Boucher was dishing out, she knew it wasn't chocolate ice cream. Mrs. Haseltine wasn't quite the pushover she had seemed the night before. I could see her slicing off Robbie's family name and sewing her husband's on.

"That's just something I wanted to reiterate again before we signed on the dotted line," Thurman said. "Which personally I'm ready to do right now. Wouldn't you say so, Tom?"

He looked at me while I pretended to consider the matter. Then, since he wasn't giving me the hands-clasped signal, I nodded.

"May I interject something here?" Leslie Whitten said.

"Go ahead," said Boucher.

"I spent half the night going over this employment agreement line by line, Thurman, and I've got problems with it."

"We've been all over that."

"All right, we have. But I have a responsibility to make my objections as forcefully as I can."

"You ever wonder why people hate lawyers, Leslie?" the Cobra said. "Ever think it might be because of something like this? When everybody agrees to something in good faith and then you guys come up with some nit-picking objection?"

"Please, Thurman, just let me get it on the table. Will understands my ethical obligations here."

"Not until I know what you're talking about, I don't," Ferguson said. "A deal's a deal."

"Here's what concerns me," Whitten said. "Under the terms of the agreement on the table, the Boucher Group is paying a very substantial sum of money to the Times-Dispatch Company, in return for which they receive the physical and goodwill assets of the paper as well as whatever monies the paper makes subsequent to the date of the sale. So far a normal business transaction. But in reality the Boucher Group relinquishes all control over whether any money is in fact going to be made, and how much. That's the reality behind an employment agreement in which the new owner abandons all operational control. Let's imagine some worst-case scenarios here. Let's suppose that—"

Thurman Boucher broke in.

"Goddamn it, Leslie, pardon my language, Christina, let's suppose nothing. I know what the employment agreement means and it's exactly what I want. This is a paper with a terrific track record. Robbie is a man with a terrific track record. Look, I'll do some supposing myself. Christina, suppose we very politely invite all the lawyers to leave the room while the nonlawyers talk like regular human beings about the *Times-Dispatch* and where we see it going in future years."

"If that's your decision," Leslie Whitten said stiffly. "You're certainly at liberty to forego legal advice."

Whitten closed his briefcase and got up to leave. Will Ferguson didn't seem pleased about it, but he didn't have much choice when Mrs. Haseltine interrupted to say it sounded fair to her, too. So Ferguson followed Whitten out, with the two junior associates trailing behind him.

"Well, that's better," Boucher said. "With those guys

around, it's like trying to run in water up to your knees. Now we can settle this thing in a hurry."

"I thought we already had it settled," Mrs. Haseltine said.

"I thought so, too. I still think so. I just wanted to get the lawyers out of the room so we could be crystal clear we were on the same wavelength, so we can tell our respective legal counsels to just get the heck out of our way. This is our deal, not theirs. Am I right?"

She nodded.

"We're agreed on the money?" Thurman asked, glancing over at me. I considered the matter carefully, and nodded.

Christina Haseltine nodded, too.

"And we're agreed that Robbie will have an absolutely free hand running the paper for the foreseeable future?" Thurman asked.

Mrs. Haseltine and I nodded again.

"Then, pardon my French, what the hell are we waiting for?" Boucher said. "Let's get the lawyers back in so we can sign their papers."

Mrs. Haseltine and I both nodded, and Boucher went to the door to call the lawyers back in. The four attorneys took their places at the table, where all the documents were laid out ready for signature.

"One thing," Whitten said.

"Oh, for God's sake," said Boucher.

"A possible problem just struck me. The Gannett agreement was drawn up to ensure that Mr. McKinney would continue to have operational control over the *New Mexican.*"

"Which is exactly what we want here," Boucher said.

"Not exactly. Mr. McKinney was the publisher."

"So?"

"In this case Robert Haseltine is not the publisher. He's related to the publisher by marriage."

"Cut to the chase," Boucher said.

"Nobody likes to think about these things, Mrs. Haseltine, but that's what we lawyers are paid to do. Much as we might like to think so, marriages are not eternal."

He had her interest now, although Boucher just looked impatient with this new foolishness.

"Suppose, God forbid, that Robbie and Marcia run into problems," Whitten went on. "You could wind up in a situation where your family paper was in the hands of your daughter's divorced husband. We wouldn't want that and neither would you, Mrs. Haseltine. But that's the way the contract reads."

"Is that right, Will?" she asked.

"Technically, yes," Ferguson said.

"Maybe it isn't important," Whitten said, "but another thing to keep in mind is that the law permits a person to change his name as many times as he wishes to."

Mrs. Haseltine thought that over for a minute, and said, "What do you suggest?"

"We can fix it right now, just write in a few words and you can both initial the change."

"What words?"

"This employment agreement may be rendered null and void at any time by the party of the first part, that's you, Mrs. Haseltine, and in the event of her death, by her heirs and assigns forever."

"Does that sound all right, Will?" Mrs. Haseltine asked.

"It certainly puts you in the driver's seat, Christina."

We were on the way out to the country club so the Bouchers could have a good-pals lunch with the Haseltines and selected retainers from both clans. Boucher was driving, with Leslie Whitten beside him on the front seat of the limo. "Well, partner," Boucher said to the lawyer, "we pulled it off, didn't we?"

"It seemed to work smoothly enough, yes," Whitten said.

Putting it that way, he left himself a lawyerly loophole in case the deal fell apart later.

"Hear that, Lissy?" Boucher said over his shoulder. "It went smooth as silk."

"Of course it did, darling. I knew you'd pull it off."

Nobody thought it was necessary to spell out for me exactly what "it" meant, and of course I was far too cool to ask. Besides, I had a pretty good idea that there was more to "it" than the negotiations we had just wrapped up.

Thurman was on a roll during lunch, dominating the table with ideas for all the fun he planned to have with his new toy. He could put in a new Goss Headliner press and ship the old one down to one of his Florida papers. He could get a new Muller-Martini inserter. He could get rid of young carriers and use part-time contractors. He could close down the paper's only bureau and shrink the circulation area to cut down on long, costly routes. On and on.

Christina Haseltine kept nodding and smiling, but Robbie wasn't buying. He didn't want to be dragged away from his TV and his warm milk to go out of the house and have some fun for a change. Thurman kept tugging and pulling, but even his enthusiasm couldn't get Robbie up off that couch. Haseltine wasn't aggressive or insistent about it, but he came up with objections to every change that the new owner proposed.

Thurman surprised me. He just listened politely and said things like "You could be right" or "We'll have to look into that." I would have expected him to shoot his new publisher down on the spot and then field dress him in front of his mother-in-law, with no more emotion than if he had been making an instructional video for hunters.

"Would you mind driving, Tom?" Alison said when we got into the rental Cadillac to head for the airport where the Learjet was waiting. "When Thurman gets like this, he can't keep his mind on the road."

She sat up front with me. Boucher sat on one of the folding seats in the back so he could lean over the front seat and keep the monologue going. Like Lyndon Johnson, he was happiest with his face right in the other person's space.

"Can you believe that Robbie?" he said to us. "Guy like that if he hit the lottery for ten million bucks his first thought would be all the taxes he'd have to pay."

Actually that seems to be the first thought of every man in the country who has ten million dollars, but I kept that to myself.

"Patience, dear," Alison said. "It won't be for long."

"Yeah, yeah, I guess."

And then Boucher was off again, nonstop, about the Mexican bond market, NAFTA, interactive TV, the profit potential in Clinton's health plan, the profit potential in commercializing the Internet, the profit potential in long-term health care . . .

As with any con artist, his true customer was himself. On topic after topic, he sat there selling himself, and everybody else got dragged along. As far as I could tell, he didn't know any more about the things he was pitching than I did from reading the papers, and a lot of what he thought he knew sounded wrong. But facts don't matter to the born salesman. Lies were just as easy to believe as the truth, and the belief itself was the thing. Only believe, and we all get rich together, or go to the White House, or to heaven.

"Look, there's a Blockbuster up there!" he said, with more enthusiasm than a video store seemed to be worth. "What's your favorite movie, Tom?"

"I don't know. *High Plains Drifter? Dr. Strangelove?*"

"You never saw *Berlin Alexanderplatz?* Well, I mean, plainly you haven't. There speaks a man who never saw *Berlin Alexanderplatz.* Pull in, okay?"

I pulled into the shopping mall where he had spotted the Blockbuster Video.

"Come on, come on," he said, hopping out of the back, opening the driver's side door for me, unstoppable and irresistible. "Let's go get 'em!"

Berlin Alexanderplatz turned out to be a fifteen-hour epic directed by the great Rainer Werner Fassbinder, who had previously escaped my attention. Boucher grabbed the whole set of cassettes and headed for the checkout counter.

"I totally understand where you're coming from," the assistant manager said when Boucher had explained what he wanted. "But it's against company policy. These videos are part of our rental inventory."

"I know they're part of your rental inventory, but how long has it been since they were out?" Thurman Boucher asked. "I mean, we're not talking *Home Alone* here."

"They're in our catalog, though. Somebody might come in and ask for one of them."

"Tell them it's out. Look, here's what we'll do. I'll rent them on my credit card and you can bill me for the replacement cost when I don't return them. Or I could just write you a personal check for the money right now."

"Our policy is if you rent them you have to return them. Otherwise we charge your card for the full replacement cost plus shipping and handling."

"Good policy. Visa okay?"

"We need a picture ID."

On the way out of the store with a shopping bag full of cassettes, Boucher said, "That idiot just tossed away a pocketful of money, did you see that? He should have taken my check and kept his mouth shut. I'd never hire a man like that, would you?"

"I never hired anybody."

"Yeah, but a man that stupid?"

"Some jobs you want stupid."

"Well, that's true. As nobody should know better than me. I've hired enough reporters."

"Did you get your precious *Alexanderputz?*" Alison asked when we got back to the car.

"She knows it's *platz*," Thurman said. "She just doesn't like the movie."

"Bo-ring," Alison said.

"To answer your question, sweetheart, of course I got it. When I'm hot, I'm hot."

She patted his hand and smiled at him fondly. They had an easy way with each other. They gave every sign of being in love. It was hard to square with the thought of her in the wrestling room. Or the memory of her cries last night, coming from the room marked DADDY AND MOMMY.

Different strokes.

There's an old John O'Hara story where a couple of rich kids ride around the Pennsylvania countryside looking for farm girls. When they come across one, they pull over and ask her what she'll do for five dollars. Sometimes the farm girls don't give up so much as a feel for five dollars, even though that was a pile of money then. But sometimes the rich boys would find one who would do anything at all.

In large organizations with dirty little minds, a process like that goes on, too. The men in charge flash five-dollar bills around discreetly to find out who keeps their panties on and who goes all the way. If the criminal enterprise is the White House, good little girls like Adlai Stevenson, Pierre Salinger, and William Safire are kept out of the loop. Their feelings may be hurt, but at least they don't wind up in jail with Charles Colson and Jeb Magruder.

I had made it into the Boucher Group loop the moment I put Terry Dineen on the ground. My boss thought so highly of me from then on that he automatically gave me credit, on the basis of no evidence at all, for later pushing the poor bastard in front of a train.

So at the moment I was still walking on water, but I was afraid I might start sinking because of the wrestling sessions. How long can a boss stay fond of somebody who beats up on him, three or four evenings a week?

I was thinking about that the following week, having just slammed Thurman on his back once again. Harder than I meant to. "You okay?" I said. It was probably time for him to get a lot better and me to get a lot worse, although it would take careful handling to seem convincing.

"I'm fine," Thurman said. "Shit, will I ever learn to keep that ankle away from you?"

"Actually you will," I said. "You improve every time I wrestle you. You just don't notice it because I can still stay a step or two ahead of you. But it's getting harder for me every session."

"What's getting harder?" a voice said.

Alison was standing in the doorway, looking good in a little beige thing.

"Staying ahead of your husband," I said, pretending not to notice the bait she had thrown out. I was afraid she might want another lesson herself. She probably didn't believe my nonsense about being afraid of losing control. Maybe I could tell her I was conserving my precious bodily fluids like General Jack D. Ripper, and hope she had never seen *Dr. Strangelove*.

"Harvey Love called just now," she said to her husband.

"Who's Harvey Love?" Thurman asked.

"Didn't I tell you? That's the name I told Robbie to use if he called and somebody else answered, which of course somebody did. Martha."

Martha was their maid.

"Harvey *Love?*" Boucher said. "You're too much, Lissy."

"Well, you know how Robbie and I are about each other."

"What did the idiot have to say?"

"I don't know. I told Martha to say I'd call back in five

minutes, since Tom was here. I thought it would be a good chance to do it."

"Do what?" I said.

"We thought you might like to fire him," Boucher said. "Good training."

When we had finished and showered, we found Alison Boucher waiting for us in the library. She was reading a copy of *Mirabella*. I had never seen anybody reading it before, which is probably a sign that I've spent too much of my life in Cambridge. "All ready to go?" she asked, brightly and enthusiastically. Like a cheerleader giving a little verbal pat on the butt to the quarterback.

My smile was mostly fake, but not entirely. Robbie had a number of things not going for him, in my book. I dialed the number he had left with the maid. Alison had put down her magazine. Thurman was standing beside her chair. Both of them were on full alert while the phone was ringing, like setters on point.

"This Harvey Love?" I said when Robbie Haseltine answered.

"Huh?" he said, and then shut up while he thought things over. At last he said, "You must have the wrong number. There's nobody by that name here."

"That's funny, because Harvey called the Boucher home a little while ago and left this number. I'm calling back for Mrs. Boucher."

"Oh, I see. I'll take the message, then."

"The message is that Mr. Boucher is pretty upset."

"Mr. Boucher? . . . Who is this, anyway?"

"You don't recognize the voice? It's Tom Bethany." He went silent, so I poked him. "Say something, Robbie. Talk to me."

"Tom? I don't understand what's going on. I don't have anything to say to you."

"You could say you're sorry. This is the man's wife we're talking about. He's not real happy."

"Say I'm sorry to who? You? Why are you calling me? What the hell is going on, anyway?"

"What's going on is you're fired."

"You people can't fire me. I have a contract."

"Good for you, Robbie. Why don't you take your contract out and read the son of a bitch? We can't fire you, but your mother-in-law can. If you're not off the premises by close of business Friday, she learns what you've been up to with Mr. Boucher's wife. So either you walk off and at least stay close to all her money, or she runs you off and you never see a penny. Your choice, Robbie."

"What's going on here? What have you done to Alison? Has that bastard hurt her?"

"No, that bastard hasn't hurt her. He's standing right here beside her, Robbie. She's the one who asked me to call you."

"You're lying."

"No, I'm not lying. Think about it. How would I know Harvey Love called? Who would have told me to call you?"

He didn't say anything, and I gave him a moment to fit the pieces together.

"Well, what about it, Robbie?" I said. "You see where we're going here? You going to clean out that desk?"

"Where would I go? What would I do?"

"Come on. As long as the Bouchers keep their mouth shut, the old lady isn't going to let you starve. You're the father of her grandchildren."

"Oh, you bastards, you bastards."

His voice sounded choked, as if he would have started crying if he hadn't hung up instead. I was about to hang up myself, but then I had a better idea. The Bouchers had gotten a good show out of me, but not yet a great one. So I started talking to the dial tone.

"Oh, yeah? Well, it's up to you, Robbie. Either way you're

out of there, the only difference is whether you're pushed or you jump . . . Because we let your wife listen to the tape, that's why. The thing is that it was in your own bed, you know? The two of you's bed. They never forgive that. That bastard did it right here in our bed, where my babies were conceived. That's the way they think, women . . . Hey, we don't really give a rat's ass what you do with the rest of your life, long as you clear out of that office by Friday, period."

I slammed the phone down on the dial tone and tried to look like an Ayn Rand hero who has just scored another slam dunk for economic Darwinism. The Alan Greenspan look, but with more hair.

"What was all that stuff about the marriage bed?" Alison Boucher asked. "How did you know what bed it was?"

"I heard somebody out in the hall, so I went to take a look."

"See, Lissy?" Boucher said. "You can't slip anything past Tom. That's the point, sweetheart. That's why he's on board."

"How did you know there was a tape, though?" Alison asked. "You couldn't have seen my cunning little tape recorder, because I was carrying it in my cunning little green clutch."

"I didn't see you at all, but I figured Robbie wouldn't have known whether you had a tape recorder or not. And I assumed you probably did."

"Why did you assume that?"

"I don't know. I guess because I would have."

They laughed. They liked that.

15

ON THURSDAY CHRISTINA HASEL-
tine called from Canton with the news that her son-in-law
was going through some kind of midlife crisis and was quitting so he could get a doctorate in journalism. She didn't
know what was the matter with him.

Boucher told her not to worry, these things happen, no
inconvenience at all, he would just send up somebody from
Florida to hold things together till Robbie came to his senses.
Mrs. Haseltine would like him. He was a top man, one of
the best young publishers in America.

"I wasn't kidding, what I told the old biddy," Thurman
said to me later. "Billy Epson's only thirty-one, but he's a
real barracuda. He'll shake that shop up. You know how
long it takes those lazy bastards in Canton to compose a
page? More than two hours!"

"That's bad, huh?"

"It's terrible. Down in Florida, Billy got them down below
an hour and a half, consistently. Sometimes an hour-

twenty-five. Canton is a hell of a mess right now. They've got one guy who does nothing but write editorials. Reporters only do two or three stories a day. What we shoot for is seven, absolute minimum. Billy will get eight to ten out of them. Christ, newsroom expenses are running fourteen percent of total budget. We'll get that down to ten before long. Got to. Matter of survival."

"Isn't the paper surviving now?"

"It was, but from now on it can't. The price I paid, debt service alone comes to more than the Haseltines made from the paper in the best year they ever had."

"If this guy of yours gets practically twice as many stories out of each reporter, does it work out that you can get by with half as many reporters?"

"Maybe even better. Our paper in Middletown has about the same circulation as Canton with only one full-time reporter and a part-time news contractor."

"Can you get by with that?" I asked.

"Put it this way, Tom. The Middletown paper manages to come out every single day, just like the *New York Times*. Unlike the *Times*, however, it returns forty-two percent on gross."

"Wow," I said, and meant it. The Mafia doesn't do that well. "Could you get by with no reporters at all?"

"I've been toying with the idea. Relying entirely on news contractors, submissions, press releases, boilerplate. So far I've held off, but that's where the business is heading. Newspapers as we know them are dinosaurs."

"How come we just bought another one, then?"

"You ever hear of Nauru?"

I had, but I shook my head.

"Well, Nauru is a pile of seagull shit in the Pacific. Literally. It's solid guano, practically pure phosphate. The Nauruvians, whatever the hell you call them, are sitting on a gold mine. But the faster they sell it off, the faster their island disappears."

"They could sell the whole place and move to the Riviera."

"That's what you and I would do, but they think of this pile of birdshit as home. So they're selling it off slow, which runs the risk that world prices will go down or demand will dry up. To put it in business terms, the dumb bastards are selling off their principal without getting interest on it."

"Okay, I see that."

"So what I do is, I look around for Naurus and cash them out quick. That's why I can pay more than other people for properties like Canton, because I have no emotional investment in what happens to the island. Phosphate means nothing to me. Nauru means nothing to me. Nor does a newspaper. It's just a goose that lays golden eggs.

"The funny thing about that kind of goose, though, the more you starve it, the bigger the eggs get. But only up to a point. Getting back to your question, that point might be reached if you got rid of reporters entirely. You risk killing the goose."

"But the goose can stay alive with one reporter huh?"

"And stay alive very profitably. The fact of the matter, Tom, is that poor quality is the natural and necessary result of sound financial management. That's the big secret they never come right out and say in the business schools."

"There's got to be some limit, though, doesn't there?"

"In terms of editorial quality? Not much. Who cares if it's poorly written? You get your readership and your advertisers from delivering information, not from delivering high literary quality. You know the only place you find good writing?"

"I never stopped to think."

"In the supermarket tabloids that have to live off newsstand sales. The *Star*, the *National Enquirer*, the *Mirror*, the *Globe*. They can't afford bad writing, and so they have to pay their reporters top dollar. Consequently the papers are written so well that any goddamn idiot can understand what they're writing, which means huge circulations. And huge circulations mean that they're free from the tyranny of the major advertiser."

"What tyranny is that?" As far as I could tell, major advertisers allowed the daily press to range freely all the way from Newt Gingrich on the left to Jesse Helms on the right. There was plenty of room in that spectrum for Thurman Boucher.

"I gave a speech about it at the American Association of Newspaper Publishers once," Boucher said. "Called my speech 'The Three B's,' for Big Business Bullying. There's nothing more gutless than a major corporation. Afraid of their goddamned shadows, all of them. Won't touch controversy. If I could figure out a way to get loose from those spineless bastards, I'd put out a national daily that would deliver a bigger audience than *USA Today* and the *Wall Street Journal* and the *Christian Science Monitor* and the *New York Times* combined. You know who my editors would be?"

"Who?"

"Howard Stern and Rush Limbaugh."

"I thought they hated each other."

"All the better. Conflict is what sells, look at 'The McLaughlin Group.' Maybe I'd let Howard edit half the paper and give the other half of it to Rush, let them throw bombs back and forth. God, how I'd love to put out a paper like that. The combination of sex and politics would be irresistible. Of course it's just a dream."

"Why?"

"I could never get Limbaugh and Stern. From the electronic media to print would be a step backward for them."

"Be some paper though," I said, "wouldn't it?"

And it would. It occurred to me for the first time that Thurman Boucher was stupid enough and crazy enough and rich enough to cause serious damage some day. Certainly the last thing we needed was a national rag to pump more porn and primitive politics into inquiring minds.

Thurman and I were in his office, where I had gone to see what I could do to bring him down from the high he had been on ever since he conned the Haseltines.

"Gladys has been able to dig out most of the information you wanted," I told him.

"Gladys? Oh, the girl we put over at the *Cambridge Trader*."

"Gladys Williams, yeah."

"You have her outside?"

"I didn't think it was a good idea." Actually, she was on rounds till six at the hospital. "We don't know who's on our side around this place and who isn't. I thought if she came by the house nobody would see you with her. Six-thirty all right?"

When we got to the Bouchers' house, her car was already parked in the driveway. Gladys got out when I pulled the Rolls up behind her. "The maid said you weren't home yet," she said. "I told her I'd wait out here."

She had her demure clothes on, and her manner matched. Normally she would have barged right past the maid and helped herself to a beer.

"I'm sorry we're late," Boucher said. His own manner was soft-spoken and polite, as it usually was. "Come on in. My wife, Alison, ought to be around somewhere. The maid should have told you she was here."

It turned out that Alison was out back in the garden. Thurman sent the maid after her while we waited in a book-lined room off the entrance hall. The books were all in their dust jackets and looked new. I pulled one called *On Bended*

Knee. It turned out to be a book about the obsequious way the press covered Ronald Reagan, by a guy named Mark Hertsgaard. It didn't seem to be the kind of thing Boucher would have in his library.

"This any good?" I asked the Cobra.

"I haven't read any of them," he said. "Don't have the time. If you've got shelves you need books, though, so I get my editors to send me the review copies that come in."

"Do some of our other papers review books?" I asked. I had never seen a review in the *Banner*.

"No, but the books still come in," he said. "What the editors don't send along to me, they're free to keep or pass out to the staff. It's a little perk that they appreciate."

"Isn't that clever!" Gladys said. One of her recent boyfriends had been a nice young kid who had written six novels before getting the seventh published. It hadn't gotten even one review. "Don't you think that's clever, Tom?"

"I'd've never thought of it," I said.

"Help yourself if you see anything you like," Boucher said. "Alison just throws them out, now that the shelves are full."

"Yes, do help yourselves," Alison herself said from the door of the reading room. "I inquired about selling them once, but it turns out you only get a few pennies for books."

She smiled at Gladys, the sincere smile of a pretty woman meeting a plain one. "I take it you're our little secret agent, dear," Alison said.

"Well, I wouldn't know about that, Mrs. Boucher."

"It's all right, Gladys," Thurman said. "Mrs. Boucher knows about our arrangement. Let's all sit down and hear what you've come up with."

"Well, then . . . ," Gladys said, and started passing out the wildly inflated figures we had cooked up with Jonathan Paul.

"I'm sure these figure aren't impressive to a person such

as yourself," Gladys said. "What with so many larger papers that you're used to dealing with, but I thought it was interesting because of the trend. I mean, of course I don't have any idea what's normal but the improvement this quarter is twenty-six percent, and of course carried out that would mean more than double on a yearly basis. If I'm doing the arithmetic correctly."

"I'm afraid you are, Gladys," Mr. Boucher said. He pulled a yellow pad out of a drawer in a reading table, and jotted down the numbers. "The growth rate is bound to slow down some over time, so let's figure it at half of what it is now. Projected over the next two years . . ."

He did the calculations in his head, from the numbers he had written down.

"Household penetration could reach a hundred percent, theoretically, but let's say ninety-five thousand households for the moment. Let's see, say fifteen hundred column inches an issue, eighty percent of it ads, twenty dollars a column inch. One million two would be the annual revenue . . . average of five employees projected for the period, thirty-five thousand each including benefits . . . Delivery at seven cents apiece, figure three hundred and sixty-five thousand per year. Figure twenty thousand salary plus fifteen percent commission for your ad people, comes to a hundred and fifty altogether. Of course you've got insurance, rent, printing and paper . . ."

He jotted down a few more estimates.

"Not too far down the line we could be looking at a net of close to three hundred thousand a year," Boucher said.

"That pathetic little rag," Mrs. Boucher said. "The advertisers must be total fools to think anybody could possibly read it."

"Isn't it amazing!" Gladys said. "Now these lists here, you'd think I was employed in Fort Knox, Kentucky, the trouble I had getting my hands on them, and I'm the bookkeeper. You'd think they would make all relevant figures available to the bookkeeper, wouldn't you? I mean, if a person is expected to do her job properly, she needs access, wouldn't you say?''

"I would say you seem to have managed the access part just fine," Boucher said.

"Well, it was a trial, let me tell you. To get the right key for Mr. Paul's desk I had to call up the desk company in North Carolina and then send them the serial number of the stupid thing on company stationery signed by an officer of the requesting corporation.''

"How did you manage the signature?"

"I signed it myself, and typed 'vice president for financial operations' under my name.''

"Someday you may be exactly that," Boucher said. "Stranger things have happened.''

Gladys gave him a look that managed to combine "What, little me?" with "You better believe it, Buster.''

What she actually said was, "I don't see what the big secret was, I really don't. They're nothing but lists of names with the monthly payments after each one.''

"No way to tell what the payments are for," Boucher said after glancing over the lists.

"I ran down the first four names," I said. "I didn't bother with the rest, because I figured they'd check out the same. The first four, three of them are building supers and one has a newsstand at Kendall Square. That big stand by the T.''

"Let me guess. The three buildings are locations where we've been having delivery problems?''

"And the newsstand has the *Banner* out of sight," I said. "The only way you can get it is to ask for it.''

"This is a pretty significant amount of money, when you total all these numbers," Boucher said.

"One thousand one hundred and twenty last month," said Gladys, the little girl in the front row who always has her hand up first. Actually I would have bet she never raised her hand and always sat in the back row. That's where you find the really smart kids.

"That's a lot of money for a brand-new little shopper to be throwing around every month," Boucher said. "I wonder where he gets it."

"Maybe from his investors?" Gladys said.

"What investors?"

"There were these three men who came last week. They toured everything, not that there's much to tour, and then Mr. Paul went off with them somewhere all afternoon."

"What makes you think they were investors?"

"Just the way they acted, and the way Mr. Paul treated them. They acted like people from headquarters, you know? Except there is no headquarters, the *Trader* is so tiny, so I thought maybe they were rich backers or something. I told their names to Mr. Bethany."

"You were right about them, Gladys," I said. "A guy I know at Widener Library was looking into it for me, just got back to me this afternoon. Anderson isn't listed, but Raymond Gill and Arthur Braxton are in the directory of the American Investment Bankers Association. Both of them work for Tingley, Davis."

"Son of a bitch," Boucher said.

"Exactly," I said.

Tingley, Davis was the firm run by Felicia's old beau. Earlier I had told the Cobra that Jonathan Paul's Rolls used to belong to Tingley, Davis.

"Weren't you going to call that awful Tingley man and ask him what Jonathan Paul was doing with his car?" Alison Boucher asked her husband.

"Louise has been trying for weeks, but our friend Mr. Tingley is too good to call me back. One day Mr. Tingley will regret that. If you sit by the window long enough with a brick in your hand, eventually everybody passes by down below."

"Isn't that the truth, Mr. Boucher!" Gladys said. "What goes around, comes around, doesn't it?"

"If you have enough patience it does. Personally, I like to speed things up a little. George Tingley. He has no history at all with newspapers. What interest could he possibly have in a two-bit neighborhood shopper operating out of the back of a drugstore?"

"Maybe he's fronting for somebody," I said, to make sure the suspicion got planted. I'm like Boucher. I like to speed things up, too.

"Who, though?" Boucher said.

"I was thinking maybe the old owners," I said. "The Cushing family."

"Mrs. Cushing signed a noncompete agreement."

"Contracts get broken."

"Nobody to break it," he said. "Christ, Linda Cushing is dead."

Then he paused a moment to think it through, as I had hoped he would.

"Of course she might have set something up before she died," Thurman said. "Possibly put some or all of her money with Tingley, Davis on the basis of a quiet understanding with old George."

He paused again to think.

"Could be done in spite of the noncompete agreement," he said. "Probably not too hard to build some kind of fire wall between her money and this apparently unrelated new venture that they're just happening to back. Whether it would stand up in court is another matter. It might. Tingley's old Boston, probably went to school with half the judges in town. Even without that he might win. These handshake deals are hard to smoke out. There's no paper trail."

"May not even be a deal," I said. "We don't really have much to go on."

"Oh, I bet there's some sort of an arrangement. That god-damn Jonathan Paul, he's an absolute zero. No ambition, no brains, no guts. Soft, useless. Just another nice guy. I was amazed he had enough drive to start that little rag of his in the first place, and of course now it looks like I was right. He didn't. There's somebody behind the son of a bitch, somebody with deep pockets."

"One of the other chains, maybe?"

"Wouldn't be worth it for them to go head to head, not in a market like this one. It'd cost you a fortune and if you won you'd still have the *Globe* looking over your shoulder. No, it's like I said. Somehow, that ridiculous woman is be-hind it."

By now, the idea I had planted only a moment before had become completely his. It's always a treat to watch a socio-path at work. For a man like Thurman Boucher, memory as the rest of us understand it just doesn't exist. The past is rearranged and reinterpreted every second to satisfy the or-ganism's changing needs. So once the idea had started to look good to him, it became his.

"Why would Linda Cushing set up something like this and then kill herself before she had a chance to watch it work?" I asked.

"She was a dreary, droopy woman," Alison Boucher said. "Very unstable. Crazy people are capable of anything."

"Some mess," I said.

"Just a problem to solve," Boucher said. "No matter why she did it, or how, or even if, the problem remains. We have to remove Jonathan Paul from our path, that's all."

"Maybe now isn't the time to bring it up," I said, "but maybe it is. There could be a Jonathan Paul connection. Take a look at this garbage one of my maintenance guys got in the mail."

I handed Thurman a leaflet I had printed up with my Mac a couple of nights before. *Banner* personnel would start finding it in their mailboxes tomorrow.

" 'Unjustified and illegal discharges'?" Boucher said once he had scanned it. " 'Degrading and un-American surveillance? Police state tactics? Salaries slashed to the bone? Journalistic integrity and quality slashed in the name of higher profits? Carpetbagger ownership? Doubled workload? Loyalty is not a one-way street?' What the hell is this, Tom?"

"The beginning of an organizing drive?" I said. "That's the way it looks to me."

"It's unsigned."

"Well, sure. Who'd sign something like that?"

"If it's a union they'd have to," Boucher said. "The regulations are strict. You haven't been picking up any hints of union activity, have you?"

"Not yet. I'll shake a few of my trees tomorrow, though."

"Go ahead, but this isn't how unions start an organizing drive. I think you're right, that this is a little something cooked up by our good friend Jonathan Paul. You're over there every day, Gladys. Did you run across any hint of this leaflet?"

"No, sir."

"Of course he probably wouldn't do something like this at the office," I said. "This is the kind of thing where you don't want anybody to know."

"Mr. Paul is starting to irritate me seriously," Boucher said.

"There's things we could do," I said. "Various forms of payback."

"Such as?"

"Harassment, things breaking down, things getting lost, constant problems around the shop. I could think about it."

"Do that."

"We've got somebody in place, remember. Gladys could do a lot of damage in her position."

"That might be a little more than she bargained for," Thurman said.

"I'd help any way I can, Mr. Boucher," she said. "As long as I knew that there was a position with your organization waiting for me if anything went wrong."

GLADYS GAVE ME A LIFT BACK, but not to my apartment on Ware Street. We went instead to Felicia's house on Bond Street. Jonathan Paul and Serena Cushing were waiting there to debrief their field agents.

I started off with the trip to Canton and my long-distance firing of Robbie Haseltine. "That's kind of an amazing story," Gladys said when I was finished. "The Cobra pimped out his own wife."

"Amazing, but not surprising. She came on to me one evening when I was giving her husband a wrestling lesson. He was right there looking at us, is what I'm saying."

"Watching what? She got it on with you?"

"Not quite, but close. He was just smiling, like watching the cute kids playing in the park. So I assume they're into swapping, group activities, that kind of thing."

"Unlike you."

"Well, I'm kind of bashful."

"Yeah, right."

222

"Hey, I begged off, didn't I? At least I'm that bashful. Anyway, my point is that if the Bouchers swing for fun, they've pretty much gotten over that jealousy problem already. So why not swing for profit?"

"I'm sorry," Gladys said, "but turning your wife out is still amazing."

"You have to be around them. They're a unit, the two of them against the world. They're very close. I think it's love, actually. Yes, actually I do. Seen from the viewpoint of the unit, it made sense to back Robbie Haseltine into a corner. So why not do it? No big thing. You've both been operating as a sexual team for years, probably scouting prospects for each other or for group action. How is this any different?"

"It's the money element," Gladys said. "I don't know, it's just different."

"Without the element of money there'd be a lot fewer marriages."

"You're a hard man, Tom," said Felicia.

"Besides, the Bouchers want money a lot worse than you and me, Felicia. That's why they've got so much more of it than we do."

"Hey, greed is good," Gladys said. "Isn't that what Reagan said?"

"It was the unspeakable Ivan Boesky, actually," Felicia said.

"I knew it was one of those guys."

Serena looked unamused, and so did Jonathan Paul. Politics had never come up with either of them, but my guess was that Jonathan was a JFK conservative and Serena was a Bush conservative. Gladys cultivated her own garden, Felicia was basically an anarchist, and I was against whoever was in power. Most of the time this made me look like a liberal, since nobody but conservatives ever come to power in America. The only disagreement between the two parties is over how unfair they can be and still get reelected.

"Well, the sex life of the Bouchers is irrelevant anyway," I said. "I just figured you'd be interested. They could do it with kangaroos and it wouldn't help me get them out of Cambridge any faster."

"So where do we go from here?" Jonathan Paul said. "Tom and the rest of you have put in a lot of time already. I don't mind driving around in a Rolls-Royce, but is this thing really doable?"

"Maybe not," I said. "But I don't mind driving around in a Rolls, either, and I'm willing to hang in a little bit longer."

I passed around copies of the attack leaflet I had showed Boucher earlier. "The point of this is to goad the guy into doing something dumb," I said when they had looked it over. "He thinks Jonathan is behind it . . ."

"Oh, great," the editor said.

"And he thinks Tingley, Davis is behind Jonathan, and he thinks Cushing money is behind the Tingley, Davis involvement. He thinks it's payback time, and he wants Gladys and me to get to work. Fundamentally, Jonathan, we're supposed to sabotage the hell out of you."

"Wonderful."

"Hey, it won't be so bad. We'll just come up with a bunch of petty stuff, and you'll write editorials about what dirty pool it all is. Blaming it on unnamed business rivals, but how many business rivals have you got? Nobody's going to think it was the *Globe*."

"What kind of petty stuff? I've got a business to run."

"None of it's going to happen, Jonathan. All we need to do is make him think it happened."

"I don't see how this hurts Boucher. Won't it just make him feel good?"

"To start with, yes. But the point is to produce escalation. I'll sabotage the *Banner*, and he'll think it's you striking back.

By then he ought to be mad enough so I can get him to approve some really major thing against you. Then I can develop a conscience and go to the police with it, or set something up that can be traced back to Boucher. Hell, I don't know exactly, Jonathan. Staff morale at the paper is already pretty much down the tubes. I'm just trying to stir things up, keep the pressure on."

The truth was that I was running out of ideas. You couldn't blackmail a man who didn't have any shame. You couldn't make things so unpleasant for him that he'd give up and move on; Boucher was proud of being hated and he enjoyed conflict. It gave him an excuse to hurt people and push them around, which seemed to be his main aims in life. The money was nice, but its main use was to allow him to push more people around. It was like rank in the military. So it was tough to find a pressure point that would hurt.

But I wasn't quite ready to give up yet.

So we worked out, Jonathan and Gladys and I, a program of dirty tricks that we would pretend to be carrying out against the *Cambridge Trader*. And I outlined the series of retaliatory acts that I planned to carry out for real against the *Banner*.

"His weak spot is his rage," I said. "If we can get the bastard mad enough, maybe he'll self-destruct."

Nobody argued, but nobody nodded in agreement, either. No wonder I was losing my audience. In effect I was telling them that the way to whip Mike Tyson was to get him mad at you.

Jonathan Paul left first, with Serena Cushing. Then Gladys took off, after I told her I didn't need a ride. It was only a fifteen-minute walk home.

"What do you think?" Felicia asked when we were alone.

"I'm discouraged."

"I thought you might be."

"You knew Linda Cushing pretty well," I said. "Would you describe her as droopy?"

"No one beats gravity. Or were you referring to emotional droopiness?"

"I don't know. Alison Boucher described her as a 'dreary, droopy woman.' It just seemed like an odd word to use."

"I doubt if she was any more droopy than most women her age, speaking physically. Speaking emotionally, though, she certainly was. After all, she committed suicide."

"You've given up on the possibility of murder?"

"Murder doesn't seem very likely, does it?" Felicia said. "Or at least not the sort of murder the law recognizes."

"What do you mean?"

"I still think that Mr. Boucher somehow drove her to it."

Thurman Boucher came out of the house the next morning with his tan summerweight jacket slung over his shoulder and a song in his heart, probably. In any event, he was whistling. There wasn't any tune to it, but he couldn't help that. Most of us baby boomers whistle tunelessly because the songs we grew up with didn't have tunes. But we're like a baby banging on his high chair with a spoon. We all got rhythm.

So the sound Thurman was producing was the best he could do, as a musical postliterate. It had no structure, no melody, no relation to any place or period or human society or musical heritage. It meant nothing except that Thurman Boucher was feeling good about life.

He bounced into the front seat beside me, opened today's *Bummer*, and started to page through it as we rolled along toward the office. Then all of a sudden he stopped feeling good. "Pull over!" he practically hollered, for no reason I could see. At the moment we were in heavy traffic on Memorial Drive, just crossing JFK Street. You couldn't pull over, at least not legally, so I did the necessary. I bounced over the curb and into the patch of dirt in front of Weld Boat House where the coaches park during crew season.

Boucher didn't say anything. He just sat there with the paper open in his lap. He was reading an editorial headlined "Common Decency."

"Look at this goddamned thing," he said when he was done.

I took the paper and started to read the editorial myself:

I am the former owner of the *Cambridge Daily Banner*, which my husband, Michael Cushing, left me upon his death. Subsequently and to my deep regret I made the mistake of selling it to Thurman Boucher, president and chairman of the board of the Boucher Group. I owe it to friends and supporters of the paper to reveal the details of that fraudulent sale.

Several months after Mr. Cushing's tragic and untimely death, Thurman Boucher appeared in Cambridge and rented a suite in the Charles Hotel. He expressed interest in purchasing the *Banner*, which I informed him was not for sale. He then said that he planned to be in Cambridge on other business for several weeks and would help me in any way he could with professional advice in the operation of the paper. He expressed the belief that the paper could be made much more profitable with a number of minor changes that he would explain to me. He understood that the paper was not for sale at the moment, and any help he could offer would be merely a professional courtesy among publishers. Only a fool·would have believed this, but I was that fool.

I was a lonely widow in late middle years, emotionally vulnerable and with no worldly experience apart from marriage and motherhood. He told me he was lonely too, his wife having left him and begun divorce proceedings, or so he said. I quickly came to trust him and depend on this experienced and successful younger man who seemed so helpful and attentive. I see now what easy prey I must have seemed.

When he renewed his offer to purchase the paper at a very attractive price, I was receptive this time. I insisted only on continuity of management, as the managing editor of the *Banner* was a lifelong employee who enjoyed my complete trust, confidence, and respect. If the paper could continue under the competent management of this editor, Jonathan Paul, I was content to give up the responsibilities of ownership. Thurman Boucher agreed to a contract that specified that Mr. Paul would remain as chief news executive as long as he desired.

Nevertheless, one of the first acts of the new publisher was to fire Mr. Paul and replace him with an outsider with no knowledge of this community or its newspaper. This was done without my consultation or knowledge. When I reproached Thurman Boucher for his action, he threatened to reveal certain material of a private nature to Mr. Paul. After months of anguish, I decided that I would rather die than live with the shame of having betrayed the memory of my husband and ruined the future of a man I hold in such high regard as Mr. Paul. I therefore reached a decision to end my life.

It is my hope that my daughter, Serena, will devote a portion of the proceeds from the sale of the *Banner* to the support of Mr. Paul and the *Cambridge Trader*, which he established in the hope of one day providing the Cambridge community with a responsible, professional alternative to my late husband's paper. I could not support him myself because a condition of my sale of the *Banner* to the Boucher Group was that I not compete with it for a ten-year period.

However if my daughter sees fit to support Mr. Paul's struggling paper, I would hope that the many loyal lifelong friends of the *Banner* will support it as well, with their readership and their advertising.

I beg the forgiveness of God and the forgiveness of my daughter and my friends, and all others I may have hurt by my action, especially and above all, for what might have been, I beg the pardon of my valued and respected friend of so many years, Jonathan Paul. And I also beg God to forgive Thurman Boucher for his cruelty and betrayal and to lead him into a better path.

That was the end of the letter, which was signed Linda Cushing. But I pretended to read it for a moment longer, while I got hold of myself. I wanted to drag Boucher from the car and give him a final wrestling lesson. I wanted to break his arms and legs and leave the son of a bitch on the ground like a fly with his wings pulled off.

After a while I was able to hand the paper back to him and say, "Jesus, Thurman, you must've really run a number on her." I hoped I sounded admiring.

"That cunt," he said. "That lousy dried-up old pig. I want to know how this fucking thing got in the paper, Tom, and I want to know yesterday."

"I'll find out," I said. "There's plenty of people I've got on the tapes that I can squeeze."

"Do whatever you have to," he said. "Anything."

"Leave it to me, Thurman. You and Fogel stay out of it. Things could get rough, and you guys don't want to be involved."

"Rough?" Boucher said, and smiled. "I'll show them rough." His voice was cold and calm.

My first call was to Jonathan Paul, who sounded hard hit. "That poor, poor woman," he said. "If only she had felt she could come to me, tell me about it. I would have understood. At least I think I would have. I hope I would have. Poor Linda. That prick. That absolute prick."

"Do you know who put the editorial in the paper for her?"

"I have no idea."

"Any suspicions?"

"A dozen people would have done it if she had asked them. Everyone loved her. She was the real spirit of the paper."

Paul was the only one who remembered her this way, as far as I could tell from people at the *Banner*. The publisher's wife had been a pleasant but dim figure to most of them, even after she took over from her husband.

"Is it a hard thing to do?" I asked. "Slipping something like that into the paper?"

"Not if you know the routine."

"You'd think Fogel would check everything that goes into the paper. Wouldn't he have spotted it?"

"He probably would have glanced at the editorial page before he went home, sure. But then there would have been a legitimate editorial in that hole. During the evening somebody slipped in a substitution."

"You?"

"No, not me. You think I would have let something like that run?"

"Who then?"

"I don't know. Practically any of the holdovers on the staff would have."

"How many people were in a position to do it?"

"The night city editor, the style section editor, the proofreader. Everybody on the editorial and production staffs, really."

"Good. The wider I can spread suspicion around, the better."

Next I called Felicia, who was fully devious enough to

have thought of a scheme like this. Although the editorial certainly sounded authentic.

"I've just read it, yes," she said when I asked. "Perfectly extraordinary."

"I can't go flying around blind, Felicia," I said. "If you have any knowledge of this at all, you've got to tell me."

"I wish I had thought of it, but I didn't."

"That's a lawyer's answer. I didn't ask whether you had thought of it."

"That's a lawyer's answer to my answer, Tom. I neither thought of it, nor did I nor do I have any knowledge of it. I do, however, have a new respect for Linda Cushing. She has put the unspeakable Mr. Boucher in the absurd position of having no possible redress except suing his own paper for libel."

"Truth is a defense against libel anyway," I said. "Do you think Mrs. Cushing was telling the truth?"

"Oh, indeed I do. Linda was a sweet soul, but totally lacking in imagination. She could no more have made up a thing like this than she could have written Shakespeare's sonnets."

"Do you think her daughter could have had anything to do with it?"

"If possible, Serena is even less imaginative than her mother was. No, I think this is just what it seems to be. A belated suicide note and public act of contrition."

"Revenge, too, I guess."

"Probably, but I doubt that she would have seen it that way. She would have successfully disguised it to herself as a public-spirited warning. Something like shouting 'Fire' in a theater crowded with other publishers' widows."

"Sounds a little cynical, Felicia."

"It's not meant to be. I very much envy the Linda Cushings of this world the ability to deceive themselves so effectively. It's the first requirement for mental health."

"Do you think anybody else could have made up that article?"

"What do you think?" she asked.

"I think not."

"I agree," Felicia said. "Perhaps she inserted it into the bowels of the computer somehow, like one of those viruses programmed to pop up at Christmas all around the world."

"Was she good enough with computers to do that?"

"Of course not, now that you mention it. Linda couldn't even change the setting on a toaster."

"So we're left with her as the one who wrote the editorial. But somebody else had to handle the technical side. Some loyalist at the paper, presumably."

"Presumably, but why does it matter? You don't intend to find this person, do you?"

"I'd be curious to know, that's all. I certainly wouldn't turn him in to Boucher."

"I should hope not. What has been Mr. Boucher's response so far?"

"He hollered a little just at first, and then he kind of geared down and started muttering. Like when a dog stops barking and makes that low noise in its throat."

"Do you suppose the dog's heartbeat slows down?"

"I don't know. Why?"

"Because I read this fascinating thing about wife beaters recently. Apparently the most violent of them don't lose their tempers at all. They become super calm and their pulse actually slows way down."

"That's him, all right. That's my Cobra."

For the rest of the day the *Banner* was like the headquarters of a political campaign right after the candidate has made a major blooper. The editors and reporters were whispering in the corners or into the phones, trying to find out what the hell was going on. Outsiders with briefcases disappeared into Boucher's office and then came out again, and others went in. Camera crews were in the parking lot, kept outside by the rent-a-cops I had hired that morning on Boucher's instructions. Other camera crews were staking out Boucher's house.

Boucher himself was unavailable to the press. Instead he tossed them Alan Fogel, who had the presence and charisma of Senator Nunn. But Alan had something that was probably better under the circumstances. He was boring and bureaucratic, forgettable and entirely unquoteworthy. You'd have better luck finding a sound bite in IBM's annual report.

The official line was the usual one when a woman accuses a man of doing her wrong. Linda Cushing had been flighty, hysterical, unstable, deeply disturbed, disappointed in love, delusional, and under psychiatric care, all of which had made the poor woman unable to tell shit from Shinola.

Normally this argument works, or Clarence Thomas wouldn't be on the Supreme Court. But this time, to judge by the early TV and radio reports, it wasn't flying. Maybe it was because some of the announcers actually knew the man and the woman involved, at least by reputation. Whatever it was, the reports made it sound as if Linda Cushing really might have had an affair with millionaire media mogul Thurman Boucher, and that he might even have treated her so badly as to have contributed to her death.

I, meanwhile, was trying to track down the treacherous son of a bitch responsible for slipping this lying message into the paper. I started with the city editor. Wally Briggs was about thirty, one of the young guys promoted by Alan Fogel to replace older guys who made more money. Briggs had been the paper's City Hall reporter. City Hall was now covered by an even younger reporter who also had to cover police and fire and schools.

"What I'm trying to figure out, Wally," I said to the city editor, "is how this thing could have happened. Walk me through it from the beginning, will you? How does an editorial get into the paper in the first place?"

"Well, if it's staff written we'd normally have it by deadline. If it's canned, like tomorrow's lead editorial, we'd already have it on hand."

"What does 'canned' mean?"

"A lot of our editorials come from an editorial service, kind of generic editorials."

"So tomorrow's editorial is in the system now? How about calling it up so I can get an idea."

Briggs brought tomorrow's editorial up on the screen of his Mac. The headline was "Sharing the Burden."

"Could you make changes in that right now, if you wanted to?" I asked. "Or replace it with something else?"

"Sure."

"Who else could?"

"Anybody on the network. There's about twenty Macs in editorial alone, plus you've got production."

"Of all those people, whose actual job would it be to edit it, though? Yours?"

"Alan Fogel picked out this one to run, so he might have edited it. It's not my department. I probably wouldn't even glance at it."

"Wouldn't somebody look it over for misspellings or something?"

"Normally the copy editor. Marcia Bogan."

"Would it go straight in the paper from her?"

"The proofreader checks it for errors, and marks it 'good' or 'okay.'"

"Who's that?"

"Russ Wiggins."

"And after that nobody can change it?"

"No, pretty near anybody could access any page and change it."

"It's the honor system?"

"I guess in a way."

"You get the feeling Mr. T is going to want to put in a few controls from now on?"

"I don't know how practical that would be. The system depends on a free flow of information. The more roadblocks you put in, the slower the system is going to work."

"Let me give you a little hint, Wally. If I were you, I'd be thinking about ways to do it, not reasons it couldn't be done. This was a major fuckup."

"I know that. Thank God I'm out of the line of fire."

"How do you figure?"

"I told you. Editorials aren't the city editor's responsibility."

"Everybody who could have slipped this thing into the paper is in the line of fire, and that includes you."

"It does?"

"Why not? Now listen, Wally, the way investigations work, we have to build a wall between each person interviewed. That way we can cross-check one against another, be sure people aren't getting together to cook up some bullshit story. We wouldn't want that, would we?

"So I'm going to start by questioning the people you just mentioned, Wally, and I'm counting on you not to warn them. The element of surprise can be key in an investigation. Okay?"

I punched him on the shoulder a little too hard to be hearty, but not quite hard enough to really hurt. Then I told him I was going out to grab a sandwich, which would give him time to tell Bogan and Wiggins they were next on my list. I wanted them to have time to cook up a solid story. Otherwise I might crack the case.

After my sandwich, the first person I talked to was Marcia Bogan, the copy editor. She seemed flustered, but then she always seemed flustered.

"So you didn't see a thing?" I said when she had answered all my questions. I had asked a lot of very detailed questions, because of course I was looking for ways to get into the system myself and secretly mess things up.

"Nothing out of the ordinary," she answered.

"And . . . Hey, look, I have to ask this . . . naturally you didn't do it yourself?"

"Of course not."

"Of course not. Well, I know you're busy, but thanks for your time."

The next person I talked to was Russ Wiggins, the proofreader.

"So you didn't do it, and you don't know who did, and you wouldn't tell me if you did," I said at the end. "That about sums it up?"

"That's it, and if the front office doesn't like it, they can take this job and stuff it."

"Hey, no need to be hostile, Russ. I share your concern."

Then I talked to a couple of other people on the staff, just to put a few more people on edge.

The first was a newly hired reporter who had just graduated from Northeastern. She took it personally and started to cry after I asked her two or three innocuous questions.

"For God's sake, what's the matter?" I said. "Don't cry. It's not like you're a suspect. You told me you didn't do it, I believe it. Case closed, far as you're concerned. Really, please. Come on, a little smile. There, that's better."

The second was a guy in the production department.

"You want to know what I think, here's what I think," he said. "That little shit Clancy, that's exactly the kind of shit that little shit would pull. I don't care he was off the last two days, he done it somehow."

"Sounds like a strong possibility," I said. "I'll try to nail it down, and don't worry about a thing. He'll never know it came from you. I don't work that way."

17

EITHER IT WAS A SLOW NEWS day, or a lot of people in the business had just been waiting for Thurman Boucher to stumble. In any event, the reporters were still staking out the parking lot when it was time to go home. So I told Thurman to wait for me at the loading dock while I brought the car around to him. Nobody paid any attention to me when I walked out of a side door, but that changed when I got behind the wheel of the Rolls.

"Hey!" one of the cameramen shouted, and then everybody began to run toward the car. I wasn't the press lord himself, but I was the only game in town for the moment.

I could have peeled out of the parking lot, gone around the block, and come back through the rear gate. That way I could have picked up Boucher at the loading dock unnoticed. But then none of the news mob would have known that the Cobra was out of his hole. So instead I drove around the building to the loading dock, slowly enough so that they'd have time to get to the corner and catch a glimpse of their prey escaping. Thurman jumped in before anybody could reach us.

"The bastards won't be able to make much of that on the news," Boucher said when we were out of the lot. "All they got was a shot of a car driving away."

"Channel Four still has a team at your house, though," I said. "And shit, here come the others, on our tail."

At last. I couldn't have driven much slower without Thurman starting to wonder just whose side I was on. For the same reason, I couldn't let the media mob actually catch him. But I could arrange it so Boucher would have to crawl a little. I stepped on the gas and the Rolls surged ahead until our pursuers were out of sight. When we were eight or ten blocks from Boucher's house, I pulled into a side street and parked.

"What gives?" Boucher said.

"The bastards will be all around your house. We don't want news clips with you hiding your face like some Mafia guy. In fact we don't want any news clips of you at all. So what I thought was you could hop in the trunk and I'd drive you right into the garage."

"Isn't there some other way?"

"Well, we could just not go home at all, leave Alison there alone."

"Shit. The trunk's probably full of carbon monoxide."

"No, it's got to be safe. That's the way they test these things, put an inspector in the trunk and drive around a while."

"What the hell for?"

"So he can listen for rattles and shit."

"Is that really true?"

"I don't know. It's in one of those books that came with the car."

I opened the trunk. "What the hell are those things?" he said.

"You never looked in here before?"

"Why would I?"

"Those are little lamb's wool rugs you can put down. In case passengers want to kick their shoes off."

Riding in the trunk wasn't going to be hard duty. It was lined with pristine Wilton carpeting, with the stack of lamb's wool rugs for a pillow. It wasn't the kind of trunk you'd toss a filthy lug wrench into.

"I still don't like the idea," he said, but he climbed in.

"Won't be long," I said as I closed the lid gently. After all, he was the boss.

The Channel Four crew was waiting outside the grounds when we arrived, and a couple of other cars had joined their van. They were cars that had been in the *Banner*'s parking lot, cars I had shaken off earlier. Presumably the drivers had figured out that we would eventually head home.

"Come on, guys," I said out the window. "Give me some room to get past."

"Where's Boucher?" one of the TV blow-dries said.

"I let him off."

"Is it true he fucked the widow out of her paper?" said somebody else. "Literally?"

"Hey, I just drive the car, all right?"

"Where'd you let him off?"

"For God's sake, the man's having supper. Can't a man have supper in peace?"

"Supper where?"

"You'd just go pester the poor guy if I told you."

"No, we wouldn't. We just need to know for the story."

"Would you promise not to pester him?"

"Sure."

"All of you?"

They all nodded.

"He's at the Harvard Faculty Club."

"What's he doing there?"

"Having supper with one of the professors who writes for the paper. Remember now, you guys promised to let them alone."

Safe inside the garage, I let Boucher loose and went into the house with him. He rounded up Alison, and I waited downstairs while they packed for a few days away from home. I had convinced Thurman to stay at the Charles Hotel with his wife till the press lost interest in him and moved along to the next big thing. One of the *Banner*'s circulation trucks could pick him up each morning and bring him in to the office unobserved. At the end of the day he could slip out the same way.

"Christ, here I am sneaking around like a spy in my own town," Thurman said. "Did you get anywhere finding out who planted that goddamned thing in my paper?"

I told him nobody had cracked under my interrogation. "My impression is that they're all hiding something," I said. "Wouldn't surprise me if the whole damned news staff and production staff were in on it."

"I should have fired the entire goddamned staff the day I took over," Boucher said. "You try to be a good guy, people just walk all over you."

"I'll get the son of a bitch," I said. "Give me another day or two."

"Doesn't matter which one of the treacherous bastards actually put the thing in the paper," Thurman said. "Who gave the orders, that's the point. The only way to kill a snake is to cut off its head."

"Jonathan Paul, you mean?"

"Who else could it be? Bastard made me hide in the trunk of my own Rolls. Ought to put him in the trunk of that goddamned Rolls he drives, leave him there to rot."

"Or lock him up in your trunk, maybe," I said. "He could check for rattles."

"If he was alive he could," the Cobra said.

* * *

Next day things got even worse. The *Globe* ran an editorial that basically said, There but for the grace of God go I. Innocent publishers were all at the mercy of the new technologies and could be victimized at any time by disgruntled or irresponsible employees. In fact, although the editorial didn't bring the matter up, that exact thing had happened back in the 1970s to the *Globe* itself when somebody put "Mush from the Wimp" on top of an editorial about President Carter's budget message. The original headline had been, "All Must Bear the Burden."

The *Globe*'s news staff had dug out the old stories of the sale of the *Banner* and Linda Cushing's death, and supplemented them with mush from the Cobra's wimp, Alan Fogel. And there was a lot of stuff about Boucher's newspaper career, which managed without quite saying so to leave the impression that he was a greedy, ruthless, power-mad swine.

The *Boston Herald* gave the same impression, but even more openly. They had managed this by quoting various anonymous sources within the newspaper industry. They also quoted Felicia Lamport, identified as an old family friend of the Cushings. Presumably the paper had tracked down Serena Cushing and she had passed the ball off to Felicia.

"I have no special knowledge of Mr. Boucher beyond the generally unfavorable reputation he seems to have earned for himself," she was quoted. "Nor did Mrs. Cushing ever speak of her intimate affairs with me. Thus I cannot go beyond her eloquent last words. I can only say that she was making a strong recovery from the tragedy of her husband's death until she had the misfortune to come under the influence of Mr. Boucher. Shortly after that she had turned into a shattered woman under psychiatric care who soon took her own life. I hope Mr. Boucher reads her delayed suicide note carefully, and that he is capable of shame."

Felicia was somebody you really didn't want to have mad at you. It wasn't just that her ad libs sounded like most people's prepared statements; it was also that she knew all the people who counted in Cambridge, and most of them in Boston. What she said carried weight.

Nor had the editors at the *Herald* forgotten the staged photos of Terry Dineen's death that Boucher had caught them running. Their editorial said, "Thurman Boucher is not above offering moral instruction to other newspapers, this one among them. It is a pity that the highly regarded Linda Cushing crossed his path before he became an expert on ethics. We have no doubt that the endlessly acquisitive Mr. Boucher broke no law. A heart is another matter."

This was amazingly rough stuff for a newspaper to say about another newspaper publisher. Normally they cover for each other the same way doctors and cops and Mafiosi do. Or maybe being called endlessly acquisitive was a compliment in publishing circles, like being called hungry by a shrew.

Boucher didn't see it that way, though. "Pious, hypocritical sons of bitches," he said. "They wouldn't have run garbage like that if Rupert still owned the paper. Come on, I need to talk with you. Let's take a walk."

"A walk?" I said. We were alone in his office at the paper.

"I know you've had everything swept in here," he said, "but let's take a walk anyway."

A guy carrying a bag full of electronic gear and tools had come in three weeks before, sure enough, but it was only one of Gladys's boyfriends who was a computer nerd. He pretended to look for bugs for a couple of hours, and charged the paper $400, which I immediately sent to Terry Dineen's widow. So Boucher was right to be careful.

"You don't mean walk outside, do you?" I asked. "Because there's still some reporters hanging around. A woman from *People* and two or three others. They're keeping their heads down, but they're out there."

"Where can we go?"

"How about the pressroom? No bug would work in all that noise." The presses were running. You could feel the vibration anywhere in the building. We could have talked just as safely in some hallway, but Boucher seemed to want theatrics. So we went downstairs, nodded to the pressmen, and huddled in a corner. "It's time we got rid of the Jonathan Paul problem," he said, almost in my ear.

"That's affirmative, Thurman," I said, feeling that a little jargon from the Nam was appropriate. "How?"

"How is up to you. You've done these things before."

"You saying what I think you're saying?"

"I'm sure I am."

"You want me to waste the fucker?"

"Do you have a problem with that?"

"Just that I work for you. You don't want it that close to you."

"Well, then, what?"

"I could ask around."

"You know who to ask, I take it?"

"I know a couple people. It's a cash business, naturally. A lot of cash."

"How much?"

"Been a while, I'd have to see. Twenty, twenty-five, I'd guess."

"No problem. I keep more than that in the safe at home."

"Mad money, huh?"

"That's a good word for it. I'm mad, all right."

"You got a right to be, Thurman. The prick is just begging for it."

"Not bad, Bethany," Billy Curtin said when we had finished eating. "Naturally you didn't cook it."

"All I know is the newspaper business, Lieutenant. The Bouchers' cook does the cooking."

"I don't see a cook."

He hadn't seen a maid, either. I had brought out the cold sorrel soup, salmon in aspic, new potatoes, and baby peas myself. The two of us had just finished the raspberry sherbet the cook had frozen up for us that afternoon.

"The cook is Oswald something or other," I told Curtin. "French guy. I told him to fix up dinner for two and then go home. I didn't want anybody to see you here."

"Yeah? Why not?"

"Maybe you shouldn't be in the guy's house without a warrant or something, what do I know?"

"I'm a guest. You asked me in. This cook, does he live in?"

"Everybody goes home at night, the maid and the gardener, too. What I think it is, I think the Bouchers need a lot of privacy for their games. This is two pretty weird people."

"They got to be a little off center, they let a guy like you house-sit for them."

"Hey, somebody has to keep the press out. They're awful. They don't even flush when they take dumps."

Curtin didn't smile, but that didn't mean anything one way or another. Detective Lieutenant William X. Curtin was practically no laughs at all. On the other hand he was very, very tough and absolutely honest according to his own rules. They were stricter rules than the legal system had, but so far he had got away with enforcing them. He had even risen to be assistant chief of detectives in the Cambridge police. Billy Curtin essentially ran the detective division, since he was twice as smart as the chief of detectives. That also meant he'd never rise any higher than he was. Really smart guys make the dummies on top nervous.

"Why don't they make you chief of police, Lieutenant?" I asked.

"Fuck that. You got to hang around with retards like politicians and other police chiefs all the time. What are we doing here anyway, Bethany? Career counseling?"

"I got some stuff upstairs I want to show you."

I took him to a study off the master bedroom. The master bedroom was a little bit interesting. It had a giant bed eight feet square, and there were mirrors all over the place. It also had a hidden video camera aimed at the bed, maybe shooting footage for the Bouchers to enjoy in their old age. Or maybe they loaned their bed to friends.

The bathroom was a little bit interesting, too. It had a shower stall big enough to hold a basketball team, with nozzles on all three walls, overhead, at waist level, and knee-high. It also had his and hers bidets, facing each other.

But I had taken the day off to search the house from attic to cellar, and the most interesting thing was the study.

"Place looks like an ad," Curtin said when I showed him in.

And it did. One of those Ralph Lauren ads showing the young squire relaxing in his den. Priceless Oriental rugs tossed casually on the floor. A fly rod in the corner. A Purdy shotgun. Maybe a sextant or a globe, to suggest expeditions. Prints on the wall of sailing vessels and Thoroughbred horses. Leather-bound volumes, maroon and green. A meerschaum pipe, a bottle of ruby port. Nineteenth-century when-men-were-men stuff.

Boucher didn't have all those things in his study, or even most of them. But that was the idea. What dominated the room was an extraordinary antique desk, full of pigeonholes and dozens of little drawers. The only time most of us see a piece of furniture like that, it's behind a velvet rope in a museum. You could buy a whole house for what that desk had cost.

Naturally I had gone through every one of those drawers and slots and pigeonholes. Most of them had been empty, although I found a few business cards, paper clips, rubber bands, pencil stubs, matchbooks, notepads. The usual desk junk. I had been about to move on when my eye was caught by a slight irregularity in the green leather desk top where it met the first row of little pigeonholes. When I poked around with one of the paper clips I found a couple of small brass hinges hidden between the leather and the wood. The desk top wouldn't rise up, though, and there was no keyhole to indicate a lock. So I poked around under the desk until I found a tiny block of wood that slid when I pushed it. Then I had been able to lift the whole writing surface up, like the top of an old-fashioned school desk.

Now I showed Lieutenant Curtin how the secret catch worked, and took a gilt-bordered black calfskin album out of the desk. I put it on the huge bed for him to read, and then brought over the other things I had found in the desk. Two of them were unlabeled videocassettes. The other was a small gray lump, heavy for its size, in a clear plastic bag that zipped closed. A number was handwritten on a slip of paper inside the bag.

"Is that what I think it is?" I asked.

"A bullet, sure. Looks like it came from an evidence room."

He turned back to the album.

He read slowly, skipping nothing.

The album held a collection of newspaper clippings, court records, reports from private detective agencies, memos, correspondence, government papers, and company records. Photographs were mounted here and there among the written material. The album had four sections, each of them headed with a person's name.

The first section was marked "Elvis Clopton."

It dealt with a printers' strike at one of the Cobra's papers in western Maryland. By the third week the level of violence had risen high enough so that Boucher had been able to convince the governor to bring in the National Guard.

The union denied it was responsible for the tire slashings and plant sabotage and beatings of replacement workers by strangers from out of town. The union said that management was framing it. The union also denied responsibility for the flash grenade that went off among the National Guard MPs and the city police one night, causing the cops to go a little nuts.

When it was all over, a printer named Elvis Clopton was dead. During a police beating he fell in the path of a National Guard armored personnel carrier and his head was crushed under the wheels.

After the newspaper clipping somebody had pasted in a page from a high school yearbook with Clopton's senior class picture on it. It was neatly mounted, like all the items in the album. Was the Cobra that neat? I wondered if one of the two Louises had done it. Or more likely Alison Boucher. This stuff was too confidential even for confidential secretaries.

The next section was headed "Ernest Gibbons, Jr." Most of the material was dated the previous year. Gibbons had been an expert in preventive labor relations, which is to say a union buster. Then he went into midlife crisis and came out as a union organizer for the American Newspaper Guild. His first assignment was to organize a Boucher Group paper in southern Illinois.

He did a good job, knowing management's little tricks as well as he did. After winning the National Labor Relations Board election, he set to work hammering out a contract for the newly organized shop. But right in the middle of negotiations, he was arrested for taking a million-dollar bribe from Thurman Boucher. The money was payment for selling out his membership with a sweetheart contract. Boucher had brought it in an aluminum suitcase along with, as it turned out, a microphone hidden on his body. The first night Gibbons was free on bail, he checked into a motel and killed himself with a .38 caliber bullet in the temple. He left a wife, and three kids in college.

"Think that's a thirty-eight?" I asked Curtin, pointing to the lead lump in the plastic bag.

"Looks like it."

"How do you suppose Boucher got hold of the thing?"

"Guy's dead. The case is closed. No reason for the property clerk to keep it around. Maybe your pal paid him a million bucks for the goddamned thing. Who ever heard of a million-dollar bribe, anyway?"

"Doesn't matter how big the bribe is if you're not going to pay it," I said. "That suitcase full of cash was just window dressing so Boucher could get Gibbons to talk into the mike."

"Your pal's a real prince," Curtin said. "Piles money up in front of this Gibbons guy till he finally caves in, then runs straight to the cops to get himself fitted for a wire. That's cold."

"Soon as you finish with this stuff, Lieutenant, I'll show you colder than that."

The third section of the album was Linda Cushing's. The lead item was handwritten on heavy, cream-colored note paper folded like a Christmas card. *Mrs. Michael Patrick Cushing* was printed on the outside in raised letters. It read:

Dear Mr. Boucher:

You are very kind to offer to share your advice. Heaven knows I certainly need it! Tuesday next is convenient for me as well. See you at one o'clock.

Sincerely,
Linda Cushing

The paper trail continued through their relationship. Mr. Boucher became Thurman in the note that followed their first meeting. "Sincerely" became "gratefully," and then "warmly," and then "fondly." "Linda Cushing" became "Linda" and then "L." The last note had no salutation and no signature. It was just the words: "Last night something wonderful happened," written in her neat, good-little-girl handwriting on a scrap of plain paper. "Something I never thought would come into my life again. Thank you, Love, L."

Then came clippings, dated a couple of weeks afterward, about the Boucher Group's purchase of the *Cambridge Daily Banner*. Next was a very brief story from the paper about Alan Fogel replacing Jonathan Paul as managing editor. The Linda Cushing section ended with clippings from the *Banner* and the two Boston papers about her death.

The last section in the album was Terry Dineen's. Mostly it was newspaper clippings about his boxing career and his death under the wheels of the subway train. There was also an office memo from Alan Fogel firing the ex-fighter from his job in the sports department, and another re-hiring him as a chauffeur. I was in the Dineen section, too.

"What's this thing?" Lieutenant Curtin asked, tapping a finger on a carefully mounted Cambridge parking ticket.

"I parked Boucher's Rolls in front of a fire hydrant on Mem. Drive."

"I can see that. Why's it in here?"

I told him about my failed attempt to save Terry Dineen.

"Why'd you run?" Curtin asked.

"Jesus, Lieutenant, the guy was cut in half. What was I supposed to do? Stick around and give him CPR?"

He gave me an uncomfortably long look. He knew I wasn't in the phone book and had no known address and until recently no visible means of support. As a cop he didn't like it that I did my best to move through life without leaving a paper trail. But even if he didn't like it, he knew it gave me a good reason for leaving the scene.

"That still doesn't tell me why the ticket is in this album," he said.

"Because Boucher thinks it means I pushed Terry under the train."

"Why didn't you just pay the damned thing so he wouldn't see it?"

I told him how the ticket had blown loose as I drove away. "It never occurred to me that somebody would find the ticket and send it to Boucher," I said. "How would they even know who to send it to?"

"Think about it," Curtin said. "The meter maid is working her way up the street and she sees a ticket she just wrote lying in the road. Some rich son of a bitch in a Rolls thinks he can blow her off, huh? We'll see about that. She runs the owner's plate number when her shift's over, probably has the ticket in the mail to him that same night."

"Could be."

"Trust me. I've written enough tickets myself to know how you feel, some wiseass throws one in the gutter."

"I guess."

"But that still doesn't tell me what's going on here," the lieutenant said. "What if you *were* there? Why would that mean you killed Dineen?"

"Because Dineen got some guy to make threatening phone calls to me and Boucher both."

"Then what? Boucher told you to push him under a train?"

"He never told me that, no. He never told me he had this ticket, either. But he kept hinting around that I went out and killed the guy on my own."

"And you didn't tell him any different?"

"I told him, but not very hard. I could tell he wanted it to be true. It made his dick longer if he had a murderer working for him."

"Explain this scrapbook to me. All these people, what're they doing in here?"

"It's a trophy album. They're all people who crossed Thurman Boucher, and they all wound up dead."

"You're saying he killed them?"

"Well, didn't he? Not legally, maybe, but really?"

"The ones who killed themselves didn't have to. The guy that got his head squashed, it was an accident."

"All right, fine, but you asked what the scrapbook is all about and that's what I think it is. Scalps from his victims. He gets off on thinking he caused the death of all these people. Look what kind of guy he is. He fired Terry and then hired him back when he learned the way Boom-Boom Greer died. Then I come along and whip the guy that killed Boom-Boom and so he hires me instead. Basically this is a murder groupie."

Boucher's fancy VCR was in the master bedroom, placed so you could look at movies while lying in bed. Any ten-year-old in America could have figured out the control panel, but there hadn't been any ten-year-olds around when I tried to view the tapes yesterday. Eventually I managed it, but now I was having trouble again.

"Shit, Bethany, let me do it," Curtin said after he got tired of watching me mess things up. "I got one at home."

"So do I, but all it's got is on and off, forward and reverse."

"Hold on to it, it'll be worth something someday. You still got the original box?"

I didn't say anything. My experience with people like cops and noncoms is you don't try for snappy comebacks.

The first tape was unedited news footage taken by a Baltimore TV station. Violence seldom looks as stark and uncomplicated as the Rodney King tape did. Mostly it's just a big, confusing muddle. Cops and guardsmen and strikers were all mixed up, pushing and shoving at each other. Clubs were swinging, but when they hit you couldn't hear the noise and the person didn't drop like a stone.

The picketer who turned out to be Elvis Clopton dropped to one knee, and then disappeared from view. The armored personnel carrier was rolling very slowly, and then stopped. Plainly the cameraman didn't know anything special had happened. He kept on filming the milling crowd for a minute or so. Then the picture started swinging and zooming all over the place as the cameraman realized something was up and pushed his way into the mob. You saw backs and ground and sky for a minute, and then you saw the victim's body, with a policeman kneeling beside it. The left front wheel of the vehicle had gone over Clopton's head and stopped a couple of yards farther on. There was blood, but the head didn't seem to have been squashed flat or even broken open.

"Maybe it mostly went over his neck," Lieutenant Curtin said when I asked about that. "Some fatals you see damage you wouldn't believe, sometimes it's nothing. I've seen jumpers, you'd swear they just stretched out for a nap."

"This guy is almost like that," I said. "Must have been a big disappointment to the Cobra."

"What Cobra?"

"It's what the other publishers call Boucher."

"I'm starting to see why. What's on the other tape? Terry under the train? Gibbons blowing his brains out?"

"Boucher and Linda Cushing."

"What are you saying? Dirty movies?"

"They're dirty, all right."

"I knew Mrs. Cushing a little bit, over the years. I don't need to see these movies, I'll take your word for it."

"I think you ought to at least take a look, Lieutenant. Otherwise you won't really know the kind of guy we're dealing with here."

18

THE CAMERA SHOWED THE same eight-by-eight bed that Curtin and I were sitting on. Thurman Boucher was sitting on it in the video. He took off his shoes and his socks, and stood up to finish undressing. Then he got under the covers and lay on his back with his hands clasped behind his head, not moving.

A woman came onto the screen from the direction of the bathroom, wearing a man's bathrobe that trailed on the floor. The picture wasn't sharp enough to show the small signs of age—the fine wrinkles, the lost tautness of the skin. Except for the graying hair, Linda Cushing could almost have been a child dressed up in her father's robe. The robe was belted, but she held the lapels closed with her hands, too.

"Let me see you," Boucher said.

"You don't want to look at me," Linda said. She got under the covers quickly, and began to maneuver herself out of the robe.

"You're silly, do you know that?" Boucher said. "You have a beautiful figure."

"An old figure."

"Beautiful," he said, and kissed her cheek gently. "Not too young and not too old."

"You're sweet, Thurman, but I know just how old I am. Every wrinkle."

"Only fools think young is beautiful, Linda. Beauty has to be grown into. Earned."

"I wish I believed you."

"You can. My wife, soon to be ex-wife, thank God, anyway she's younger than I am. Most men would call her beautiful. But she's just like a pretty package with nothing inside. Men don't want that, not really. At least I don't. I've learned that much from Alison, so I guess I have to thank her for that. Next time around I want a woman that's comfortable, a woman who's kind, and gentle, and pretty, and soft where . . . No, don't move. Just tell me exactly where it feels best. Up? Down? In my lady's chamber?"

"Right there. There is fine."

"Good. You mustn't be shy about telling me exactly what you like, darling, otherwise how am I going to know how to make my pretty lady happy?" His hand was busy under the covers. She moaned.

"Jesus," Lieutenant Curtin said, "this guy's slick as goose grease."

"Oh," Linda Cushing's voice said. "Oh, oh, oh."

"You wouldn't think it would work," I said.

"Why not? It's been working for thousands of years."

"I guess it has at that."

On the screen, Boucher shifted position and took Linda's face in both his hands and kissed her. Then he lifted her left hand to his lips and kissed her palm, and then kissed her wrist. "Pretty little wrist," he murmured. "Lovely wrist, lovely lady. I feel the lovely lady's pulse. It's like I'm kissing her heart."

"Fucking amazing," Lieutenant Curtin said.

"Let me look at the lovely lady," Thurman Boucher said, and he swept the covers to one side. The camera went in tight on the naked woman, and Lieutenant Curtin moved slightly, as if surprised. I had been surprised, too, the first time I watched the tape. Until that point it hadn't occurred to me that somebody was operating the camera.

From then on it became obvious. Boucher would hitch his partner and himself around to give a clear view of whatever he was doing to her at the moment, or had got her to do to him. When she wasn't looking, he mugged for the camera, rolling his eyes, sticking out his tongue, pretending he was overcome with passion, pretending to retch.

"Who's taking the pictures?" Curtin asked.

"His wife."

"His *wife!*"

"They've got what you might call an open marriage."

"Jesus, Bethany, is there any point in watching this shit? I already told you I knew the lady. I don't need this."

"I guess we've seen enough. I just wanted you to get an idea what was on it."

Curtin went over and killed the picture. I heard the rewind start up slow, and then get up to full speed after a few seconds.

"You think of any reason not to erase that thing?" he asked.

"Not really."

"What did you show it to me for?"

"Background."

"Does this tie in with this Mrs. Cushing's death?" the detective asked. "You got any reason to think it wasn't suicide?"

"None. Do you?"

"Not so far. Particularly not with that letter that ran in the paper. Even though anybody could have written the damned thing. With computers, there's no way to tell."

"I'm pretty sure she wrote it and got somebody to slip it in the paper."

"Who?"

"I don't know. I don't think it makes much difference."

"Why did she do it?"

"Same reason she killed herself in the first place. That's why I wanted you to see the tape."

"Go ahead. Explain."

So I told Lieutenant Curtin about the trip to Canton and the blackmailing of Robbie Haseltine.

"This is what they do, Lieutenant," I said. "If it's a man, she takes over. If it's a woman, well, you just saw the movie. They had that tape put aside in case Mrs. Cushing ever gave them trouble. Which she eventually did."

"Over what?"

"When she found out her old friend Jonathan Paul had been fired in direct violation of the contract, she walked into Boucher's office and confronted him. She came out in tears, and later she absolutely refused to tell Jonathan what had happened in there. Now we know what it was.

"Boucher must have told her he had her on videotape and he'd show it to her old admirer if she didn't keep her mouth shut. The bottom line is that this guy she was probably secretly in love with for years, he's out on the street because she betrayed him with a shit like Boucher. Now she's lost her husband, her paper, her self-respect. Lost her chance at true love, too. She goes into a tailspin to the point where suicide looks like the only way to solve her problems. So she ends the noncompete agreement by dying, and she leaves a suicide note asking her daughter to help Jonathan run the Cobra out of business."

"By suicide note, you mean the thing that ran in the paper?" Curtin asked.

"Sure."

"Why not just a regular note?"

"We'll never really know, but look at it from her point of view. She's getting ready to die and she's got a couple of things she wants to take care of. She wants to help Jonathan Paul with as much public support as she can, and she wants to humiliate the man who humiliated her. But if she leaves a conventional suicide note with those accusations against Boucher in it, her family and friends are going to suppress the whole thing. Who needs the scandal? Who needs people laughing at Mom?

"So she found somebody at the paper who agreed to get her whole message out to the world unedited, and everything worked like a charm. Now the one everybody's laughing at is Boucher."

"Why wait so long to do it?" Curtin asked.

"Again it's just a guess, but how about this? Whoever she asked for help isn't just risking his job if he gets caught. Boucher's probably going to sue his ass, too. Bankrupt the guy with legal costs, no matter who wins. The guy's scared. He can slip her message into the paper and there won't be anything in the computer system to tell who did it. But there's going to be a record of *when* it was done. He stalls. He won't take a chance till everything's just right, and nobody could possibly suspect he was around. Maybe months pass until the perfect opportunity comes along."

"Maybe."

"Besides, it doesn't really matter why it happened or when it happened or who did it. The only point is it happened and Boucher thinks Jonathan Paul did it."

"Why does he think that?"

"Because I keep telling him Jonathan Paul is at the bottom of all his troubles."

"Why have you been telling him that?"

I told him why, leaving out the kickbacks for Terry's family, the vandalism in the entryway, and my plans for sabotage. I tried to leave the impression that I was mostly a harmless infiltrator and prankster, certainly not a criminal. And in fact, except for the two things I left out, I hadn't done anything illegal that I could think of.

"The Cushing family is paying you money for this foolishness?" Curtin said when I was done.

"They rented the Rolls-Royce, that's all. Boucher is paying my salary."

"This is the goofiest shit I ever heard of, Bethany."

"I was starting to think so, too, Lieutenant. Now I don't anymore."

The VCR clicked as the tape finished rewinding. Lieutenant Curtin went over and worked the controls. The red numbers on the counter started back up from zero as the machine began to erase the tape.

"You know what that video really is?" I said. "It's a snuff flick."

"How do you figure?"

"We saw her being killed right there, really. It didn't happen on film, but it happened because of the film. That tape amounted to a murder weapon, the way he used it."

"That's not how the law looks at it, Bethany."

"Hell with the law. That's how Boucher works, you can see it in his little collection. He breaks people, and sometimes it doesn't kill them and sometimes it does. When it does, the one who really killed them is him. Listen, Lieutenant, suppose this was some street punk who mugged somebody and the guy died? What if he told you, 'Hey, I was just slapping the guy around a little. I didn't mean for him to die.' You tell me, Lieutenant. How far would he get?"

"Not far, but what else is new. For guys like Boucher, the

law doesn't work that way. For them it works like a rubber glove. It keeps their hands clean."

"What if you could catch this particular guy with his rubber gloves off?"

"How do you mean?"

"He wants me to hire somebody to kill Jonathan Paul."

"Is that a fact?"

"Yeah, it is. I told him it could cost as much as twenty-five thousand. I thought you might know somebody who could help the guy out."

The lieutenant considered matters for a moment.

"All I got working for me is morons mostly," he said. "Christ, I got to do everything myself."

Lieutenant Curtin sat for a long time without saying anything more while we listened to the VCR whir. Now and then he would glance my way, but mostly he just looked off into space. With his fingers laced together he was flexing one hand against another in what might have been some kind of strength or flexibility drill. But he didn't seem to be aware of what he was doing.

Finally he snapped back into focus and turned to me.

"You're the wild card here, Bethany," he said. "It just doesn't compute. You spent months on this guy's payroll and for what? Another guy, I'd say it was for the paycheck, simple as that. Not you, Bethany. You got no more to do with money than an alley cat."

"Him offering me a job was just an accident, like I told you," I said. "Me taking it? Tell you the truth, it just tickled me. Take a look at the newspaper business, why not? I thought it'd be fun, working for the guy and laughing at him. Bust his balls a little and see what happened. Then I kind of got into it when I started to see what a world-class prick I was dealing with."

"That undercover shit's no good for a person, Bethany. After a while you start turning into the bad guys."

"Yeah, maybe. It could be happening. Boucher thinks it is. He wants to make me a publisher someday."

"You going to do it?"

"Jesus, I hope not."

"Why not?"

"Same reason you don't want to be a police chief. The company you have to keep."

"So far you're giving the right answers, Bethany."

The VCR clicked. Curtin took out the now-blank tape and tossed it to me. "Look," he said, "if I'm going to involve myself in this hit man crap, I'm going to be more or less standing on your shoulders. I've got to be sure you're solid."

"You mean will I come out of my hole and testify?"

"Let's start with that, yeah."

"I won't like it, but I'll do it. After what Boucher did to Mrs. Cushing, I feel obliged."

"It'd be a big trial, Bethany. Huge trial. Millionaire stuff. Spy story stuff."

"Couldn't you keep the spy stuff out of it?"

"You tell me how."

"I'm just an anonymous guy, some nobody who got hired by a fluke. I'm going along doing my job when suddenly my boss gives me this outrageous assignment to carry out. I'm horrified. I go to the police like any honest citizen."

"How many people know what you're really up to?"

"Felicia Lamport, Gladys Williams, Mrs. Cushing's daughter, and Jonathan Paul."

"Mrs. Lamport I've heard of. Jonathan I know, and naturally Gladys from when she worked for the department. How about this daughter?" he asked.

"She's in the same boat as Jonathan Paul. They both want to run Boucher out of town and take back the paper."

"So?"

"If they let it out there was a sabotage campaign, Boucher would haul their ass into court and probably win."

"You know Mrs. Lamport a long time?"

"More than ten years. She's a rock."

"Well, maybe the lid would stay on. Nobody at the paper suspects about you?"

"No. I made myself into pretty much prick-of-the-year down there, so they figure I'm just part of the management team."

"I was thinking Boucher might suspect something."

"Because it's tough to bullshit a bullshitter, huh? Actually it's the other way around, it's easy. They believe each other's crap. It's like they were extending professional courtesy."

"I got to think about that a while."

And he actually sat there and thought about it, doing the business with his fingers again. Tell most people something new to them and they just automatically figure you're lying. Not Curtin. He'd pick up the new thing, turn it upside down, shake it, maybe scrape a little bit of the paint off to see what was underneath.

In this case, he would be running through the great bullshitters he had known and making matches. Who were the people they trusted and believed? Other bullshitters? Non-bullshitters? Did this new notion of mine check with reality or not?

"There's something in that," he said after a minute or two. "I noticed a long time ago that ass-kissers like their ass kissed, but I never thought about bullshitters liking bullshit. For instance, I saw this guy Ollie North on the TV. You and I meet a guy like that, we'd know he was lying the minute he opened his mouth. Why would a president fall for him?"

"It answers itself, Lieutenant."

"I guess it does. Professional courtesy, like you said."

He tossed the cassette onto the bed and said, "All right,

then, let's assume you're right and he's been buying your bullshit."

"He sold it to himself. He wanted to have a stone killer working for him, so he turned me into one."

"Don't tell me you weren't an easy lay."

"I won't tell you that, no."

"But even if Boucher believes you, we have to assume that it could come out somehow. What you were really up to at the *Bummer*, I mean."

"Be a real circus then, wouldn't it?" I said. "Well, so what? I'll run the risk, for the pleasure of seeing this prick hung out to dry."

"Will I run the risk, though?" Curtin said. "That's the point."

"What's the risk for you?"

"The risk is I don't know what you've really been up to over there. I don't want some lawyer sandbagging my case, saying Your Honor, this guy was a saboteur. He was slashing tires, throwing wrenches in the machinery. Your Honor, this witness is nothing but a goddamn common criminal. You can't believe a word he says."

"It won't happen, Lieutenant, you've got my word. There's nothing like that they can throw at me."

Could a mob lawyer have come up with a better answer than that? All right, I spray painted the lobby and shook down suppliers for kickbacks, but that's nothing like slashing tires, is it? Besides, they couldn't throw those things at me unless they found out about them, and how could they find out?

So I wasn't exactly lying. What the hell, there's a little bit of lawyer in all of us. Or maybe it's the other way around.

The press had gone on to other things, and nobody was staking out the paper or the house anymore. The Bouchers were due to move out of the Charles the next day, and I'd go back to my apartment. This was my last shot at mansion living. Once Curtin had gone back to wherever he went at night, I made a farewell tour, basement to attic. I didn't turn up anything new, so I made do with what I had already discovered.

I returned the tape of Linda Cushing, now erased, to its secret place in the desk. Then I got a bunch of other tapes from the closet where the video cam had been concealed behind a two-way mirror. The closet had been locked, but I had found the key in the desk's secret compartment.

I had already run off copies of most of the tape collection I had found in the locked closet. Each was labeled with the date and initials, often just "A & T." They were building a film library of memories for their golden years, maybe. The non-Boucher participants on the other tapes were identified only with initials that didn't mean anything to me. Nor did the first names on the sound tracks.

Thurman Boucher was in most of the tapes, laboring away. He was long-winded, but it couldn't have been much fun for his partners. Like being attacked by a locomotive.

I thought of something a friend of mine named Wanda Vollmer once told me. Wanda started out in the job market as a teenage hooker. Her least favorite customers, even worse than computer nerds, were Arabs. The nerds were just awkward and inept. "But Arab guys," she said, "most of them treated you like you weren't even alive, like you were just a big piece of meat they were handling." The Cobra was like that, too. A meat handler.

Alison, on the other hand, had the true touch. From the tapes with her in them, you could tell she liked everything about men—the way they sounded, looked, felt, smelled, tasted. She was the initiator, in control of every encounter on the screen, yet I doubt if any of the men ever knew it. She even managed to make her control-freak husband look good in spite of himself. Alison was an appreciator, an enthusiast, a student of her partner—and she came practically on contact. It almost made me wish I hadn't been such a fuddy-duddy, that evening in the wrestling room. Maybe if we had got something going she would have brought me up here to the home studio. It would have been fun to have a tape of the two of us for my own golden years.

19

"I MAYBE COULD HAVE GOT him to come down some if you were Joe Blow," I said to Boucher the next day. "But the trouble is you're Thurman Boucher, and the guy reads the papers. He knows you're loaded. He wouldn't budge."

"When it comes to something like this, I don't mind paying top dollar," the Cobra said.

"Well, still. At least I kept him to twenty-five. He tried for thirty, but I told him, shit, Billy, we both of us know twenty-five is what you get. Just because the guy's got money's no reason. He says it's good enough reason for doctors, isn't it? They got that sliding scale, don't they? So I go, Billy, what are you, a brain surgeon? Any asshole can waste somebody. You and I were places where a hundred bucks got the job done."

"That would be Vietnam?"

"Southeast Asia anyway. That's where we met."

"Special Forces?"

265

"Let's say we worked for the government. Anyway, long story short, I finally got the son of a bitch to settle for the usual."

"How does it work? Half now and half on completion?"

"Most guys yes, but Billy doesn't bother with front money. You don't owe anything till after the guy is whacked."

Boucher thought about that for a minute, tapping his fingers on the blotter of his desk. Cambridge Louise was outside the office. Beyond her the reporters and editors were going about their business in the newsroom, missing the real story of the day. But then reporters are generally the last ones to learn what management is really up to.

"Presumably he'll have to put in a certain amount of time studying the habits and movements of our friend Mr. Paul," Boucher said. "If this is supposed to look like a routine mugging, you can't just bust in on him and shoot him in his office or at home."

"No, it'll take at least a few days to set the thing up right," I said.

"During which time he's working for nothing."

"All part of the service."

"How does he know I'll pay him once the job is done?"

"I doubt he's worried. You owe your old grandma money, you might stiff her. You owe your bookie money, you might even stiff him. But nobody stiffs a hit man. It goes without saying."

"I guess it does. When do I get to meet him?"

"You want to meet him?" This was better than I had hoped. I had some bullshit story ready about how Curtin always insisted on being paid by his clients face-to-face, but now I wouldn't have to use it.

"I like to know who I'm doing business with," Boucher said.

"I know he won't talk to you beforehand, because part of

the deal is that the customer stays completely out of it. No interference. I just give him the name and that's it."

"Understandable."

"But maybe he'd see you afterward. I don't know. I could ask."

"He has to come by for his money, doesn't he?"

"True enough," I said.

That evening wasn't our regular wrestling night, but Boucher had been cooped up in the hotel for more than a week and was in a hurry to get back to his workouts. So I wasn't able to get together with our little study group until the next evening, at Felicia's house.

We ate first, like civilized people. "I never do business on a filling stomach," Felicia said when I was unmannerly enough to mention the *Banner* while Josephine was clearing away the soup plates. So we talked about the medical school admissions process, which led into the story of a premed who had stolen another premed's lab report from a professor's In box, copied it as his own, thrown out the other guy's, and been punished for his conduct by getting his M.D. last spring. Which led to service academy cheating, which led to body counts in the Vietnam War, which led to Ollie North's campaign in Virginia, which led to Bob Dole's recent public planting of a big wet one right on Ollie's lips. All of which struck me as a good deal less suitable for the dinner table than an uplifting story of disinformation and sabotage at the *Bummer*, but what did I know about manners?

After dinner, in the living room, Felicia turned to me and said, "Now, Tom, as you were saying . . ."

"As I was saying, this thing of ours may be working out after all."

"What's up?" Gladys Williams asked.

"I'm not supposed to tell you the exact details."

"Says who?"

"That's one of the details I'm not supposed to tell you. But it looks like we've finally driven the Cobra pretty much around the bend. He's about to step on his own . . . well, let's say blow his own foot off."

"In what sense?" Jonathan Paul asked.

"I can't say how, but it's a major thing that could give him major difficulties. And it's better for everyone if you don't know any more than that. Later you'll understand why. For now, though, I have a couple of favors to ask. First, Jonathan. If Serena and you manage to get the paper back, would you be able to find a job and day care for Terry Dineen's widow?"

Jonathan Paul looked at Serena, who nodded. "I was thinking of it anyway," Jonathan said. "With her boy, she needs to get back on health insurance."

"Okay, fine. Remember at the beginning when I said nobody had to pay me, I'd figure some way to pay myself? Well, this is the way I'll be paying myself."

"Seems to me like it's paying Terry's widow, not you," Paul said.

"Comes to the same thing. I owe her."

"You don't, of course," Felicia said.

"I feel like I do, so I do. Humor me."

"Of course we will," Felicia said.

"All right, fine. Apart from that, nobody has to do anything but sit tight for a few more weeks. I'm sorry to be so mysterious, but I've got to be."

"Since we don't have the slightest clue what's going on," Felicia said, "it's hard to ask intelligent questions. But can you give us an idea of the general purpose of all this mystery?"

"The general purpose is so you can honestly deny that you knew anything about what's going to happen soon."

"Is anyone likely to ask us?"

"I'm about ninety-nine percent sure nobody will."

The one percent was Lieutenant Curtin, who was the only outsider to know what my role was at the *Banner*.

Eventually, of course, Jonathan Paul would have to be told about the plot against his life, but it could wait till the last minute. And Lieutenant Curtin would make sure the editor kept his mouth shut.

Next day I called up Wanda Vollmer, the woman who had told me about Arabs as lovers. Back when she ran a massage parlor out by the Alewife T-stop, she and I had got together to bring the true spirit of Christ to a Virginia televangelist. When it was all done, she wound up in Virginia Beach running the guy's Christian theme park for him while he delivered the sermons. And she was in charge of receipts, so he wouldn't steal it all for himself anymore. Instead Wanda used it to set up schools and orphanages and clinics.

"Sister Wanda," I said when I had got past her secretary.

"Brother Tom," she said. "When are you coming down to Lordland? We got a new ride called Jacob's Ladder. You slide up it."

"Is this for real?"

"The ride's for real. You don't slide up it, naturally. Any dumb fuck knows you can't slide uphill."

"I knew it sounded fishy."

"See, what did I tell you? A dumb fuck did know."

"Are we finished with the abuse here, Wanda? I'm calling to make some money for you, but I could change my mind."

"Money, huh? Well, maybe I could listen for a minute."

"You know all about this financial shit now, don't you? Futures, currency markets, stocks and bonds?" Actually Wanda had been an investor for years, even before her massage parlor days. She started back when she was tending bar at a hangout for bankers and brokers. But now, at Lordland, she had real money to play with.

"I'm learning every day," she said.

"Okay, suppose you knew that a company was about to take a major hit on a certain day, could you make money off that?"

"A publicly held company?"

"Controlled by an individual, but the stock is traded publicly."

"Yeah, you could probably make money off that. Depending on the situation."

I told her the situation.

"You'd have to sell short," she said at the end.

"That's what I thought, but I don't understand the process too well."

"I'd need some time to make it look good. I'd have to call around to various brokers, establish short positions in other newspaper stocks so that establishing a position in Boucher wouldn't be entirely out of left field, you know?"

"Would anybody even bother to look at you?"

"The SEC? They might. Selling short isn't all that common, and to make real dough off this asshole's company I'd have to go short on a whole lot of its stock. I mean, short sales are leveraged, but still."

"How much time would you need to cover your tracks?"

"I'll have to look into it and let you know."

"Good enough."

"And look, Tom, you got to remember I'm not playing with my own money here. It's the church money, and there's no limit to how much you can lose selling short if the stock goes the other way."

"The company's basically this one guy, Wanda. With him out of the picture, it's got to go down."

"Not as much as you might think. All those papers are going to keep on generating cash flow whether he's around or not. They can be sold."

"For how much, though? Isn't that the point?"

"That's my point, all right. What's your point, Tom?"

"He's in the middle of trying to raise sixty million in sub-ordinated debt, if I've got the term right. Only his books are cooked and he hasn't got a damned thing to back up the offering, really."

"He must have some assets."

"His own lawyer told him the company couldn't possibly meet the dividend payments on the new bonds, and the bondholders would win if they went to court about it."

"Okay, I promise not to buy his junk bonds. How does that make the stock go down, though?"

"I've got a copy of the lawyer's letter. Boucher left his briefcase behind when he moved to the Charles to duck the reporters. Well, actually he didn't exactly leave it behind. I left it in the car on purpose and drove off. By the time I supposedly noticed it and took it back to the hotel, I had stopped by Kinko's and copied everything inside."

"What are you going to do with this letter?"

"My thought was, I'd send anonymous copies to the papers and to the media analysts at a bunch of the big brokerages."

"When?"

"Probably the day before the main shit hits the fan, so they'll get it a day or two afterward."

"That should help."

"What do you mean, should? Look, first the company loses its CEO and then a few days later it turns out he was trying to raise money by floating worthless securities. Which way can the stock go? Up? It's got to go down, Wanda. The only question is how far."

"How do you know Boucher won't pull out, Tom?"

"On this hit man bullshit? Well, I guess he could get cold feet. But I've still got that letter, and I'll send it out regardless. That way there's not a chance the stock will go up, which is the only way you guys can lose money. Right? At least that's the way I understand this whole procedure."

After a while we came to an agreement that the church would put up as much money as Gladys was comfortable with, and keep 80 percent of any profits. The other 20 would go to me as a finder's fee. Not that it would look like a finder's fee, of course. It would look like a payment to an outfit called Infotek, which was me, for research services rendered to a much bigger outfit called CORR, Inc. Which was the corporate umbrella of Lordland and the Church of Our Redeemer Risen, both of them run by Wanda Vollmer.

Time passed while Wanda made her stock market arrangements and Lieutenant Curtin made his police arrangements. I didn't have much to do myself. I could have been tipping Jonathan Paul off to upcoming *Banner* stories so he could get them into print first. Or fiddling with files in the newsroom directories, now that I knew how easy it was. Or slipping impossibly low prices into big display ads, or making classified ads disappear before they ran, or trashing the digitized images of full-page color ads an hour before press time, when it would be too late to reconstruct them. Or taking a powerful magnet into the computer room and erasing huge chunks of data. Those were some of the things I had planned on doing one of these days, but they weren't worth the bother now that Boucher was marching himself toward the cliff.

One way and another, it had taken more than two weeks for Lieutenant Curtin and me to set up Jonathan Paul's murder. When the designated evening came, I was in the sauna with Boucher after a hard workout. Sweating. Waiting for our hit man's signal.

"How do you think your friend will do it?" the Cobra asked.

"Choke hold is the simplest. Ask any cop. You need special training *not* to kill people when you use a choke hold. A few seconds, the guy's out. A few more, he's gone."

"He told you a choke hold?"

"I'm just guessing. Billy doesn't talk about his business, and you don't ask. Could be a knife, gun, ball bat. Anything. We'll know soon."

"I'm surprised he'd risk using the phone, something like this."

"No risk with this kind of signal. Unless the call is completed, the phone company's got no record."

"Presumably we can trust him."

"For what?"

"That he's really done it."

"He wouldn't expect us to trust him. The signal is just a courtesy, like. We don't pay him till we know from the cops that the job's done."

"What if the cops don't find the body?"

"Billy'll see to it they find it. That way he knows you know the job's done and you're going to pay him so he can disappear. He won't keep us waiting long. He's got to spend most of the night driving somewhere, so he can catch a morning flight."

"Driving where?"

"I don't know."

"So presumably you don't know where he's flying, either?"

"I'd guess the Coast, but who knows? Billy's vague about shit like that, which you can imagine he would be."

The temperature was cranked up around two hundred degrees. We had been in the sauna ten minutes or so when the phone rang. Boucher had his private line hooked up everywhere on the premises where he spent much time, even in the upstairs bathroom off the master bedroom.

Neither of us moved to answer. The phone rang three times and stopped. We both watched it, waiting for the second part of the signal. After a few seconds it began to ring again, this time four rings.

"He really did it," Thurman Boucher said. "I wonder what it feels like. What *does* it feel like?"

"I wouldn't know."

"Yeah, right."

"You could ask Billy when he comes to get his money."

"I could if I wanted to sound like some kid from the high school paper."

"Geraldo would ask him."

"That's different," the Cobra said. "Geraldo makes his living being an asshole."

I couldn't see the difference myself, but I kept my mouth shut about it.

Usually we had three sauna sessions of about fifteen minutes each. I had the feeling Boucher didn't really like the heat as well as I did, but he hated to be bested at anything. So he always waited for me to call it quits first. That meant he had to tough it out in the sauna while I was cooling down under the only shower. When I went back in for more heat, he'd duck out for his own shower. Since this meant his last session would always be a few minutes longer than mine, he had it arranged so that I could never get ahead of him in our personal bake-off.

It was a dumb game, but then he was an American male and that's the kind of game we're raised to play. In fact I would have played it myself, hanging tough till we died side by side, medium-rare, if it hadn't been for the other game I was already playing.

The third phone call was a real one. We were cooling down after the heat, on the slatted cedar lounges I had ordered for the purpose. There was a phone outside the sauna, too, handy to Boucher's lounge. He reached out from under the sheet that covered him from neck to toes and answered the phone.

"My God, Alan," he said after a moment. "Are they sure? . . . Well, it couldn't have happened to a nicer guy, could it? Hell of a story, too. Do the cops have any theory yet?"

Thurman listened for some time without interrupting, and then said, "All we can do is tell our guys to keep their mouths shut and hope the cops do the same thing. I'd love to see the *Herald* and the *Globe* running second on this, wouldn't you? Especially the *Herald.*"

Boucher hung up, tossed the sheet off, and reached for the clothes he had hung on a chair.

"Son of a bitch pulled it off," he said. "What's more, we've got an exclusive tip on Paul's identity. As far as the Boston papers know, he's still an unidentified holdup victim mugged somewhere on Mass. Ave."

"Billy must have decided to do it outside when Paul came home," I said. "He lived out toward Central Square."

"Could be. Anyway, the Boston papers didn't bother to send anybody to the scene, because what went out on the radio was just a report of an unconscious man in an alley. By the time the dispatcher said over the air that the man was dead, he was already at the hospital and it was too late for the TV crews to get those stretcher pictures they love to run. Besides, who gives a shit? Just some anonymous dead guy. Luckily for us one of the cops slipped the victim's identity to our police guy, what's his name? I always think of galoshes."

"Galetta. Joe Galetta."

"Joe Galoshes. He should have been a mobster. Bottom line, we've got the rest of the night to wrap the whole thing up and jam it down the *Herald*'s throat in the morning."

Lieutenant Curtin and I had come up with this charade as a way to avoid getting the Boston papers all steamed up over being fed false information. We didn't really care whether the Cobra got steamed up.

"What do you think?" I said. "Want me to give Billy the signal we're on our way?"

"I'll do it," Boucher said. He was the quarterback, and now that we were so close he'd run the ball over himself.

He dialed a number, waited a moment, and hung up. Then dialed it again and did the same thing. At the other end would be Billy Curtin, sitting in his office with a bunch of other cops, all of them looking at the phone ringing first three times and then four.

We finished dressing and headed out for our rendezvous. I was driving the Rolls and Thurman was sitting beside me. A canvas shopping bag with the *Banner* logo on it, left over from some circulation promotion, was between us on the seat. Bundles of fifties and hundreds were in it.

"You think he'll want to count the money?" Boucher said. He sounded offhand, but it was the question of a curious and excited kid.

"I doubt it. He knows where to find you if it's short."

"You think he minded what I said about the gun?" Boucher had told me to ask Curtin not to bring a gun to our meeting.

"I don't think so. If he had one, he probably already got rid of it, anyway. He's got a plane to catch later."

"He could get rid of the gun on the way to the airport."

"If he's got one, he'll leave it outside. He knows I'm going to pat him down."

"He must have been offended."

"Why? The man's a pro. All he said when I told him was you can't be too careful. In fact he was going to check us, too."

"I know. You told me that. No matter what he says, though, don't you think it must bother him that we don't trust him?"

"Not much bothers him."

"I'm sure it doesn't," the Cobra said. "Imagine how it must feel to be him. Every person you see, you say to yourself, That person owes his life to me. He exists at my sufferance. If I decide he goes, just like that, he goes." Thurman snapped his fingers. "Like the camp commandant in *Schindler's List*, whatchamacallit . . ."

"Amon Goeth."

"Him, yeah. Nothing bothered him, sitting up there with his gun. He didn't have to get *mad* at people, he was above that. Above and beyond."

"He got mad at the girl, though, didn't he?"

"That's what made that scene so shocking. She dragged him down to her level."

"I guess that's right. I never thought of it that way."

Our meeting was down the street from the *Banner*, in a small, windowless one-story building that was used partly for storage and partly for phone solicitations. I had included it in my general surveillance camera frenzy, and Curtin's technician had installed microphones yesterday. I hadn't spotted the lieutenant on the way in, but he was out there in the dark somewhere. Once we were safely inside the windowless building, he would signal his men into position and then join us.

During circulation drives, temps would be operating the phones in each of the cubbyholes that ran in two lines, back to back, down the center of the room. There were phones in the cubbyholes. On the top corner of each divider a little red light lit up when that phone was in use, so the supervisor could tell if anybody was dogging it. Cartons and boxes were piled against the walls, full of stuff not quite useful enough to keep handy in the main building and not quite useless enough to throw out.

Thurman Boucher set his bag of money down in one of the cubbyholes, and looked around the room. "I don't see your camera," he said.

"Up there in that exit sign."

"Oh, yes. I hope it's off."

"You better believe it."

"Although it would be fun to have this on tape, wouldn't it?"

"I might run into Billy if I went back to the plant to turn it on."

"I'm not serious, of course. Although it *would* be fun. Remember those FBI tapes of DeLorean?"

"Well, they were fun for the FBI at least."

"In this case the tape would be mine."

And it would have been fun for the Cobra, too. It would have gone right into his trophy drawer, an exhibit in the new Jonathan Paul collection.

"I wonder where your man is," Thurman said. "He had time to get here before us."

"He probably did. He's probably checking the neighborhood. He's in business this long because he's careful."

Three knocks came on the door, then a pause, then four more. Our little gang's secret code. I went and opened the door for Billy Curtin. He stepped through and stood there without saying a word while I closed it behind him. I shot the bolt, just in case anybody wandered over from the main plant for some reason. The last thing I wanted was for some maintenance guy to blunder into the middle of our show.

My stone killer had to be a disappointment to Boucher. Curtin was of average height or a little less. He was wearing a Kmart sports shirt with the tails out, the way cops do when they want to hide a gun. His pants were polyester, or some kind of plastic anyway, with a crease so sharp it had to be permanent. He was in his early fifties, and the hair on the top of his head had mostly gone south. His neck was too skinny for his collar, and the arms sticking out of his short-sleeved shirt were somewhere between wiry and scrawny. But tough isn't muscle.

"So this is Billy," the Cobra said. "I don't suppose last names are appropriate?"

The lieutenant didn't bother to answer.

"Tom?" Boucher said, making a little gesture with his head toward Billy Curtin.

"Sorry, Billy," I said, walking up to the lieutenant.

He held his arms away from his body and said, "Help yourself."

I patted the gun holstered in the small of his back and the handcuffs next to it and kept on patting, first his pants pockets and then down his legs like a tailor checking the fit.

"Nothing," I said.

"Sorry about that," Thurman said to Curtin.

"Sorry about what? You're careful, I'm glad to see it. I'm careful, too."

Curtin turned to me and I held the same stupid wing-flapping pose while he patted me down. Then he did the same to Boucher, who seemed more interested than offended.

"Now we're all friends," Curtin said to us.

"You're in an interesting business, Billy," the Cobra said.

"Same business as a soldier, nothing special."

"Were you a soldier?"

"I was in the service, yeah. Can we hurry it along here? Are you satisfied I killed this Jonathan Paul guy?"

"Very satisfied."

"Then where's my money for it?"

"It's here."

"Where here?"

Thurman Boucher took a step toward the cubbyhole where the money was, but Curtin said, "Hey." The lieutenant didn't shout, but the way he said it, Boucher stopped like he had hit a wall.

"I'll get it, okay?" Curtin said, moving past Boucher quickly, and taking the shopping bag.

"I'd want to count it, too," Boucher said, trying to regain control. "Be my guest."

"You counted it already, didn't you?"

"Oh, yes. I counted it."

"Twenty-five thousand, right?"

"Right."

"No reason to do it all over again, then. I bet you count money better than I do."

"I'm sure you do fine."

"Plus if it's short I know where to find you."

Lieutenant Curtin turned toward the door, with the bag tucked under his arm. He was going to join his men down the block, and they were going to handcuff the Cobra when he came out of the building.

"Billy?" Boucher said.

The lieutenant turned, and asked a question with his eyebrows.

"You did a hell of a job for me," Boucher said. "Mind if I shake your hand?"

MAYBE SOMEBODY ELSE would have read the past better and seen what was about to happen. But I didn't. All I saw was a homicide groupie, smiling, holding out his hand to his hero. Billy Curtin, after a baffled moment, taking it.

Then the Cobra did just the way I taught him, and Curtin went flying perfectly through the air while the canvas shopping bag went flying, too, spilling bundles of fifties and hundreds everywhere.

Here there was no four-inch mat, though, and the lieutenant smacked onto the hardwood floor with a sound that was sickeningly final. Curtin didn't even twitch, just lay there like roadkill. I ran to the body and knelt down.

"Jesus, Thurman," I said. "I think he's dead."

"I certainly hope so." He was standing there, curious, like a bystander after an accident. Like the wife beaters Felicia had told me about, the ones whose pulse rate slows way down as they carry out their unpleasant disciplinary duties.

"What the hell are you doing?" I said. "Are you crazy?"

"I think not. You were the one who told me to make sure there wasn't any link between me and the murder."

"Not by committing a murder yourself, for Christ's sake!"

"We don't know yet that he's dead, do we, Tom?" he said. "Check for a pulse, or whatever it is you do."

"Jesus, Thurman," I said, but checking for a pulse was a good idea. I couldn't find one, but I didn't try for long. Seeing all the money scattered around us on the floor, a question suddenly came to me. If the crazy son of a bitch meant to kill Curtin all along, why did he bother to bring along the money? Why didn't he just blow the guy away as soon as he came in the door? Who was the money meant to fool? Why?

The answers didn't come to me right away, at least not on any conscious level. But the questions must have shown on my face, because when I looked up at Boucher he suddenly broke for the junk-cluttered wall behind him and reached up for something out of sight on top of a pile of paper towel cartons.

I felt under Curtin for the gun I knew he was lying on. By the time I got to it and tugged at the handle and discovered the holster was snapped, Boucher had located his own gun, the one he must have stashed on top of the cartons. But he was in as big a hurry as I was and grabbed it by the barrel instead of the handle.

Then I did another wrong thing. The first one had been going for Curtin's gun instead of going straight for Boucher. The second was vaulting over the row of phone booths instead of going for Boucher.

Now he had things straightened out and all he had to do was climb up onto the working surface of one of the booths, and there he was, pointing his gun down at the defenseless idiot crouched in front of him. Boucher didn't seem to be in any hurry. Probably his pulse was in the low forties.

"You were right about links," he said. "Can't have links."

This was what I should have figured out as soon as he attacked Lieutenant Curtin. The tip-off was the money. Why bother with bringing the money along if the idea was to kill only the hit man? An empty briefcase would have done just as well. The point of the money was to convince *me* that the deal was going through as planned. That way I would make sure Curtin wasn't carrying a gun, and Curtin would make sure I wasn't. It had worked just fine. Boucher had plenty of time to reach his own gun, which was now aimed at my chest.

I couldn't get to him before he shot me, and he wouldn't believe me if I told him the Cambridge police were listening to every word. My only chance was to stall till the cops were banging on the door, and hope that he didn't shoot me then out of pure frustration. The Cobra wasn't a good loser.

"This is crazy shit, Thurman," I said, trying to sound calm and unafraid.

"Not at all. I've got a bunch of Hefty bags behind the boxes, and there's plenty of room in the trunk of the Rolls. Nobody knows that better than I, if you remember."

"Then what?"

"I've worked it all out so there's very little chance anyone will ever find you and your friend, don't worry. Besides, why would anyone even bother to look? Neither of you is going to leave much of a void behind, are you?"

Where were the cops, I wondered. Were they deaf? Dumb?

"Billy will," I said. "His real name is Lieutenant Billy Curtin. He's a Cambridge cop."

"Sure he is."

Then Billy Curtin himself appeared, rising up behind Thurman Boucher. He looked undead, but not much better than that. Still, he had good position. I babbled on, for fear that Boucher might hear him.

"It's the truth, Thurman. I'm not shitting you. The cops made me do it, I'm sorry . . ."

Billy's hands flickered out, grabbed Boucher's ankles, and yanked back. The gun flew out of his hand as he tried to break his fall. The Cobra toppled toward me, over the divider that separated the two lines of phone booths. Boucher kept on in the direction of his momentum but managed to twist around so that he landed on his feet. I was between him and the gun. Curtin was on the other side of the line of booths, presumably with his own gun.

Boucher came at me too fast and too mad. Spider Mead, my old high school coach, used to hammer it into us. "Only explode on purpose," he'd say over and over, "or the only one you blow up is yourself."

Like Boucher now, who was in such a hurry to get his hands on me that he was overbalanced in my direction. So I was able to guide his head under my right armpit, shoot both my arms under his, and lock him up with a wrestler's grip in back.

I let his charge carry me to the ground, with him on top and probably feeling pretty good about it for a fraction of a second. Then I did my own exploding, hooking my left foot under his right thigh and elevating him right over onto his back. At the end I had him tied up in a double grapevine and a bar lock. He was in a spread eagle, his legs forced apart and his arms flailing helplessly on both sides.

"Jesus, Lieutenant," I grunted out, "where are you?"

Boucher was twisting around like a snake trying to escape, and I wouldn't be able to keep him spread-eagled forever. I was barely keeping my hold on him when Curtin finally showed up with his handcuffs. Boucher fought the cuffs the best he could, but the bar lock kept him from using his strength.

When the cuffs were on I got to my feet, leaving Boucher

sitting on the floor. "Jesus, Lieutenant," I said, "why didn't you shoot the son of a bitch?"

"I couldn't hit a bull in the ass with a snow shovel," he said. "Even if I could, you can't tell what somebody will do if you shoot him while he's holding a gun. Lot of times that'll start him shooting. Trip a man, though, and he'll throw out his hands for balance every time."

Just then the cavalry arrived, late.

"Open up," a voice hollered. "Police." A hammering on the door started.

"Here comes your friends," I said to Curtin. "Where they been, eating doughnuts?"

"They're doing all right. They're waiting down the block, okay? No shots are fired, who the hell can tell what's going on? What's it been since this guy broke bad, anyway? Maybe a minute or two, no more."

The hammering and shouting kept on.

"Hold it for a fucking minute, will you!" Curtin shouted back. "Everything's under control here. Be right there, for Christ's sake."

"Is the TV out there?" I asked.

"Of course they're out there. I tell them we're arresting this guy's ass in time for the eleven o'clock news, how they not going to be out there?"

"Shame you didn't shoot him a little," I said. "If it bleeds, it leads."

Curtin pulled out his handkerchief and bent to pick up Boucher's gun. The line of phone booths hid him from the surveillance camera.

"Hey!" Boucher said, seeing what was coming before I did.

"Come back here, you!" the lieutenant hollered, although Boucher wasn't moving. The lieutenant was shouting for the benefit of the mike, although I only figured that out a second later, when he clubbed Boucher with the gun barrel.

The front sight tore his scalp, and blood ran down his face in rivers.

"That's for Mrs. Cushing," Curtin whispered, not for the mike. "I know the lady a long time."

"Guy shouldn't have tried to get up and run," Curtin said to me in a normal tone. "Looks like he cut himself on that chair, wouldn't you say?"

"Yeah, I'd say so, too."

I kept hold of Boucher while Lieutenant Curtin unbolted the door. "You okay, Billy?" said one of the cops outside.

"Actually I feel like shit. Asshole back there knocked me cold. But, yeah, I'm okay now."

"What happened to the guy?"

"Asshole tried to run, you know what I mean?"

"That's going to be your new name from now on," I told Boucher under my breath. "Everybody's going to call you that."

"I hope you understand that I'm going to have both of you killed," Thurman whispered back. "That's a promise."

"Give me a break," I said. "Asshole."

"Well, we better take asshole downtown," the cop at the door said.

"See?" I said to Boucher.

"TV cameras out there?" Curtin asked.

"Yes, sir."

"Let's go, then, asshole," said Curtin, shoving the Cobra in the direction of the door. "Gonna make you a star."

"You might want to put your hands up in front of your face," I said. "Makes a good shot, with the handcuffs and the blood."

"Fuck you."

"Hey, it was just a suggestion."

I hung back when the others went outside. I'd be on public view when the trial began, and that would be soon enough. Maybe I'd have time to grow a beard. It wouldn't be much of a disguise, but it would be something. At least strangers wouldn't recognize me on the street, once I shaved it off.

The TV cameramen were outside the building, along with reporters. Among them was the recently dead Jonathan Paul, looking very pleased with life. The police had leaked news of the arrest to him and to the Boston media, but not to anyone at the *Banner*, just down the street.

"Hey, Thurman, surprised to see me?" Paul hollered out.

Thurman Boucher knew better than to answer on camera, so he shot Paul a fast eye-fuck instead.

"Any comment on your arrest for trying to kill me?" Paul shouted, loud enough so all the mikes could pick up their sound bite for the eleven o'clock news. Again, Boucher knew better than to add to the fun.

He kept on not answering press questions while Billy Curtin had the medics bandage his head on camera. Eventually the reporters gave up and turned to Jonathan Paul and Curtin himself. Curtin limited himself to listing the charges—soliciting the commission of a murder, resisting arrest, assaulting a police officer, possibly more to come—but Paul was just as forthcoming as he could be with his fellow journalists.

Short of mentioning his connection to me, of course.

NO NEED TO GO TO WORK THE next morning, since Thurman Boucher would be tied up with arraignment and whatnot. Even when he got out on bond, he might not want me around. In fact I felt that way about him, ever since he told me about those Hefty bags. Still, it was going to be tough to give up my new gym.

For breakfast, I nuked a container of the lamb stew I make and freeze every Sunday. While eating it, I hopped from channel to channel enjoying the first-day coverage. The Cobra wasn't a TV star yet, in spite of the bloody arrest pictures. He would be, though, once the stations got hold of the tapes from the *Banner*'s security monitors. Naturally the camera in the exit sign had been running, no matter what I had told Thurman Boucher.

The phone rang. It was Wanda Vollmer, of Lordland and the Church of Our Redeemer Risen, Inc.

"I been watching the tube," Wanda said. "You do nice work, Bethany."

"It's the Lord's work, sister."

"Yeah, right."

"At least I hope it is. You got your bets down, didn't you?"

"Put it this way. Every point that stock drops, we make eighteen thousand dollars."

"You must have really gone into it heavy."

"It was a sure thing, why not? Mean son of a bitch like you says he's going to fuck a guy, that guy gets fucked."

"Well, thank you, Wanda. I guess."

"The only thing is knowing when to cash out, but it ought to drop a good ten points, anyway. From what I've been hearing, the whole Boucher Group is kind of a house of cards. Maybe it'll even drop more than ten."

"Gosh, I'd hate to see that happen, Wanda."

"Likewise, I'm sure."

"But if it does, it's nice to know that the church won't suffer."

"And nor will you, Bethany."

"We do well by doing good."

"You could do even more good by not doing quite so well."

"Wait a minute, Wanda, what's this?"

"It's the bite, Tom. How would you feel about taking fifteen percent?"

"We said twenty."

"I know what we said. But I thought you might want to help us out with this walk-in clinic we're setting up in Richmond."

"Is this for orphans and shit like that? Sick, pitiful little kids with big eyes?"

"You got it."

"A man would have to be a mean son of a bitch to say no to that."

"Who ever said you were a mean son of a bitch?"

So I let her Christian me down to 15 percent.

Then I called Hope in Washington. She was already at work, naturally. Every morning she rowed on the Potomac, but she still managed to be the first one in the office most days. Today she must have beat the receptionist, because she answered the phone herself.

"American Civil Liberties Union," she said. "Hope Edwards speaking."

"Hope Edwards, huh? I've heard of you."

"Oh, Tom, I was just thinking of you. Naturally. There you were on the morning news, in the background of course. Behind our bloody friend, Boucher. It occurred to me that his civil liberties might have been violated."

"Billy Curtin did it, but you pinkos will never nail him. I intend to lie about it on the stand."

"Well, I'm afraid there's nothing this office can do, then. Hey, you guys did good. What actually happened?"

I told her, and then asked whether there was any way Thurman Boucher could wriggle out.

"I don't see how," Hope said at the end. "His lawyers will argue entrapment, but it's pretty hopeless. The police or their agents have to be the ones to entrap the defendant, not private citizens. Did the police ask you to propose killing Jonathan Paul?"

"They didn't ask me and I didn't propose it. The Cobra proposed it to me. He wanted to be like the big boys, commit his very own murders."

"Then entrapment won't fly. What's left? Temporary insanity, maybe, but that won't fly, either. No, I think you got him."

"He got himself."

"Did he? Would any of this have happened without you?"

"True," he said modestly. "But it's also true that it

290

wouldn't have happened if Boucher hadn't been a murderous son of a bitch to begin with."

"And it's equally true that he would have gone right on being a murderous son of a bitch if you hadn't stopped him. He seems to have liked causing pain to people. That kind of behavior has a tendency to escalate unless somebody stops it."

"Keep going. I love it when you give positive reinforcement."

"Well, it's true. What does Lieutenant Curtin think is going to happen to him?"

"Probably not enough. He could be out in a couple of years."

"What about what's-her-name?"

"That Boucher woman? I've got to say, Hope, this jealousy of yours is very unbecoming."

"Well, what about her?"

"My guess is what's-her-name will stand by her man."

"You kind of liked her, didn't you?"

"I kind of did, in a weird way. She was funny, and she laughed at herself. Unlike the Cobra. She would have been okay, if she hadn't got her head all messed up."

"With what?"

"You know. That love stuff."

"She loved him, huh?"

"Hard to picture, isn't it?"

"Not that hard. We're brought up to love rich bullies."

"With her it took," I said. "I think she'll drive out to Walpole every visiting day and bring him a cake. When he finally comes home, she'll have his slippers and his pipe all laid out beside his favorite chair."

"Think she'll stay in Cambridge?"

"Well, the bank's probably going to take over her old family place in Brewster, since she sold it to the Boucher Group for a headquarters. And the Cambridge house is in her name, the Cobra told me once."

"She's got a nice little gym out there, I heard."

"I know, but I guess I'll stick with the Malkin Athletic Center. Harvard's got this hundred-and-sixty-pound junior, kid named Mastrangelo. I think he might do something at the NCAAs this year."

"What's his first name?"

"Tony."

"Nice name. I like it better than Alison."

It was weeks later and Thurman Boucher was loose on bail, which made me just as glad my home phone was unlisted. And unlisted under a phony name, too. If he was going to jail for hiring one killer, he might as well hire another. Or maybe he couldn't afford one anymore. His investment bank had pulled the plug on him, and now they were selling off all his former papers.

Ellsworth Court, the old gentleman on the hill in Sperryville, Virginia, was the broker handling the sales for the bankers. The autumn leaves were past their prime in New England, but the colors ought to be just about peaking in Virginia.

"I thought we might take a drive," I was saying to Hope, who was returning my call between meetings. On a typical day, she seemed to have a total of about three minutes of free time between meetings.

"A drive where?"

"Well, we could go out to Sperryville and see if Mr. Court has sold the *Banner* to Serena Cushing yet."

"The closing's set for day after tomorrow," Hope said. "I just spoke with him this morning."

"We could at least wave as we went through Sperryville, couldn't we? Then on down the Skyline Drive. What I figured, we could go down as far as Charlottesville and maybe hang a left for Virginia Beach."

"I'm going to need some convincing on Virginia Beach in October. Virginia Beach anytime, really. The whole point of Virginia Beach has always escaped me."

"Virginia Beach is the coconut cream pie capital of America."

"You're going to have to do better than that, Bethany."

"All right, it's the home of Lordland, where they have a new ride everybody's been talking about. It's called Jacob's Ladder."

"You're making a little more sense now. You want to visit Wanda."

"Want to visit Wanda. It's got a nice swing to it. Wander down Wanda way. Want to wander Wanda way with me?"

"If it'll shut you up."

"The thing is, Wanda is getting ready to send me this major check for my work as a security consultant. She's been having a lot of security problems in the department where the donations come in. I thought I ought to at least look at the place."

"In case the IRS ever asks?"

"Well, that too. But actually Wanda says the operation is really worth seeing. They have these little wagons that armed guards wheel around this huge room all day long. They collect the cash from the various letter-opening stations and carry it to the vault."

"Is this true? Money wagons?"

"Apparently they need wagons. The money just rains down from heaven, Wanda says."

And it *was* true. An amazing place. We got there late in the afternoon and only had time to peek through the door of the money room as it was closing. "Come back tomorrow and I'll give you the full treatment," Wanda said to us. "The biggest pipe organ in the world, the new rides at Lordland . . ."

"Jacob's Ladder?" Hope asked.

"We got an even better one we're opening up in the spring," Wanda said. "The Road to Tarsus. It's not a ride, exactly. It's computer stuff. Virtual reality. You think you're going along this actual Roman road and you have this out-of-body conversion experience. It's hard to describe, but it messes the living shit out of your head. One guy took the trip, he went straight from Lordland to the police station and turned himself in for killing his wife eighteen years ago. And that was just the beta version."

"Beta version?" I said.

"That's like an early version of the software. A rough draft, sort of. That's what a beta version is, you ignorant fuck."

"I know what a beta version is, Wanda. I was just amazed you knew."

"We got to keep on top, us big executives. What's the matter, you think Jesus wouldn't have used computers?"

She stopped for a minute, considering. "Shit, I'll give that idea to Howard," she said. "Make a good sermon."

Howard Orrin was the televangelist who fronted for the organization while Wanda ran it.

"Come on, let's get out of here and get something to eat," Wanda said, grabbing us both and hustling us along. "You don't know how good it is to talk with a couple of heathens for a change. Most of the time I got to pretend I'm like this nun."

"Not much of a stretch," I said. "You're mean enough."

"Up yours, too, Bethany. So listen, Hope, you must follow all this shit up in Washington. What's the story on this election next month? This guy Gingrich, he really going to get Tip O'Neill's job?"

"Tom Foley's job," I said.

"To me it'll always be Tip's job. Hey, I'm from Boston. Anyway I'm talking to Hope. Is it possible this Georgia guy is going to get it? I mean, the fucker looks like Chuckie-doll."

"I think we have to be fair about the thing," Hope said. "Don't you think Foley looks a little like the Addams family butler?"

Hope didn't like Foley's chances, but she thought the Democrats would hang on to the Senate, at least.

Wanda took us to a restaurant where they set up an easel by your table. Then a male waitperson lugged out a big blackboard and propped it on the easel. The menu was handwritten in colored chalks on the blackboard in tiny writing. They had practically everything an eatperson might want, except coconut cream pie.

"Christ, next thing you'll want lime Jell-O or butterscotch pudding," Wanda said. "Nobody serves coconut cream pie anymore."

"Why not?"

"Because only old farts eat it, Bethany."

"I resemble that."

"Only old farts say 'I resemble that.' Get the grasshopper pie instead."

"What's grasshopper pie?"

"It's just like coconut cream except for the filling and the icing."

So I shut up and got the grasshopper pie, and I guess it was okay, but it would have been better with coconut cream filling and meringue on top.

JEROME DOOLITTLE

TOM BETHANY MYSTERIES

BODY SCISSORS
STRANGE HOLD
BEAR HUG
HEAD LOCK
HALF NELSON
KILL STORY

AVAILABLE FROM POCKET BOOKS

POCKET
BOOKS

582-04